"Hello, Jules." His  hesitant step toward him as if he'd pulled on an invisible thread. A swarm of bees erupted in her chest.

He stood, and she couldn't help herself; she took him in from hair to soft leather loafers. Their gazes locked. His startling gray eyes should have been cool given the color, but the emotion swimming in their depths held her fixed in place. Riveted. The silvery center rimmed in a blue so dark it was nearly black, and thick lashes, a lush sable brown like the roots of his hair. This Beck was as familiar as home and at the same time different as night from day. Gone was the boyish promise of good looks, and in its place, a devastatingly handsome man. The shoulders she used to love were broader, his waist honed. The flat stomach she'd caressed with curious, questing fingers was now an impressive six-pack of muscle revealed by the cling of his T-shirt. His chest, when he drew in a deep breath, strained the white fabric.

Her body seemed to disconnect from her mind, and the power of speech deserted her. When she finally mustered the wherewithal to reply, her voice resembled the grate of a rusty screen door. "What are you doing here?" She cleared her throat. "I mean, hello yourself. I didn't know you were back in Charleston." She fought the urge to sling herself across the distance and jump into his arms. Her fists clenched to drag back control. *Pull yourself together, Juliette. He trashed your stupid heart and didn't think twice about it, remember?*

Praise for Jayne York and...

IF WISHES WERE HORSES, Jayne York's first novel, a contemporary romance set in the Colorado Rockies, a story of love, loss, retribution, and redemption:

"An outstanding first novel by Ms. York. A well-rounded story that will keep you reading until the exciting end."

~Sharon G., NetGalley Reviewer

~*~

"This is a new author to me...will keep you reading to a surprise ending."

~Ann R., NetGalley Reviewer

~*~

"This was a surprising book that takes the reader on a journey. There were a few surprising twists and turns along the way and kept me turning the pages to the end."

~Debra LM., NetGalley Reviewer

Midnight Acquisition

by

Jayne York

Midnight Acquisition

Cover Art by *Rae Monet, Inc. Design*

The Wild Rose Press, Inc.
PO Box 708
Adams Basin, NY 14410-0708
Visit us at www.thewildrosepress.com

Publishing History
First Crimson Rose Edition, 2021
Trade Paperback ISBN 978-1-5092-3493-6
Digital ISBN 978-1-5092-3494-3

Published in the United States of America

Dedication

To Mr. C for teaching me the joy of creation
and the importance of acceptance

Chapter One

"Welcome To Charleston!"

Juliette Rochambeau scowled at the bright blue-and-white banner hanging above the baggage carousel. South Carolina's humidity only took a moment to kink her carefully straightened hair back to its normal volume. She grunted out a curse as she grabbed her suitcase and wrestled it onto its wheels. *Yay, home sweet home.*

The terminal's wide windows spilled a sweltering pile of sunlight onto the terrazzo floors, creating a blinding reflection. She yanked her sunglasses into place and fired up her phone.

A text alert flashed across her screen. —*Hurry*— it read.

Huh. Generally, if one word would do, Evie Rochambeau used a dozen. A skitter of alarm kicked her heart.

Juliette hustled to the curb and issued a shrill, double-fingered whistle for a cab. Unlike the stream of taxis that zipped by her Manhattan apartment, this driver hopped out and loaded her bags into a back seat reeking of incense and homegrown ganja. She dropped in beside them and shouted the address over the pulsing reggae pouring from his speakers. She got a lopsided smile and a thumbs up in return.

"Hey." She tapped the driver. "Turn that down,

would you? I need to make a call."

The driver nodded, and the decibels retreated a couple notches.

She plugged one ear and listened to her mother's line ring. And ring. No answer. "Can you step on it? I need to get to Rochambeau, Inc. double-quick."

The cabbie glanced at her and grinned. She slammed into the seat as they raced away from the airport toward downtown.

She cinched her seatbelt tighter and dipped back into her bag for a tissue to wipe the sweat collected at her hairline. Her fingers brushed a copy of the *Charleston Post Examiner* tucked inside. The headline was tough to miss. "Rochambeau Family to Lend Historic Necklace." The family's heirloom necklace would get the long-awaited recognition it deserved, and from the Smithsonian no less. Quite the plum bit of press for the oldest family-owned jewelry store in North America. Her father was probably busting his buttons with pride. She smiled with satisfaction; it wouldn't hurt her reputation, either. And she got to appraise the pigeon-egg-sized ruby with its swath of diamonds—lucky her.

As the traffic whizzed by, she tried her mother's phone two more times. Her father's line, same story—no answer. As a last resort, she tried her "favorite" uncle, Roland, though she prayed he wouldn't answer. The misguided loyalty that kept his misogynistic, creepy ass an active part of Rochambeau, Inc. was a mystery to her. Finally, she tried the store phone. It went to voicemail. Strange for a late Saturday afternoon. The store should be hopping. Five minutes more and she'd have her answers.

The taxi finally rounded the turn onto Meeting Street and came to a screeching halt. A wedge of police cars blocked the road. Shocked, she gaped at the red-and-blue lights streaking color across the store entrance. Fear slammed her, and she grabbed the cabbie's shoulder. "Pull over and let me out." She shoved a couple of twenties at him and vaulted into the street.

No fewer than six cops milled about on the sidewalk. One burly, round-bellied uniform stepped forward. He raised a palm to stop her from charging up the marble steps leading to the showroom doors.

Her mouth was as dry as week-old cornbread as she moved to shoulder past him. "Oh, my God. What's happened? Was there a robbery?"

"Whoa now, missy. This here's a crime scene. Nobody goes in." His face was ruddy in the heat. Sweat stained his light blue shirt's underarms and dripped from his buzz cut.

"I'm Juliette Rochambeau. Sound familiar? My parents own this store." She pushed past him, and he grabbed her arm. She shook off his grip and glared at him. "You'll have to arrest me to keep me from seeing to them. Now get out of my way." Her chin jutted skyward.

The cop shot her a mulish glare. For a second, she thought he'd take her up on the threat.

An older cop whistled him down. "Let her through, Clinton. She's family." The second cop tipped his hat and waved her forward. "Go on up, Ms. Rochambeau. We'll collect your bags for you."

"Thank you." She didn't spare Clinton another glance as she charged up the steps two at a time and skidded to a stop in the showroom. The scene was

3

chaotic.

The showroom lights blazed unusually bright, delineating the destruction in stark detail. The primary island of display cases was awash with crushed glass and scattered forms. Beside her, the handmade antique tower displays lay in pieces on the burgundy Aubusson carpet. Delicate vases of fresh flowers wilted in fractured heaps on the hardwood walkways. The destruction was as severe as if somebody had used a battle-ax. As if more than simple greed was behind the havoc.

Wide-eyed with confusion, Juliette turned in a slow circle as she registered the carnage. "Oh, my God." Her voice was small and childlike in the spacious room.

Charles Forman, their sales manager, spun on his heels. "Miss Juliette?" His eyes were bright with unshed tears as he reached for her. "I'm so sorry."

She went willingly into his embrace and hid for a moment in his soft shoulder, then pushed back till their gazes locked. "Charles...?" Fear etched her question. "What... When?"

"I can't believe this happened. Not here. Not to Rochambeau." His usually booming baritone voice was a rough, cobbled grate. Charles's jowls wobbled, and his gaze flitted from one destroyed fixture to the next. He swept a hand over his face and winced as his fingers met a bloodied piece of gauze on his cheek.

She reached out a tentative hand.

He grimaced away; his rounded shoulders crept toward his ears. "It's nothing." His thinning hair stood on end in tufted spikes of salt and pepper.

"Jesus, Charles." She turned in a slow circle. "Did this just happen?" Her hand pressed to her lips to hold in a shocked sob. "The staff, everyone, are they all right?" She scanned the crowd.

The police grouped around her Uncle Roland as he slumped in a chair. Their employees huddled together off to one side, avoiding the crowd of blue uniforms. Her folks were nowhere to be seen.

"A couple of hours ago. They...they came in fast and held us at gunpoint. Then they started smashing cases and grabbing whatever they could get their filthy hands on. Gabby managed to hit the silent alarm. When we heard the sirens, the bastards ran. Terrible. Just terrible." Charles's voice hitched, and he stopped abruptly.

"Where are my parents?"

His face crumpled, and he shook his head. Her heart stopped beating.

"Mr. Edward, he took the brunt of it. They were after the necklace, and your daddy, he wouldn't let go. They...they hit him real hard. He says he's fine, but he wouldn't go to the hospital. Miss Evie, she tried. He just wouldn't listen. Miss Juliette, you'd best go upstairs. Your mama needs you."

"Damn stubborn man." She took off at a dead run. The back of the store and the stairs to her home looked a million miles away.

****

Becket Ford sat obscured in the deep shade of an ancient plane tree. He'd been summoned, and that was never good when London's crime kingpin was involved. He could feel his deal with Fanish Singh evaporating like water on a hot griddle.

He kept his gaze on swivel as he watched the big man's townhome. London's Berkeley Square reminded him strongly of the quaint gardens in Charleston. The cold, damp air was different here, though, even in the height of summer. It didn't hold the punishing, oppressive swelter accepted as normal in America's South. He missed the sun, the humidity, and the heady smell of coffee strong enough to strip paint. Fifteen years gone was a long time.

He yawned and stretched. The night had been tedious—profitable, long, and dissatisfying. The mark never knew what hit him; the diamonds were firmly in Yosef's capable hands. Nothing had gone wrong. No frightening glitches, no bowel-gripping moments, no breath-stealing incidents, no screaming sirens. Old hat, really. No fun at all.

He checked his bank app; his account was one hundred fifty thousand dollars richer, approximately twenty-five percent of the take. He was another step closer to paying off Renée's debt to Fanish Singh. He knew going in his efforts would never be as simple as the bottom line on a balance sheet. Singh had a long reach and a well-deserved reputation as a man who believed in hanging on to his property. Beck detested being considered just that—property. It made his blood sizzle with irritation. The sooner he got out from under him, the better. *Damn Renée.* What was she playing at by taking on a job so far out of her league?

The only thing Beck could figure was that Singh was dissatisfied with how quickly he was getting the job done. Like he hadn't just made the dude close to half a million dollars last night. What the fuck was his problem, anyway? And why attach a link to a news story about the Rochambeau necklace to his demand for a meeting? If Singh wanted him to make a play for that bit of fluff, closer pros could accomplish the job. The guy was just turning the screw. Letting Beck know who was in control, his "Beck and call boy," as it were. He huffed out a mirthless laugh. He'd been called worse.

His head needed to be in the game, not thousands of miles away and years in the past. He focused his attention back on his objective—staking out Singh's complex across the crowded street.

Mayfair's Berkeley Square was a convenient vantage point and a good foil for just such a job. During the time he lounged on the park bench, several people had come and gone from the Georgian residential portion of Singh's network of businesses. One of them Beck recognized, a woman he'd dealt with recently. Pashmina Mirin, a beauty whose dusky skin and startling, pale-blue eyes were a sure draw in any scam they ran.

Beck glanced at his phone and silenced the reminder tone that signaled his departure from his lookout post. "Teatime," he said and rose to stretch out the kinks from his time in the shade. He strolled the length of the green space and exited the square down the block from Singh's home, then doubled back along the sidewalk.

Like most of the older places on the edges of the square, shops carved out the street level, and dwellings took up the stories above. The marble steps leading from the street had a timeworn depression sculpting the tread, a testament to the hundreds of years of traffic to the door at the top. He glanced both directions down the street before lifting the heavy brass knocker. New money, dirty as it was, kept the brass gleaming in the watery sunlight.

The door swung open with a grating protest from the hinges. "What do you want?" Singh's doorman growled up at Becket. The man couldn't have been over four feet tall. He called to mind an angry bulldog, all slavering jowls and protruding teeth.

Beck nodded at him and suppressed a grin, tremendously grateful the spit stayed put inside the mutt's mouth. "Becket Ford. Your master called me."

The man's eyes narrowed. Clearly, he got the inference. "Up the stairs, arsehole. End of the hall. No detours along the way."

A grand staircase coiled up from the checkerboard marble on the foyer's floor. Beck ran an appreciative hand along the glossy mahogany banister as he climbed toward the landing. Beside him, the satin-smooth plaster of the curved wall held an impressive collection of old oil portraits and modern landscapes. He itched to stop and study them, touch them. His "spidey-sense" tickled the back of his neck. Doubtlessly, the little man on the ground floor watched his every move. He gave the doorman an apologetic shrug and continued up the stairs.

At the end of a long hall, he paused and gave a perfunctory knock at tall double doors. He pushed them open and stepped into Fanish Singh's office.

Singh sat comfortably reclined on a richly upholstered damask sofa. Casually, he watched the arc of a long-bladed knife as he flipped it from handle to tip and back again. His suit jacket draped in elegant precision from broad shoulders; his tie perfectly matched the gleaming black of his eyes. The knife split the air as it passed his face, destroying the image of a wealthy businessman relaxing after a hard day's work.

Beck's gaze dropped to the crumpled shape on the carpet at Singh's feet. Blood-matted hair and dark-crimson stains stood in stark contrast against the man's waxy pallor.

Singh flipped the knife again and buried the blade deep in the dead man's chest. "Did you enjoy your time in the square, Mr. Ford? The weather is lovely. Don't you agree?" His gaze rose slowly from the old target to the new.

Becket flinched slightly, then squared his shoulders. Bile burned his throat. He was surprised they'd spotted him, but advertising his error wasn't recommended if living was on the agenda. "Surely you don't begrudge me some reconnaissance."

"Hardly." Singh stood smoothly and stepped over the corpse. He pressed a button on his desk phone, and his watchdog entered the doors behind Becket, accompanied by two enormous helpers. Singh nodded to the body. Efficiently, the men bundled it up in the plastic sheet beneath it and carried the corpse out like yesterday's garbage.

"I believe I offered you tea, Mr. Ford. Do sit down." He glanced at the servant, and the man inclined his head as he turned to leave.

Beck gladly dropped into the chair nearest the desk—and as far removed from the recent carnage as possible. He forced his hands to relax and his breath to even out. If he showed the slightest weakness, he knew the killer across the desk from him would sense it. "That was quite a show. Did you stage it for my benefit?"

"Just a happy coincidence." Singh skirted the desk and sat in his high-backed chair. The leather creaked as he settled. He rested his elbows on the dark surface and linked his long, tapered fingers together. Blood edged the nails of his right hand. The bastard damn sure knew how to create atmosphere. "I'm glad you came by. I want to discuss your debt to me."

"You mean Renée's debt. And you got a quarter of it back last night." Becket wished for the millionth time he'd never gotten in between Renée Greenleaf and Fanish Singh. It never paid to mix personal obligations and business. Never.

"Must I remind you, Mr. Ford, you volunteered to take on her debt? So now the note is yours. Unless you default, and then, of course, you and Miss Greenleaf will pay equally for my losses." He reached into his desk drawer and withdrew an envelope. He used a red-rimmed nail to slide it across the gleaming surface to Beck. "Or we can restructure the deal. It's up to you."

"Restructure? As in what, exactly? Hit the Bank of England or something?" Two million dollars was a lot of coin to scrape together, even in the diamond business. Especially when those gems came out of other people's safes.

"Open it." Singh indicated the stiff manila envelope. "I have a proposal for you. I'm sure you'll agree closing your account quickly is preferable to dragging it out for weeks."

Becket pulled back the clasp and slid out the contents.

"As you see," Singh said, "I too believe in research. You've had quite the adventure in Europe, made a sizable reputation here in the UK especially. I found myself wondering, where does talent such as yours originate? My personal belief is that a man doesn't simply *become* a thief. One of your caliber takes a lifetime of practice."

Beck glanced up at Singh. "What's this, my greatest hits?" He unfolded the contents. In a series of succinctly typed paragraphs was his dossier, birth to the current day. A concise picture of Becket Adam Ford, American pickpocket turned European jewel thief. Then came the article from his hometown paper covering the lending of the Rochambeau ruby necklace, and a copy of a second story concerning the unsuccessful attempt to lift it. A black-and-white glossy photograph followed it. For a second, his breath stalled—a photo of Juliette Rochambeau and family. A note at the bottom identified them leaving Roper Saint Francis Hospital emergency room in Charleston, SC. The time stamp on the photo indicated it was only twenty-four hours old.

Gooseflesh rose on Beck's arms, and a drop of sweat trickled down the back of his neck. The click of a lens had wiped away every moment of the carefully constructed distance from his old life.

"As you know," Singh's mouth quirked as he continued, "I am primarily a businessman. I depend on the collection of data to keep me informed regarding everyone who works for me. You, Mr. Ford, have a unique connection to an object of interest. I want you to get it for me."

When all else fails—bluff. "The man you need is my stepbrother, Seth. If you know my history, then you should know he has whatever you need in place to get you what you want. *And* he's already on-site. Why drag me into it?"

A sly smile ghosted across Singh's lips. "Simple.

The Rochambeau girl."

Becket's jaw stiffened. "Ancient history, Singh."

The smile became a gloating sneer. "Given your penchant for rescuing damsels and your connection to Ms. Rochambeau, it's hard to believe you'd want Seth Santos within arm's reach of her. You know how he is with women. So little respect." Singh shook his head in mock regret.

His stomach soured. The bastard was right. Beck wanted his stepbrother as far away from the Rochambeau family as possible. "Can't say I give a flying fuck how Seth is with the ladies in his life, but he used to be a damn fine crook. And he's got an ax to grind. His pops died in the jail cell where Rochambeau put him. My stepbrother holds a grudge like nobody's business." Regret tightened muscles already straining to feign disinterest.

"Yes, so I was given to understand. Santos was recommended for the job. Unfortunately, hiring him proved an unreliable choice. An unsuccessful attempt to acquire the item in question was made yesterday." He tapped the picture. "That was the result." He coolly appraised Beck's reaction to the photo. "Apparently, the senior Mr. Rochambeau put up a valiant struggle, and the necklace remains in his possession. I'd like you to change that."

Beck swallowed hard, fighting the panicky urge to charge back down the stairs. "I'm listening." He couldn't afford to jump before he knew the details.

Singh's scrutiny was unwavering. "What I offer is simple. I will wipe clean your debt, as well as Ms. Greenleaf's, in exchange for the Rochambeau necklace. Get it for me, and you're a free man." He reminded

Beck of the cobras that fascinated him as a kid—cunning, focused, and emotionless. "You may, of course, decline. However, if you accept, I'll ensure that Seth Santos is at your disposal to assist in whatever capacity you may require. My sole desire is that the necklace is delivered into my hands. The decision is yours."

Beck blew out a long breath and rocked his head. Vertebrae crackled, but the tension remained. He'd hoped, once the parameters of the deal were made clear, he'd be able to figure a way out. No such luck. They couldn't run—Renée didn't have the grit to completely disappear. Singh would find her, and when he did, she wouldn't live long enough to scream. But fuck, working with Seth? That was a truckload of problems all by its lonesome. *Obligation sucks.*

Singh pushed back in his seat. "Well, Mr. Ford, what's it to be?"

Beck slapped his hands on the smooth leather of his chair and rose to his feet. "There's no love lost between Seth and me. Call it elemental differences. I prefer a quick and silent in and out. Seth thinks with a crowbar in hand." He blew out a long breath. "I can tell you he's not gonna like playing second fiddle to me. What's to stop him from getting in my way?"

"Are you questioning me?" The only change in his expression was a narrowing of his eyes. Threat received.

"I'm not stupid enough to do that." Becket backpedaled. Well, shit. "I don't have a real choice in this; you know I'll do it." He paused and watched his employer. "Answer me this, though. Why this *particular* necklace? What's so special about it? I mean, I know the story about its history, and the center stone's a whopper of a ruby, no doubt there. What I don't get is why you're so interested."

Singh's steady gaze flickered for a moment. Beck's attention sharpened. What was that? Relief? Satisfaction? No. Vindication.

"Suffice it to say, monetary gain is not my sole motivation. You have until the Smithsonian takes possession. Two weeks, Mr. Ford."

Chapter Two

Juliette stood in the doorway to her parents' bedroom. The rest of the day after the robbery had been long and hard. Now, finally home from the hospital, her father was sleeping, the blankets tucked neatly around him. He was peaceful for the moment as if he hadn't a care in the world.

The police had released the property back to them, and the insurance adjusters had finished their assessment of the physical damage to the fixtures. Uncle Roland and Charles were knee-deep in paperwork, listing the losses to their inventory. They'd been at it all day. The rest of the staff had fled to their homes and would return tomorrow for the major cleanup of the battle zone. She should be downstairs helping, but Charles had run her off when they returned from the hospital. Admittedly, she hadn't fought very hard. Exhaustion dragged on every muscle. Tomorrow was soon enough to get involved in piecing together the remains of the store.

She couldn't wrap her head around the level of violence that had laid waste to Rochambeau, Inc. The attack had been so vicious, as if the bastards were intent on causing as much ruin as they could manage in their allotted time. As if the merchandise was an afterthought. Just so unbelievably destructive. They'd even pulled china displays from the walls. She couldn't fathom a reason for such wantonly pointless vandalism.

The one who'd assaulted her dad—he must have been a real piece of shit. Gabby, their flamboyant French designer, told the police she'd hit her panic button, sending out the silent alarm the moment they shouted their intent. Their leader, hiding behind his skeleton mask, screamed at the staff to lie face down on the carpet. Two others, also in Halloween masks, destroyed case after case and laughed while they did it.

The one in the skeleton mask switched focus to Juliette's father. Unfortunately, Edward held the large, rectangular, leather box that housed the Rochambeau necklace. According to Gabby, the thug acted like he knew her father was the only one allowed to touch the necklace, and he wouldn't stop until Edward turned it over. The thief pointed his gun directly at Edward's head and told him to drop it. Any sane man would have done as he was told. Her father, however, clutched the box closer to his chest and refused to give in. They wrestled over the prize and managed to trip the box's latch. The necklace spilled free, and Edward scooped up the jewelry before it hit the ground. He shoved the man away. The thief used his pistol barrel like a club on Edward's head and made another move to snatch it away.

Her father, injured and furious, clutched the precious jewels for all he was worth. The gold links holding the piece together gave way during the struggle, and her dad tumbled backward with the necklace in his hands. One of the staff finally managed to trigger the exterior alarms. Their piercing wail filled the air, and for the blink of an eye, everyone froze. The leader roared out his frustration and kicked Edward hard, while the older man grasped the necklace like an endangered child. Above the noise of the alarm, the scream of police sirens added to the din. The thief and his crew had bolted for the rear door just as the police charged into the showroom.

The thief focused on Daddy. Those words rang and echoed in Juliette's head. Of course, the news article pinned the location of the necklace to the store, but how had he known it was in that particular box?

The question made chills roll up the back of her neck. That snippet of information wasn't a secret inside the store. In fact, over the years, it had become a joke among the employees. *Touch the ruby and be forever cursed with unemployment.* To Juliette's knowledge, everyone took it with deference.

That left only one conclusion—someone on the staff wasn't on the same page as the rest of them. A traitor was telling tales out of school. Anger that an underhanded ingrate was hiding in their midst had Juliette grinding her teeth. If they were foolish enough to believe she'd allow her family's destruction by a coward in their ranks, they'd best think again. She *would* find out who the person was, and she'd see them strung up by their nuts.

"Not much of a welcome home, was it, Lettie?"

Juliette flinched, startled out of her silent vigil. Her mother's soft voice was accompanied by the ever-present scent of freesia.

She turned to Evie and slipped her arm around shoulders more fragile than they used to be. "You should be sleeping, Mama. Didn't the doctor give you a prescription to help?"

"I don't like bein' muzzy-headed. There's too

17

Jayne York

much to do tomorrow, like keeping a certain stubborn man out of the mess downstairs."

"Yeah, well, good luck with that. I'll be here to run interference for you. Guess there'll have to be a delay in the party planning department, huh." The stressful day weighed down every cell in her body. Her mom was probably feeling that and more. Her home, her sanctuary, her livelihood, and her family—all violated. It would be some time before the house returned to normal.

And then her mother surprised her. "You're not gettin' out of it that easy, darlin'. We've still got the Smithsonian reception in a couple weeks." She peeked into the bedroom, then whispered, "I'm usin' it to cover a surprise party for Daddy's birthday. See, I already told him we couldn't do anything this year, so he's not expectin' it." Her shoulders shook with a silent giggle.

Juliette dragged her back into the hall. "Seriously, Mama? With all we have to do, you want to pile one event on top of another?" Honestly, the woman was a menace. Always tossing water into hot grease and expecting it to turn out just peachy. "There's no way we can handle a huge to-do *and* get the store put back together in time. We're gonna have to scale down to a simple meet and greet, hand off the necklace, and pray we still have merchandise to sell when we open the doors."

Her mother's chin snapped into the air. "Now listen here, young lady, it's your daddy's seventieth birthday, and I'm not about to let it go by without a wingding. Lettie, I'm surprised at you."

Juliette winced. "First, please don't call me that. Second, we've got our hands full just getting the damn cases here, let alone going flat out into black-tie reception mode."

Evie's hands landed on her hips. "Oh, pshaw. There's a whole staff downstairs. We'll delegate the fool out of it. Besides, with you back home, we—"

"Hold it." Juliette raised a hand. "Who says I'm back home? I came to appraise the necklace, then I'm beatin' feet back to the Big Apple. I'm not, I repeat, *not* staying in Charleston. Let's not fight that battle again. Okay?" The last thing she needed right now was to revisit the brouhaha over her choice of colleges and place of residence. The first time around had practically gotten her deleted from their wills.

Evie sighed, long-suffering and well-practiced. "We'll talk about this later. I'm too tired now to get into it with you. I'm goin' to bed." Her mother swept past her like Scarlet O'Hara dismissing her maid.

"Well. Fine, then. I'll do a run downstairs to see how Charles and Roland are doing. Then I guess I'll head to bed too." Lord love a duck, the woman could be an infuriating steel magnolia when she didn't get her way.

"Fine by me. Sleep tight, don't let the bed bugs bite, darlin' Lettie." She stepped through the bedroom door and closed it with a thunk.

"Please. Drop that infernal nickname." Juliette said through gritted teeth. Evie's muffled laughter followed her down the hall to the stairs.

She paused at the main office door and listened to a battle raging in the cramped interior. She quietly cracked open a sliver of viewing room.

Charles's tone was rife with contempt as he glowered at her uncle. "I've told you repeatedly,

Roland, this accounting method is antiquated and should have been updated years ago."

Roland glared back at Charles. "Yes, well. My *brother* put me in charge of the daily operations for a reason, Charles. He trusts my judgment, and while I understand it gripes your tight ass, you're going to have to accept it."

Roland's clipped, superior tone had Juliette's stomach clenching in revulsion. Her uncle had the unpleasant habit of invoking family to justify his place in the hierarchy. The two men had worked together for years and never found an inch of common ground. She worked to control the urge to send them both to their respective corners like children in summer camp.

"That may be so," Charles snapped, "but he trusts *me* to handle the staff and to make sure customers are treated to fair and equitable dealings. I'm sure as hell not going to tell him we can't find the pieces Mrs. Harrington consigned for resale. Not until I know for certain. Hasn't he had enough to deal with?" He crumpled the list in his hand and heaved it at an overfilled trash can. "I'm pretty sure they were in the main showcase. We'll have to ask the staff tomorrow. They're damn sure not in the safe."

"So you're saying you have no idea, on a day-to-day basis, what's in the cases and what's not? Very careless of you, Charles." Roland's tone dripped false concern. "Verges on negligence, I'd say."

"Why, you pompous ass…" Charles choked out.

Time to step in before the situation got physical. She moved into the office and cleared her throat. "Boys, boys. Let's play nice, shall we?" Damn, did she have to be schoolmarm *and* referee? She slumped down into an empty chair and frowned disdainfully.

Roland smirked into the sheaf of papers in his hand. "Juliette, it's been a long day for everyone. Don't worry your pretty little head over our squabbles. Just let us handle the accounting. Okay?"

He'd love nothing better than to dismiss her as he had when she was a child. She'd learned a thing or two since then. "Thanks so much for your concern, Uncle Roland." *You condescending asshole.* "However, Daddy and I think it's time for everyone to call it a night. You won't gain any ground by staying up all hours. So lock it up and get a fresh start in the morning. Sound good to you guys?"

Charles's shoulders relaxed, and his features smoothed. She caught the glint of gratitude in his eyes. Roland was another matter.

"No. I believe we should get farther along tonight if Charles has any gas left." He never had known when to shut up.

Charles's brows drew down into a scowl. "I'll stay as long and longer than you do, Roland," he grumbled.

She slapped her hand down on the desk in front of her and leaned toward her uncle. "Christ. Give it a rest, both of you. There's no advantage to sniping at each other like old biddies. I'm telling you to lock it up and go home." She glared at Roland. "Be here at eight in the morning. Bring a cooperative attitude, or don't come at all. Clear?" Her interest in their blame game had run out along with her ability to be civil.

Charles's teeth caught his lower lip as he looked away. Roland jerked up straight in his chair, a stubborn glint in his eyes. His newly acquired backbone was another unwelcome surprise.

"Now see here, little miss…" he sputtered.

She held up her hand. "Look, I'm not going to argue this point, Roland. And before you say another word, let me point out—this is not an option. Daddy says close it down; you close it down. Clear?" She was proud of herself for making shit up on the fly like this. Edward had been down for the count since returning home. She was sure he'd agree—hard feelings and mistakes were the only things accomplished this late at night. "One final thing, though. Daddy wants the necklace where he can see it. So if you could get it, I'll take it upstairs with me."

Again, Roland barked in protest. She held up a quelling hand. Charles tried unsuccessfully to hide his smile from her as he stepped out into the showroom. A second later, he handed her the deep burgundy box with its precious cargo.

He bowed and presented it over his arm like a fine bottle of wine. "He'll sleep the better for it. I have no doubt." His smile broke loose of his heavy jowls. "Come on, Roland, you heard the lady. Let's put all this on hold."

She smiled at the rotund senior salesman. "Thanks, Charles. Now, do I need to stick around to make sure you two can tie this place up, or can I go back upstairs?"

Roland huffed, dissatisfaction at being put in his place plain on his face. He shoved the papers in his hand into a folder and punctuated his displeasure by slamming the file drawer. His nose was in the air as he strode past Juliette out of the office.

"Damn, girl," Charles whispered. "I wish I'd filmed that. When'd you grow them lady balls?" His laugh wheezed out like old bellows.

She grinned and kept her voice quiet as well. "I've picked up a few people skills."

Charles wrapped her up in a hug. "I'm glad you're here, honey. Things are going on you don't know about. I'll tell you tomorrow. Right now"—he picked up the local newspaper and tapped the front page with his fingertip—"get a load of this. We made the papers again. Quite the hero, your uncle."

"Yeah, I bet." She kissed Charles on his round cheek and retraced her steps to the staircase. She needed to take her own advice and call it a night. After some bedtime reading, that was. She tucked the newsprint under her arm.

And it would have been nice if sleep was in the cards, but Juliette tossed and turned until well past midnight. Groaning, she gave up the fight and took to wandering through the apartment. She stopped first in front of her parents' bedroom door. All was quiet. Her father probably had the ruby's case clutched to his chest.

Her stomach grumbled a request for one of her grandmother's famous golden biscuits, and she wondered if her mother had some tucked away. A buttery bite of country ham stacked between the layers of a warm biscuit might convince her churning mind to settle down and let her sleep.

Down the hall, past the stately walnut grandfather's clock, the kitchen had undergone a complete renovation. Her mother had utterly transformed the primary living area of a two-hundred-year-old apartment into a modern, welcoming haven. Why her father was dragging his feet about redecorating the showroom baffled Juliette. He needed to hold his tongue and let Evie have her way.

She sighed into the quiet room. This trip had become more than a job foisted on her by her parents. She was only beginning to sense the layers of problems and worries facing her. For instance, the fierce hostility between Charles and Roland. Then Mother's uncharacteristic notes of vulnerability and her father's lack of interaction when she'd talked to him. If she could call it that—he'd barely spoken a word to her directly and hardly made eye contact with her when he did. Initially, she'd attributed it to shock. Now his actions made her wonder if he was hiding something.

Why couldn't life be simple? Hop a flight, say "hey" to the folks, do the job, and get back to the life she'd crafted for herself. Life was easier away from the subtle disappointment and dissatisfaction palpable in her regular interactions with her parents.

She settled for a cold glass of milk and leftover potato salad. As she rinsed her glass and tidied the counter, her mind churned. She wasn't closer to sleep now than she'd been before her thousand-calorie snack. She needed a distraction to take her troubled mind out of the here and now. A mischievous smile ghosted across her lips as she zeroed in on the perfect answer.

She pushed open the hall closet and pulled the light cord dangling down the wall. A single light, high on the ceiling, revealed a strap-hinged door in the rear wall. The first time she'd found the hideaway, she was sure magical wardrobes and trips into the unknown waited on the other side. On closer inspection, she'd found no talking lions, but magic hung in the air, nonetheless. It was the perfect space to indulge in fantasy dreams while hiding from grown-up demands.

The hidden door creaked as she pulled it open and patted the wall for another pull-chain. Finally, the rough metal of the pop-bead cord brushed her fingers. Its rusty links grated in the fixture soaring above her head. The stairs revealed were steeper and decidedly narrower than she remembered.

She climbed up into the dusty air of the attic. The cavernous room's borders disappeared past the halo of light in the rafters. Juliette didn't need additional light to know her destination. At the far end of the space beneath the eaves was her hideaway. The dim yellow glow was enough to avoid stacks of boxes and bits of accumulated fixtures from the store.

A fan-detailed Palladian window leaked moonlight and the weak reflection of the streetlights three floors below. She pushed tentatively on the casement, and the window flexed outward, allowing a fresh draft of ocean-laden air to wash the scent of disuse from her nose. Tucked away in the farthest corner, a fainting couch concealed the nest of secrets accumulated during her years as a lonely kid. She breathed out a sigh of relief. They'd remained undiscovered for...well, more than a decade since she'd last hidden away up here.

She peered beneath the couch and found the box she'd stashed the morning she left for the University of South Carolina. She grabbed the edge and hauled the box out. Dust billowed in the light as she blew across the lid. The flower-covered cardboard was brittle in her hands. It had done its job keeping what she'd once held most dear safe from the pervasive, oppressive heat and humidity.

She didn't have to open it to know the contents but

couldn't curb the urge to pry open the past. Most irresistibly, a packet of innocence lost—the ribbon-bound bundle of letters that detailed her "Summer of Becket Ford." She unfolded an old turquoise scarf that served as a wrapper and pressed the stack to her nose. Notes of nutmeg and clove lingering on the envelopes were the remnants of an old-fashioned sachet she'd made for him. The oil's aromatic perfume clung tenaciously to every piece of clothing he wore—a badge proclaiming his devotion. At the time, she'd been proud he loved her enough to risk the jeers of his family. She'd been too naïve, too tied up in his body to understand that it was all just a fantasy.

She caressed the ribbon tying up her memories of that summer. Now, they were just the recorded longings of two people who'd never had a chance at more than a brief glimpse of an improbable future. They'd tried so hard to ignore the realities of their lives. She was more successful at it than Becket. In the end, he'd been the one to mete out the punishment for daring to dream of a different life. He'd walked away and never looked back.

As she laid the bundle gently on top of the other souvenirs, a glimmer of silver winked at her. She hooked a careful finger under a chain and drew out a bracelet. A murmured sound of forgotten pleasure escaped her. The charm bracelet had been a birthday gift from Becket. Suspended on the delicate chain were three small shells, all from perfect moments on secluded beaches—insulated bubbles of time.

"Becket," she whispered, "have you thought about me?" God, the countless times he wandered across her thoughts, and she'd find herself indulging in wondering *what if things had been different.*

She shook off the regrettable habit, dropped the bracelet onto the scarf, and closed the box with a determined pat. She set the carton back on the floor and scooted it beneath the daybed. She could always return for a fix of happier days if she needed it. Juliette forced herself to concentrate on the present and relegate the ghosts of the past to their proper place.

Chapter Three

Beck's bags were the last ones down the chute and onto the carousel at Charleston International. Of course, they were. Every bone in his body ached after thirteen torturous hours of cramming his six-foot, two-inch frame into a toddler-sized seat. He swore the flight was no better than a holding pen for human livestock.

Overshadowing every move was Renée, or the lack thereof. Yosef was still scouring London for the elusive nitwit. Though Beck had to admit that giving Yosef the slip at Gatwick as he was carting her to the plane was classic Greenleaf behavior. Her daddy would have been proud. While she might enjoy a moment of superiority, when Singh found out she was in the wind, it wouldn't last long.

He hoisted his backpack higher on his shoulder and snatched his bags off the shiny, steel merry-go-round. A wide yawn caused his jaw to pop. He rubbed at the joint, reminding himself to stay awake during the twenty-minute cab ride to the house courtesy of Yosef's extended family.

The short trip was an education. North Charleston was an altogether different creature from the way it used to be. Urban sprawl and reclamation had changed the landscape into a tourist town. But not all of it. In the final analysis, Charleston was a seacoast town, a shipping town. A rough town built on the tough backs of sailors and slaves. Its unsavory core had educated his family for generations. Just as it had the aristocratic Rochambeaus. Their differences hinged on the number of bills in their respective pockets.

His destination was a restored brick carriage house only a couple of blocks away from Rochambeau, Inc. A quaint and quiet home base exactly right if he was to pass as a visiting tourist. Certainly not what he truly was—a native of the slums on the bend of the Ashley River.

His cab dropped him at the curb, and he yanked out his phone to retrieve the code to the lockbox on the door. The warmth of the day had passed. The perfume of jasmine filled the small courtyard in the front of his temporary home away from home. He had a deadline, and he'd stick to it, he'd assured Singh. The hand-off to the Smithsonian happened on the twenty-third. Beck intended to be on a plane back to England long before that. In a first-class seat.

He shouldered open the door, and the quiet hum of air conditioning greeted him. The lower humidity level would be a godsend when the sun came blasting out in the morning. He dropped his bags beside a four-poster rice bed in the single bedroom and pushed open the french doors onto a small, brick-paved patio off the kitchen.

He picked up his phone and sent a note to Yosef, confirming his arrival and a reminder to keep searching for Renée. He'd do his best to put that worry out of his mind in the upcoming days, hard as it would be. Bernie Greenleaf's little girl might have turned into a giant pain in his ass, but the day Bernie turned toes up, Beck had promised to take care of her. To his ever-lovin' regret, he was still trying to fulfill that vow by allowing himself to be guilted into being her patsy when her job for Singh went tits up. The clumps of shit kept rolling downhill, landing square in his lap. Usually, he did an excellent job of keeping his temper under control. Renée had abused his white-knight tendencies for the last time.

He turned back to the tiny kitchen and hoisted his backpack onto the table for two. A thick manilla envelope lay in the center, containing a set of keys to the house and a rental car. A folded note confirmed the car, rented in the landlord's name, was parked at the curb. He grinned, wondering what leverage Yosef had on the property owner. He'd find out eventually because Yosef was shit at keeping his own secrets. Beck's confidences, however, were a different matter altogether. Yosef was at the top of a perilously short list of friends.

Right. What was he doing? Oh, yeah. He needed to do a quick drive-by on the jewelry store and get some food to fill the pit in his belly. The sleep he'd stubbornly refused on the plane would come eventually.

He pocketed the keys and left the house. Out of habit, he checked the street in both directions, committing to memory the general layout and the kinds of cars competing for parking. Nothing caught his attention. No one was loitering on the sidewalk or paying undue attention to the newcomer at the carriage house. He assumed Seth had been given a heads-up from across the pond and placed a lookout at the airport, but he hadn't picked up on anyone tailing him. His shoulders relaxed fractionally.

The nondescript sedan at the curb was well-suited

to his purposes. Not new or flashy, an ordinary, indistinct dark gray. He slipped into the driver's seat and whacked his knees on the steering wheel. Yosef's relative and Singh's mutt had challenges in common. Grumbling, he rubbed his kneecaps and adjusted the position to suit his long legs.

Rochambeau, Inc. was two turns and three blocks away. He rolled slowly by the elegant, understated opulence of the main entrance. No Day-Glo yellow tape across the front door, that was good. The cops must have completed their on-site investigation and ceded control back to Juliette's family. A discreet "closed" sign decorated the wide glass door, but he bet the inside was a beehive of activity as the staff worked to put things back to rights. He didn't resist the impulse to glance at the residence above the store. Gauzy curtains fluttered in open windows, and he wondered if she was up there. Would she be caught by a sudden urge to search out the driver of an innocuous sedan? "You're dreaming." He laughed at himself.

A few blocks along Meeting Street, he lucked into a parking spot and pulled to the curb. He locked up the car and strolled down a short side street to a well-remembered alcove. Hoping the old haunt survived with its menu intact, he wove through traffic to the restaurant that held a wealth of memories—fond and painful.

The Eggsperience Diner hadn't changed much during his absence. Its blue-and-yellow striped awning still fluttered in the persistent breeze and provided an island of shade on days of searing summer heat.

The door chime jingled brightly, and the waitress smiled in welcome as she gestured him to a table near the kitchen. He sat back and relaxed into the familiar smells of frying sausage and freshly made biscuits. A moment later and coffee in hand, he picked up that morning's copy of the *Charleston Post Examiner* and scanned from the front page to the sports section. No mention of the jewelry heist. The robbery was already old news. For his purposes, old news was good news.

****

Juliette couldn't take much more without breaking down. Cleanup was like being in the muddy aftermath of a monumental flood. Scoop up the muck and salvage whatever was recognizable. She'd been okay until her parents made a halting pass through the wreckage and went white as sheets. Her mother's hands were shaking as they lay in a protective clasp on her daddy's arm. As a team, they'd made sure to thank each member of the staff for their help. Juliette was proud of them.

Roland sniffed his disgust at his brother's fragile state while mouthing platitudes for the employees' benefit. Charles treated him to a ferocious scowl. He patted Edward's back sympathetically and reassured him they'd have the store shipshape for business in short order. Edward shook his hand gratefully.

His attention wandered back to the destruction around them. He paused at Juliette's side and placed a soft kiss on her cheek. "Thank you for taking on the brunt of this, honey. Don't know what I'd do without your help." Her laconic father's eyes were misty, and Juliette tossed her arms around his neck.

"Where else would I be, Daddy? You go rest for a while and come down later if you feel like it. We got this." She rubbed comforting circles on his back while she whispered to him, then exchanged a worried smile with her mother. Evie tightened her grip on Edward's arm, and they disappeared back behind the ancient elaborate gate of their private elevator.

As soon as they were gone, she gave Roland her own fierce glare. "Really, Roland? Really? You'd best hope you never need my help because I'll be thinking twice before I lend a hand." She ignored his sputter as she grabbed her purse, her phone, and the keys to her mother's car. The disdain flowing from him was too much to bear. "I'm gettin' y'all dinner. Be right back," she announced and beat feet away from her mind-boggling jerk of an uncle. The temptation to launch at him before God and everybody was nearly too great to resist.

After googling the phone number for The Eggsperience Diner, she ordered a butt load of comfort food as she drove. The small restaurant would always be one of her favorite places in this town. Besides, they had the best shrimp and grits in the state, and their brown gravy was so good it'd "make you want to slap your mama." Pair that up with peach cobbler, and it was a guaranteed food coma. She could use a good nap after the sleepless night she'd spent. Memories and apprehension overload made uncomfortable bedfellows.

She double-parked in front of the colorfully striped awning and flipped on the hazard lights of her mama's Cadillac. She'd only be a moment, and if she got a ticket—oh well, just one more item on the list.

The place was quiet, only a few diners catching a quick bite before working their way back to hotels on Meeting Street. She smiled brightly at the waitress behind the short counter. "Hey, Maisie," she said, reading the girl's name tag. "Picking up for

Rochambeau if it's ready. I rushed you. I'm so sorry."

"Don't fret, darlin'. I'll check with William and be right back." The girl's curly black hair bounced behind her as she scurried through the kitchen doors. Juliette dug for her wallet. Why she carried an overgrown satchel for a handbag was beyond her. The purse was always full of stuff she'd never use unless there was a tidal wave or a zombie apocalypse. As she searched, an odd brush of awareness traveled up her legs like a featherlight caress. Her hand stopped digging, and she glanced over her shoulder.

She skimmed across the occupants of the diner and almost... Her attention snapped back to a man in the rear. Were her eyes playing tricks on her? Becket? Like he'd been conjured back to life from beneath a decade's worth of consecrated dirt. Her skin heated, and she had the urge to run—toward him or out the door, she wasn't sure which.

"Hello, Jules." His lips quirked up, and she took a hesitant step toward him as if he'd pulled on an invisible thread. A swarm of bees erupted in her chest.

He stood, and she couldn't help herself; she took him in from hair to soft leather loafers. Their gazes locked. His startling gray eyes should have been cool given the color, but the emotion swimming in their depths held her fixed in place. Riveted. The silvery center rimmed in a blue so dark it was nearly black, and thick lashes, a lush sable brown like the roots of his hair. This Beck was as familiar as home and at the same time different as night from day. Gone was the boyish promise of good looks, and in its place, a devastatingly handsome man. The shoulders she used to love were broader, his waist honed. The flat stomach she'd caressed with curious, questing fingers was now an impressive six-pack of muscle revealed by the cling of his T-shirt. His chest, when he drew in a deep breath, strained the white fabric.

Her body seemed to disconnect from her mind, and the power of speech deserted her. When she finally mustered the wherewithal to reply, her voice resembled the grate of a rusty screen door. "What are you doing here?" She cleared her throat. "I mean, hello yourself. I didn't know you were back in Charleston." She fought the urge to sling herself across the distance and jump into his arms. Her fists clenched to drag back control. *Pull yourself together, Juliette. He trashed your stupid heart and didn't think twice about it, remember?* She straightened her spine and cooled her expression.

"You either," he murmured.

He stepped toward her, and she dug her toes into her sandals.

"I didn't expect to see you. Aren't you living up north somewhere?" His voice was deeper than the teenaged version, and he sounded as blown away by this situation as she was. He slowly navigated between tables.

He was close enough to touch now, and she clutched her bag till her fingers stung from the bite of the zipper. "Manhattan," she said. There it was, the delicious mix of spices. Or was it a whiff of scent from the peach cobbler she'd ordered?

"Just got back to town myself. I'm on a buying trip for my import business."

"Imports? Doesn't that stuff come from the Orient?" *Yowch*, that sounded snarky. "Sorry. God, I'm so surprised to see you that I've turned into an idiot."

She scrambled for a more relaxed tone. "I heard somewhere you were in Europe. Where's home these days?" Better. That sounded sufficiently unaffected.

"I live in London, though I spend most of my days on the road." He paused and glanced down at her hands for a blink, then he smiled again.

Damn him. She'd been arrested by that smile the first time he'd turned it toward her.

"Jules," he murmured, "come sit down for a moment. Please." He gestured to the table behind him.

Sorely tempted, she shook her head. "I've got to get back to the store. I just came to pick up dinner for the staff." She scrabbled for solid ground. Had the room gotten smaller, hotter? It was like fighting a whirlpool that wanted to suck her back into the past.

Maisie barreled through the kitchen door, hefting several large plastic bags of to-go containers. She set them down beside Juliette and wiped her brow. "Whew. That's the lot, Ms. Rochambeau. Twelve orders of shrimp and grits. A side of cobbler for each. We boxed the dessert separate, so's the two don't mix. William said ta tell ya there's a gallon of good vanilla ice cream wrapped up tight too."

Juliette smiled her thanks at the girl and handed her the card she managed to free from her wallet. She had to get the hell out here before she lost what was left of her self-control and buried her face in his neck. Or punched him for throwing her away like week-old meatloaf.

She slipped her purse strap onto her shoulder and reached for the food. Refusing to let herself meet his eyes was a solid survival tactic. "Sorry. Gotta feed the troops."

Becket stepped to her side and brushed her hands away from the sacks. She studiously ignored the flex of his arms as he jockeyed for a grip on the bags.

"I'll help you out with these, then." He sounded disappointed. Was he? Well, he should be. Showing up like this, unwanted, uninvited, and pouring fertilizer on old buried wounds.

"Thanks, but I can..." She stopped when he frowned at her over his shoulder. "Oh, okay, then. I'll get the door." Gentleman. Sometimes she forgot how nice that was.

She accepted the returned credit card and pushed open the door. "Tell William we appreciate the quick service." The waitress beamed back at her; Rochambeau had left the business a good deal richer today.

"You gonna open the trunk, or do you want it in the back seat?" Beck's voice was tight, and she regretted, just for a second, not sitting down with him.

She responded by popping the enormous trunk. Trust her mother to drive a car big enough to hide several bodies in the rear end. He loaded the bags carefully, and she used the moment to study him more closely. His hair was the same intriguing mix of color from blond to dark brown, as though the sun had affected each strand differently. Stubble darkened his jaw, accentuating the square lines. She suppressed the urge to graze his ear with a finger to make him shudder. She had no business doing anything of the kind.

"Am I so different?" His question was soft.

She jumped when their gazes connected. "Not *so* different. Changed, though. We've both changed, Becket. Grown up." She slammed the trunk closed and began to slip past him.

"Not that much, Juliette." His large hand closed around her upper arm, and he stopped her motion. "I've missed you." He took a deep breath, then let it slowly out, ruffling her hair. "I didn't mean to hurt you, Jules." And he dropped a kiss on the corner of her mouth.

Her startled gasp was pure self-preservation. "I got over it. Now, if you'll excuse me, I have to get back to the store." She brushed off his hand and darted for the car door.

"Yeah, I read about your trouble. You weren't here when it happened?"

"No, I just missed the excitement. We'll come through. We always do. Daddy's pretty rattled." Daddy wasn't the only one.

He followed her to the driver's door. "I'll be here for the next couple of weeks, Jules." He hesitated, as though he was making up his mind. Like he wasn't sure if what he was about to say was a good idea. "Let me take you to dinner. I don't want to miss the chance to spend some time with you."

Definitely not a good idea. Not if she wanted to remain in one piece. Becket had the power to take her apart from the inside out. He always had. She found herself saying, "I'll think about it. Call the store. I'll be there." She struggled to control the quiver overtaking her hands as she climbed into the driver's seat.

He nodded and closed the heavy door behind her. "I'll be sure to do that," he said as his fingers flexed on the window frame just an inch from her bare skin. A fingertip brushed her shoulder, and her hand stilled on the key.

"This was an incredible surprise. We need to talk.

I'll see you soon, Jules."

The Cadillac roared to life. She glanced at him before she took off like a scalded cat and screeched around the next corner. As soon as he was out of her rearview mirror, she slowed and pulled off the street. Mind racing and hands shaking, she couldn't get her lungs to work properly. What the hell was wrong with her? Damn it. She didn't need to be dealing with this right now. She had an important job to do, a business to put back together, a family to tend to, a life to live. She didn't need the complication of an old dream jumping back to life like a ghost from the grave.

Becket Ford was dangerous to her peace of mind and her buried heart. The first tear leaked past her eyelashes, and she dashed it away angrily.

Chapter Four

He stood like a fool drooling in the dust while the Caddy raced down the block. He couldn't gather enough rational thought to move off the spot where she'd left him. Jules didn't suffer the same problem. She'd been in a huge fucking hurry to dismiss the connections arcing between them.

The current of awareness that flashed to life at their first sight of one another hummed beneath his skin. That had always been their way. Instant chemistry, spontaneous combustion, and pain the likes of which he didn't know he'd survive a second time. Strange how the years wrapped experiences in a cotton candy blanket. They became sweeter, less devastating; then the sugar high wore off, and they took on the power to kick him to pieces.

Why couldn't she have let herself go or popped out a raft of kids? She was so much the same, with her blonde hair pulled up in a ponytail, cut off denim shorts, and legs for days. Her smile remained as breathlessly beautiful as ever, and her face was still open and unlined. At the same time, some not-so-subtle differences advertised the passage of the years. The long, lean lines and colt-like beauty of a young woman not yet at her peak were engraved on his memories. But now, softly defined muscle joined curves only hinted at years ago. Her breasts—he stopped and swallowed—

gorgeous. Spectacular. Her narrow waist flowed into hips flared in the tantalizing way he relished. He'd wanted to grab her so badly he'd had to jam his fists into his pockets.

Get a grip. He should've anticipated this. Should've been ready for the jolting strike of that first look. Seeing her again left him reeling, all his expectations blown to smithereens by the power that streaked across space and skewered him. Her eyes had flared in shocked surprise, and he'd watched her face bloom with color as she took a halting step toward him. He wanted to spring across the restaurant and consume her. Savor the softness of her mouth as he claimed it.

He tunneled his hands into his hair and kicked at an imaginary rock on the sidewalk. "Christ, this is…fucking crazy is what this is." He'd *known* he'd see her eventually; he'd have to. Planned to make it happen under precisely orchestrated terms. Calculated and controlled. Not like this, not by chance when he was so woefully unprepared to do more than stammer and stare after her like a moonstruck kid. *Smooth, Becket.* Angry at himself, he turned on his heel and straight-legged it down the street, mindlessly putting one foot in front of the other. He needed movement. Distance. Clarity.

The same way it had a decade ago, his world shifted on its axis when Jules dropped into his life. When they'd first met, raging teenage hormones ruled their lives. They'd breathed in each second as if it were their last. And now, crash bang, those feelings were alive and kicking? Stuff like that just shouldn't happen.

Still, he couldn't deny the ember lying just below the surface. It was poised and waiting for a breeze to jump back to flame. Was that what he wanted—a

41

chance to redress old injuries? The idea was inane, considering the reason he was back in town. No. Trying to pull that off was pointless. If she ever made the connection, she'd slam the door so tight he'd never pry it open again.

As far as he knew, she'd never made him for who he'd been back then. God knew he'd worked hard to keep it that way. With his stepfather, Hank Santos, building his violent gang of vagrants and thieves into "The Santos Syndicate," times hadn't lent themselves toward teenage love affairs. The day old Hank caught wind of their romance had been the day Beck knew he had to run. She was safer away from him, and he was better off a continent away from temptation.

"Christ, Becket, don't be stupid," he mumbled. "You don't get to have the main course *and* the dessert. Do the job you came here to do and buy back your life." He turned another mindless corner and stopped to get his bearings. His attempt to walk off the morass of memories and attraction landed him in a small park within throwing distance of the harbor. And right back to the central issue—could he put aside their past and do what was needed to ensure his future? If he had one.

He found an iron bench and planted his butt, long legs outstretched, arms extended along the back of the sun-warmed metal. Beyond him, the gulls cried out their frustration while they searched for their next meal. Beck could relate. He shouldn't be fretting over shit he couldn't change. He had his share of regrets. Who didn't? This town had a way of dragging them all into the light. Leaving Jules the way he had was one of the top two.

He took in his surroundings and realized he hadn't

been far from here the first time he'd seen her. She was walking the tide line. Her hair was a halo of light around her shoulders like a cape lit on fire by the setting sun. A bright turquoise scarf, meant to control her wild mass of curls, fluttered around her neck.

Hell, he'd known immediately she was too good for him. Too squeaky clean to get mixed up with a punk from a family like his. He never understood what had gotten her attention that day. Was it the bad boy outfit and the I-don't-give-a-shit attitude that was part of his appeal? Rebel without a clue—damn sure him as a teenager.

Without even knowing it, Jules handed him the chance to change his path. Had he taken it? No, he'd willingly continued to ply the only trade he knew. Why bother trying to deny it—while part of him dreamed he'd go straight, the rest of him got off on the rush like a junky jonesing for a needle. The high from a job was a fix that still took his breath away. He'd never be able to give it up. Never be more than a thief.

He scoffed at his foolishness. Once upon a time, he "coulda been a contenda" for a different life. Unfortunately, like Brando's character, he'd been so busy fighting to succeed that he lost sight of his goal. It didn't matter now. Going straight was pure fantasy— the unachievable version of Becket Ford.

But Juliette Rochambeau, damn it all, still had the power to make him long for the unattainable.

She was the most direct course to the necklace, and if he were a different man, he wouldn't think twice about using her. If only old Bernie Greenleaf hadn't impressed upon him the importance of deciding on exactly the type of man he wanted to be. Sure, he was a thief, but he still had a code to live by. Using a mark's greed against them was one thing. Fucking with an innocent woman's emotions to steal her blind was base and feckless. Seeing her again made it harder than he expected. She was temptation served up on a silver platter, no doubt there.

If he ruled out the "sweetheart scam," his only remaining option was straight-up B&E. Had she ever connected him to the Santos family? The chance was slim. If he was wrong, Fanish Singh would find a way to terminate him and Renée both. At best, a very slender thread on which to hang his continued existence.

He was so deep in his head he nearly levitated off the bench when his stepbrother's voice dropped over his shoulder.

"Well, well. If it ain't Becket fuckin' Ford. Where you been so long, bro?" Seth settled onto the bench beside him. "You out for a stroll? Takin' in the view?"

Becket folded his arms to his chest and leaned back to take in the man. His stepbrother's perpetual sneer still pegged him for a cocky, feral bastard. It became especially evident when he was applying casual intimidation.

"Livin' the good life, Seth. How 'bout you? You keepin' it real?" He didn't give a flying fuck if Seth was hale and hardy or not. The jackass had crawled out of the weeds for a reason—Singh had made good on his promise.

Seth's smile was crafty and challenging. "Oh, yeah, yeah. Business is good. You ought to try it. Matter of fact, I could find you a place in my organization. For old times' sake, you know." His "love" for Beck was plain on his severe face.

"No, thanks, *bro*. Got to give you props, though. I expected your guys to clock me, but I didn't pick up on 'em. They must be pretty good." Accurate, much as he hated to admit it. While he was at it, he'd plump up Seth's egotistical pretensions to Hank's pompous title of crime lord. Another little lesson from Bernie, *help them to underestimate you.* "I'm glad you took the time to look me up. Our mutual friend thought you might come in handy."

Seth ignored the slight. "Yeah, well, we do our best. We didn't want to get in the way of your reunion. How'd the meet and greet go with your old girlfriend?" He shook his head and let out a satisfied sound. "Mm, mmm. She's even more of a looker than I remembered, ain't she? Them legs, that rack? Damn, some things change for the better."

Beck's blood pressure increased a tick. Seth was baiting him. He kept the fact that it pissed him off to himself. He laughed humorlessly and clapped his stepbrother on the back. "Don't waste your time tryin' to get under my skin. You know I wouldn't be here unless the client sent me. His confidence in you is rocky all of a sudden. The way he tells it, you fucked up big time. I said, no way—my big bro Seth is a pro, a stand-up, stone-cold baller." Beck raised his eyebrows and smirked while he waited out Seth's reaction.

A muscle jumped in Seth's jaw. Score one for Beck. "Some things didn't go like expected, that's all. So you're gonna make another run on the necklace, huh? Gonna play her pretty ass and get more for your time than kudos from the big guy? Gotta say he's really got a hard-on for that trinket."

Beck did his best not to stiffen. Which trinket was he referring to?

"Makes me wonder if there's somethin' about it he ain't sharin'."

Relieved, Beck shrugged. "It doesn't matter to me one way or the other. I'm just doin' the big guy a favor. He asked me to come over and make sure the job was done right. No offense intended."

Seth pursed his lips and nodded as he sucked air through his front teeth. "None taken. We did all right and got a hefty cut. That's a win in my book." He slapped his scarred hands on both knees and pushed to his feet. He offered a handshake to Beck. "If you need my help, you be sure to gimme a shout. You know the number." He shook Beck's hand hard enough to leave prints behind. He jerked his chin up in farewell and strolled away along the battery. "Don't be a stranger now, ya hear?"

"I'll be sure to do that, *bro,*" Becket said to himself as Seth sauntered off. A distance down the seawall, he joined two other guys. One small and darkly dangerous. The other a tall, hard-body with sparse red hair. He filed both men in his head for future reference.

****

Juliette resolutely pushed her run-in with Becket, as well as the lingering desires accompanying them, into a corner of her mind. Her spoon grated the to-go container, making nails-on-a-chalkboard squeaks as she chased the last bite of sumptuous peach cobbler.

She'd managed to avoid Roland by slipping into her father's inner sanctum. "Office" was a kind term for the room, ten feet by twelve, windowless, and crammed full of stacked banker's boxes. The desk hunkered in a corner with barely enough space to sit down. The room more closely resembled hoarder central than the hub of a multi-million-dollar retail operation. She tsked at the antiquated methods her father clung to as stubbornly as he did the necklace. At the very least, she had to talk him into modernizing the recordkeeping and find a way to get all these files digitized—a Herculean task.

A shuffling noise drew her attention, and then a soft knock tapped the door. "Come in if you can find a place to stand," she called around the squeaking of the cobbler container's death.

Chet stuck his head through a crack in the door. His shock of white hair was held down by the magnifying headgear he wore like a forgotten Fedora. His brow wrinkled in an uncertain frown, and he glanced back over his shoulder as though afraid someone was in ear-shot. "Hey, Miss Juliette. Gabby and I were hoping to get a moment before you went back upstairs."

"Sure. There's not much room in here for a conference, but I'm all yours. What's up?"

"That's just it. We want to keep this private if you don't mind. Would you mind meeting us at the Pelican?"

She raised an eyebrow. Marvelous, what now? Warning bells started clanging in her head.

Chet and Gabby were stabilizing elements in the tightly woven club that was Rochambeau. Gabby's twenty-year tenure eclipsed Chet by two years. For the most part, the jewelry industry was a Gypsy's haven. Jewelers moved from company to company seasonally, some never finding a fit for their personality and skill level. For someone to stay attached to a business for longer than a couple of years was unusual—more than ten, a miracle.

"Uh, sure. If it's truly necessary." She swallowed hard. "Please, God, tell me you're not quitting. That would be the last straw for me today."

Chet coughed nervously and gave her an encouraging smile. "Good golly, no. There're some stuff you should know is all." Tall, with heavily muscled arms and broad work-roughened hands, his physique belied his ability to produce delicate, ephemeral jewelry. His eyes twinkled at her, reminding her that he wasn't afraid to use his good looks to get his way.

"Okay, give me a few minutes, and I'll meet you there." She frowned in concern at Chet.

His smile became relieved. "Thanks, Miss Juliette. See you soon." The door clicked shut behind him. A tickle of apprehension raised gooseflesh on her arms. What in the world? Clandestine meetings? At times this place was like a private soap opera.

She tossed the Styrofoam clamshell and wiped her fingers on the thin paper napkin. Curiosity, more than pique, got her out of the chair. Coming home was so much more complicated than she'd ever expected. The tendrils of commitment were snaking around her ankles like kudzu vines. Pervasive, tenacious, and hard to kill.

Just down the street, The Pelican Grill was more bar than grill, despite the advertising. She had to pause in the door to let her eyes adjust to the dim interior. Zydeco music played quietly on an old jukebox whose neon halo provided a soft glow to the small dancefloor at the far end of the narrow bar. She spotted the covert duo tucked into a booth in the back.

"Don't you two look cozy," she said as she dropped onto the vinyl bench seat across from Gabby.

Gabby's mouth turned down in disapproval. "He's so stubborn. I told him this was crazy." Her attachment to the lead jeweler was a widely ignored secret at the store.

"Somebody's got to know, Gab. It's not right to hold this back. Besides, the boss was going to talk to her." Chet patted Gabby's hand. "Go on, show her."

Gabby gave an elegant shrug and made a uniquely French noise of resignation. "We were trying to decide a way to tell you, but well…then *la catastrophe*." She dipped a hand into the oversized bag at her side and drew out a rectangular, leather-covered jewelry box. The company's burnished gold emblem was stamped proudly on the cover.

Juliette frowned and drew the case to her with a tentative fingertip. "What's this, then, contraband?" She pressed the small brass clasp button, and her breath caught. Nestled on the creamy silk interior lay the Rochambeau necklace. The sparkle of the stones simmered in the low light of the jukebox.

She slammed the lid closed and glanced around them. "My God," she whispered furiously. "Are you crazy? This shouldn't be out of the store!" Well over a million dollars' worth of trouble lay on a cheap Formica table in a seedy-ass bar. All she needed was to get knocked in the head by an opportunistic snoop. She clasped the leather box closed and shoved it toward Gabby. "Put that away before anyone gets nosey."

Gabby grinned broadly. "See? I told you it was good." She glanced at her partner in crime affectionately.

49

Juliette blinked at her for a second. "Now would be an excellent time to tell me what the hell is going on." She couldn't fathom why they'd be so reckless.

Chet hunched his shoulder and refused to look her in the eye. "Okay, okay. Your daddy's gonna kill me for telling you." He chugged a couple of swallows of the beer in front of him, screwed his eyes shut, and nodded to the box. "It's a copy."

She shook her head. "Uh…say what now?"

"A copy, a good one. I made it. I mean, Mr. Edward asked me to make it, and then I did. The point is—"

Juliette held up a hand and stopped him. "I really can't take much more of the drama, ya know?" Jesus H. Christ. Robberies, infighting, a father who had commissioned a copy of the family jewels and then almost got himself killed over the originals. A mother who wanted, what—she had no idea. And, oh yeah, an old freakin' boyfriend. What was next, zombies? At least she had the tools for that. A giggle rolled up her throat at the list of stupendously incongruous shit she'd been handed. The giggle became a chuckle, then a guffaw. And she lost it. Her unhinged laugh filled their booth till she had to wipe her eyes and fan herself to cool off. Day drinking suddenly sounded like a solid plan. "Barkeep? I'd like a *very* large gin and tonic, and my coconspirators will have another round." She swirled her finger over their glasses and grinned at the dumbfounded faces across from her. "Sorry, that was inappropriate. But come on. Seriously?"

Gabby tilted her head disapprovingly and tapped the silk-lined box. "It was your father's idea, and we don't know why he wanted it made." Her voice took on a defensive note. "Things have been taking some strange turns lately, and we thought someone else should know about it. We're only trying to help." Her voice faltered, and Chet broke in.

"It's okay, Gab. This is tougher than I thought it'd be." He forced out an exasperated breath. "Look, Miss Juliette, we don't want to cause you or your folks any more problems. God knows there's enough to go around." He paused and leaned forward. "This copy cost the store around ninety grand. A lot of money to spend on a whim, wouldn't you say? We can't come up with a reason aside from one—and that's just speculation." He took a deep swallow of liquid courage and plunged ahead. "I hate secrets and double-dealing. Especially when it comes in the form of family. Your daddy was planning on filling you in, but what with the robbery and all...we thought you should know before anything else happens."

The bartender dropped their drinks on the table and cast a curious eyeball at the group. Gabby's imperious wave shooed him away.

Juliette's amusement faded completely. "Anything else? Like what, for instance?"

"It's complicated, and the copy is only part of the story." Chet cleared his throat and glanced at Gabby.

She gave him an encouraging nod.

"It's been so crazy since the robbery. I don't guess you've had a chance to check out the books."

Juliette frowned at his change of direction. She grabbed for patience and squinted at him. "The books?" She'd been too busy putting out fires to get into the day-to-day. "No, not yet. I haven't had time. And who's we?"

"Charley, Gabby, and me. We started comparing notes about the same time your daddy asked me to build the copy. We feel there's no doubt; there's a weasel in the henhouse—someone's stealing from the family."

All right, so someone was getting greedy. It happened even in the best of companies. They'd have to institute better double checks on incoming shipments and tighten measures on inventory control. "Okay. You've got my attention. Who tops your list for employee of the year?"

"Don't you see? It's all part of a bigger picture." He ticked off his list. "First, the copy I had to build on the down-low. Then shortages. Then Mr. Edward agrees to lend the necklace to the Smithsonian—then all hell breaks loose with the attack. Call me paranoid, but I think the timing was very convenient for whoever's been double-dipping, don't you think?"

"Wait. What are you getting at?" Her mind jumped forward. A wild thought popped to the surface. "Are—are you saying someone planned the break-in? Staged it—as a cover-up?"

Chet cleared his throat and sucked down the last of his beer. Even in the dim light of the bar, his face was beet red.

Gabby gave Chet an encouraging pat. "Just say it, *mon cher*."

His face was so pained Juliette favored him with a sympathetic smile.

"I'm sorry to tell you this way." The words tumbled out in a rush. "We believe Roland's been using the store to bankroll his gambling losses. He's put himself in a position to do it with no interference, and your daddy has been letting it happen."

Juliette's smile disappeared. "Gambling. You know this, how?"

Chet shrugged and shot a guilty glance at Gabby. "I play cards some. Charleston is a small town with a shallow pond of enthusiasts. Word gets around." Gabby tsked and shoved his shoulder.

All the pieces fell like a trail of dominos right into her uncle's lap. Sad but true, she had little trouble accepting it. Why else would he be so busy causing a stink over the inventories and generally getting on everyone's last nerve? It certainly wasn't because he wanted to win over the staff; half of them would as soon see him strung up by his thumbs. "All right, I'll bite. If it's true, and he's been using us as his bank, he needs to convert it to cash or something, right? So who can make that happen, and where do I find them?"

"Now hold on there, Miss Juliette. That's a real bad idea. Ain't your folks got enough to worry about? They don't need you out there stumbling around in the muck."

Juliette's hearing retreated behind the waves of blood surging in her ears. Her breathing sawed in and out as she worked to control the angry pressure building inside her chest. The unmitigated, unfeeling, and callous *nerve* of Roland to use his own brother this way. Pissed off like she'd stepped in a fire-ant mound, she sprang to her feet and paced the short distance to the jukebox and back. She grabbed her glass and downed it in one go. "I'm callin' the police on the pond-suckin', slimy fucking bastard," she said furiously. Her glass cracked down on the scarred Formica, and she slid the jewelry box off the surface and into her bag. They moved to join her, and she stopped them with a glare. "First, I need to talk to my daddy. He's got some 'splaining to do."

Chapter Five

She stomped her way back to the store, telling herself to cool off and be rational. Chet had said her father was letting it happen. A connection had to exist between Roland's underhanded ways and the copy. Either that or her father was suddenly in the replica jewelry business. That idea was as farfetched as Roland abruptly becoming an Eagle Scout.

Juliette leaned against the door frame of her parents' bedroom. A nest of pillows propped her father up against his headboard. His reading glasses clung to the end of his nose. Her mother curled up in a chair, tablet in her lap and earbuds tucked neatly in her ears. She hesitated, watching them and cautioning herself to refrain from straight-up interrogation. "Hey, you guys up for a chat?"

Edward nodded and beckoned her in.

Evie plucked out her buds and smiled up at her. "Sure, sugar plum. Where you been?"

"I was in a meeting—with Chet and Gabby." Her parents glanced at each other, and Juliette narrowed her eyes suspiciously. "Want to tell me what the heck is going on? They had all kinds of interesting speculation and no answers." It was time for that "come to Jesus" moment she'd anticipated when she stepped off the plane from New York.

Edward cleared his throat uncomfortably and gave

Evie the go-ahead nod. Evie rose and moved to his side, protectively. She clasped his hand, and Juliette got the distinct impression that this wasn't going to be the type of family meeting that left her all warm and fuzzy.

"This isn't going to be easy to hear, sugar. So let's all remain calm, okay?" Evie raised her chin and took a deep breath. "I promise we'll answer whatever questions you have. Just let us have our say before you ask, okay?"

Juliette's chin automatically copied her mother's. "Jesus, more melodrama. Great, y'all. Just spit it out, please."

Edward leaned back against the cushions and crossed his arms. His brow pulled down, and he gave her what she used to call the eagle-eye glare. It was the look he only used before he laid down the law. "That will be enough attitude from you, Juliette Therese."

She flinched. He'd pulled out both names, not a good omen. Backing off a bit was the best course. "Okay, no need to look forbidding." She moved to the bedside and leaned against the plush edge.

"We intended to have this conversation with you under different circumstances, but—" His hand touched the bandage covering the sutures on his forehead. He pulled off his glasses, and his face creased with fatigue. "I hoped I'd have more time." He sighed and patted Evie's hand. "Mama said she'd tell you so I wouldn't have to. Yet here we are."

He sounded so defeated her anger evaporated. Her eyes closed. *Now what?* Her footing wavered, poised for the fall. This was about more than the copy. "Okay, now I'm officially freaked out. What is it?"

"First, let me say we weren't hiding this from you,

honey. It's been so crazy since the robbery that our plans got derailed." Evie's grip on Edward's hand tightened. "We want you to know that everything is going to be all right, and your daddy will be fine if he stops being stubborn."

Juliette's chest constricted in fear like a deer trapped in the headlights of an oncoming car. A strangled noise escaped her throat as she braced for impact.

Edward reached for her, and once her hand was in his, he sighed deeply. He studied her placidly for a moment. "I've had a health scare, sugar. A series of…they call 'em silent heart attacks." His grip tightened on hers. "The doctors say I need to make some changes, and if I don't…well, the outcome could be serious. I've been going through tests, and my doctors are working to figure it out. Stress is a big part of it. It's frightening as hell; I can tell you that."

Her legs wobbled, and her pulse galloped unevenly as her mind jumped to the worst-case scenario. Was he dying, leaving her without an anchor? Pain, sharp as a dagger, lanced her like a physical blow. Her eyes stung, and she clamped down on the urge to throw her arms around him. Her father was a man who didn't appreciate hysterics in his women. She had a role to play—controlled, respectful, distant. "I see. And you guys didn't think I needed to know. So I guess there's no need to worry, huh?" She clenched her jaw and did her best to keep her chin from quivering.

"Now, sugar, don't get your back up. I'll be fine." He offered her a soft, apologetic smile as he patted the mattress.

Her rigid shoulders dropped, and she crawled up

beside him, grateful that he understood her need to comfort and be comforted.

He laid his hand on her knee. "Ahh, Jesus, sugar, I'm sorry we dumped it on you. I truly am." His breath gusted out in a long sigh.

Juliette was sure he could see every crack in her façade. Some daughter she was. Stressors had been piling up by the bucketload at home while she'd been playing the isolation game and blaming them for its existence. She was acting like a whiney, self-centered little shit.

Evie chimed in. "And so am I, honey. Truly. Though I've got to say, I could use some help convincing him to slow down and take some time off. We'd hoped to do that after the Smithsonian people were here. Maybe take that cruise we've been putting off for years."

Juliette chimed in. "If that will do the trick, then yeah, that's exactly what you should do. I'll arrange for a leave of absence from my job and hold down the fort. Don't worry about this place. I got this." Wait, had she just offered to do what she'd avoided like the plague for the last ten years? Yup, that was what she'd done, and surprisingly, the prospect didn't feel as repugnant as she'd expected.

He reached out and tweaked her nose. "Don't get ahead of yourself, sugar. I'm cleaning up my act, and your mama is cramming rabbit food down my throat till I choke. She's even got us signed up for yoga classes. I'm a little worried about how my fanny will look in those stretchy pants, though."

An unexpected laugh burst out. "Oh, Daddy." Despite herself, a sniffle snuck past her. It was just like him to make fun of a life-threatening heart condition. "I'll help you find a getup that's not professional suicide."

"There's my girl." He patted her cheek, and she focused on his face as he composed his expression into the controlled, self-possessed man he'd always been. They both had roles to play. "Back to business. You talked to Chet, huh? Judgin' by the steam rollin' off you when you got here, he must have given you an ear full."

She took a deep breath and jumped in despite herself. "That's an understatement. A few other 'minor things' y'all didn't see fit to share." *Cool and calm.* "Like a replica of a certain French necklace? Like issues with accounting. Embezzlement level issues. Charles, Gabby, and Chet are pointing fingers at your brother. Is that a surprise, or have you been ignoring the situation for a reason?"

His eyes popped open wide. "I—uh. Well, you weren't to know about that. Chet and I will be havin' words tomorrow." He leaned against the cushions and crossed his arms.

Evie frowned at the both of them. "This is exactly the kind of situation you're supposed to be avoiding." She tossed her hands in the air and plopped back down in her chair. "I told you a year ago to fire him, and you wouldn't hear of it. How long before you'll bite the bullet and do what needs doin'?"

Whoa. Juliette could count on one hand the number of times she'd heard her parents disagree. Arguing couldn't be good for anyone's heart, especially his.

Edward's jaw clenched tight, and his color deepened. "All right, all right." He slashed the air. "It's true, Roland's been helpin' himself to more than he deserves." He gave Evie a scathing look. "Never had the proof I needed to make the charge stick. Roland isn't stupid, and he's covered his tracks. I knew I'd have to catch him red-handed and was ready to dangle a tempting carrot under his nose. He beat me to the punch."

"Are you kiddin' me?" She was shocked he'd admit it. "That's the reason you spent countless dollars having a copy made? The copy was bait."

Evie made a disgusted noise from her chair and glared at her husband. "Look up hack-brained in the dictionary, and there's his picture."

Wow, her world used to be so ordinary—now she was hip-deep in family intrigue. Roland wasn't a man who'd come out into the daylight to make his move. His criminal deceit struck her father harder than the loss of a few bucks. This level of treachery transcended sibling rivalry and pure jealousy. "So Chet is right. You think Roland's up to his eyeballs in the robbery. I don't get why you didn't just bust his ass."

"Again, I couldn't prove it. I shoulda known he'd get greedy."

"What the hell, Daddy? What happened to the guy who used to ground me for skipping class? This is a wee bit more serious than that, wouldn't you say? Chet told me you'd been carting the original around with you like a baby you were afraid to put down. Why drag your feet?"

He tossed his hands helplessly. "Who'd have imagined I'd have to plot the arrest of my *own brother*? I've always tried to make his life better, and look how he repaid me." He slumped. The hurt in his eyes belied his stiff-upper-lip demeanor.

Evie shook off her snit and moved to comfort him.

"I'd planned on making the switch the very day those goons came bustin' in. When push came to shove, the only thing I could do was hold on to the necklace for all I was worth. Roland stepped in and kept me from getting hurt worse than I did."

Damn. Roland had always been an entitled shit, taking more than he gave and expecting applause when he deserved none. "Yeah, sure, Saint Roland." Revenge wasn't an everyday indulgence for Juliette. Still, if they could prove Roland guilty, the taste would be like hot, sweet honey. She composed her smile into a less bloodthirsty version than the one that wanted to break free. Forcing Roland out was the right thing to do for everyone. She needed to take the heat off her father, not make it worse by berating. "All right, if you can't stomach having him arrested—" She waited for confirmation, and he made an oh-well gesture. "—then please, oh please, let me be the one who sacks his skinny butt. I'd love that."

She was surprised when he barked out a laugh and nodded. "Knock yourself out. I don't have it in me to deal with this now. He's more'n likely downstairs." She reached for the phone on the bedside table, and he stopped her. "Makes me look like a coward, I know." Resigned and exhausted, he adjusted his back against the cushions. "There are some other issues to discuss, but I'm just too tired tonight." He patted her cheek and closed his eyes.

"It's high time, I'd say." Evie twitched the covers up around him. "I'll see your daddy settled, and then I'll be out directly, Lettie. You don't have to worry,

Edward. We'll take care of it."

Juliette ran a hand over his hair. He'd aged in the blink of an eye. The skin on his expressive face was drawn, and the usually ruddy color was suddenly pale. "You rest, Daddy. We'll go deal with the serpent in the garden, all right?"

He nodded without opening his eyes. She kissed his forehead and righted her shoulders. She had a snake to hoe.

Her father was grumbling about being coddled when she left the bedroom for her parents' living room and the confrontation to come. Her plan was simple— drop the ax and call the cops if need be. To make sure she wasn't on her own when it fell, she called down to the shop and asked that the men remain on site. Chet and the boys were waiting in the wings to jump in if necessary.

They sure as hell didn't need her father having another heart attack while she was playing executioner. She'd never been in this position before, and she was entirely in the dark as to proper procedure when accusing a family member of outright theft. Subterfuge sounded like a good approach—perhaps a meeting to "go over the losses." And then she'd just—wing it.

She even managed to sound competent when she called for a face-to-face with the bastard. Charles answered the office line. "Charles, do me a favor. Ask Roland to bring the figures up here."

"Uh, just Roland? I think I need to be in on this too, don't you?" Charles, bless his heart, didn't want her to face the slimeball on her own.

She loved him for it. "Okay, nanny. Sure, you can guard my back."

He was chuckling when she hung up on him.

While she waited for them to arrive, her bravado began to slip. She shook out her arms and stretched her legs like she was warming up for a fight. The closest she'd ever come to a physical confrontation was avoiding being backed into a corner by a handsy customer. Her usual tactic was to use her height advantage and an imperious scowl. Let them know that if they got inappropriate during an appraisal, their "family jewels" were in danger of becoming acquainted with her knee. She hoped she wouldn't have to go further than a good old shouting match with Roland, but she just didn't know. She paced impatiently until the elevator clanked its way uphill.

"Gentlemen." Her tone was flat as she greeted them. "Let's get to it, shall we?" She indicated the couch.

Charles looked nervous as he arranged the files on the coffee table. Roland's put-out expression only served to strengthen her backbone.

"It isn't good, Miss Juliette, not good at all." Charles sat in a sad lump on the small settee and watched her pace as she listened to the report. "They got half of the loose stone inventory and most of the finished goods. We'll be hard-pressed to reopen, let alone survive the year. Some of those pieces were memo goods, and I've got my doubts as to whether the suppliers will be willing to front us more merchandise. Insurance is making noise about inadequate security. So you can bet they'll be dragging their feet about handing out money."

Roland relaxed in her father's favorite leather chair as if he owned it. "This would be the right moment to talk about the future of the store." His deep voice was concerned and fatalistic. "If there is one."

Juliette stopped her pacing and stared her uncle down. "That's the last time I want to hear drivel like *that* from anyone, especially you. We're a long way from spouting doom and gloom. We only lost a few pieces of customer merchandise, and we should be grateful it wasn't worse. As to the inventory, you've completed the assessment of loss. We've been customers of Lloyds for ninety years. That has to count, right? We'll deal with them tomorrow." She paused before delivering her coup de grace. "Now, as to how we will handle the store going forward. Daddy has asked me to take over temporary charge of the business, and I'd appreciate all the help you can give me."

Roland exploded to his feet. "He what?" His entire body tensed, poised and ready for a fight.

She stood her ground. "You heard me. I'm sorry you're upset, but in case you don't remember, this isn't a democracy. The only vote here belongs to Edward Rochambeau. As of now, and until further notice, I'm in control."

Roland took a threatening step toward her. "Where's my brother? I won't stand for this. He—he has no right to do this. I've been in charge of operations for the last two years, and he's never had cause to complain." His voice rang with self-righteous indignation.

"Daddy is resting. He asked me to handle this." Okay, physical contact wasn't out of the question.

"What's changed? Huh? You tell me." His hands balled into fists, and she eyed him warily.

"You'd best back off that attitude, Roland. You're

on very thin ice." She glared at him, not giving an inch. "If I thought for one second you were as good a man as your brother, I wouldn't have taken this step."

"What lies did you feed him to get him to do this?"

"Lies? That's a laugh." She narrowed her eyes and squared off with him. Damned if she let this slimeball cow her into being the meek kid she used to be. "In the last few hours, staff members have come to me with some interesting information, *Uncle*. The consensus is that your accounting practices are extremely creative. They told me you've been spending big bucks at some of the local clubs, specifically Longfellow's and The Cajun. Even I know those places have high-stakes poker tables and run a cutthroat business in craps and roulette." She paused for effect. He sputtered out a denial, and she shut him up with a theatrical "cut" motion beneath her chin. "Now I realize you're arrogant enough to think that nobody would dare mention seeing you there, let alone share that knowledge. It turns out that's not the case." She glanced away and caught Charles smothering a smile behind his glass of bourbon. She took his lead and backed away to pour one for herself.

Roland was determined to pile it on higher and deeper. "I've been to both those clubs, sure. Who hasn't occasionally? That proves what, exactly? Are you making an accusation, little miss? If so, you'd best make it plain, and you'd best make it stick. Because, believe you me, I'll sue your sanctimonious ass for libel and defamation of character if you can't."

She warmed to the fight. "Know what? I don't have to prove shit; all I have to do is whiff the *smell*. The laws in this state are pretty clear on that point."

She took a long sip of the smooth, burning liquor in her glass. Over his shoulder, she spotted her mother frozen in the hallway. Their gazes connected, and Evie's nod of approval was bolstering as she joined the fray. She moved past Roland and took Juliette's glass from her hand, finishing the amber-brown liquid in one swallow.

Evie turned to her brother-in-law and brandished the empty crystal tumbler. "My daughter is right, you know. And frankly, I've had enough of your posturing to last me a lifetime. In case you haven't figured it out, Roland, you're fired. Drop your keys on the table and leave these premises. Immediately."

His hand shot out and swiped at the glass. The crystal flew across the room to shatter in a glittering spray against the wall. He took a step closer to Evie, and Juliette moved in front of her mother. His hand flew up to slap her away. She struck first. One knee crunched into his groin, and the heel of her hand met the end of his nose. A shove to the ground, and he folded like a house of cards. She dusted her palms and stepped away from his moaning carcass.

Evie stared at her daughter in wide-eyed wonder. "Holy Mother of God, sugar plum, your time in the city wasn't wasted after all." She turned to Charles, who'd scrambled behind the couch and gaped on in shock. "Charley, call down to the shop, will you? Ask Chet to bring a couple of the boys up here and walk my brother-in-law off the property. Please make sure he doesn't stuff our property in his pockets on the way out."

Charles came unglued from his fort. "Yes, ma'am." He grabbed the old desk phone next to him and pushed a button on the five-line panel. His rattled request was answered directly when Chet and two men from the shop burst into the living room. They unceremoniously grabbed Roland's arms and jerked him to his feet.

"You'll be sorry for this, both of you." Roland failed to shake off their hold. "You think you've got problems now? Wait till I get done with you." His threats didn't have much punch behind them.

Juliette and her mother stepped out of the way and let the men hustle Roland down the stairs—no elevator ride for her uncle, she noticed. They sat in tense silence until the phone beside them rang, and Juliette answered. She smiled in approval as Chet let her know Roland was "spraying the street with enough crap to fertilize ten acres of Georgia clay."

Evie slumped to the nearest couch and ran her hands through her usually immaculate hair, and a big smile lit up her face. "My gracious, that felt—good." She took Juliette's hand. "Now tell me, was what you said just Yankee bull, or are you actually taking over for your daddy?"

Her mouth was suddenly as dry as dust. "There's no way Daddy'll turn loose of this store. Least of all to me. I took advantage of an opportunity, that's all." The challenge of a business like theirs was daunting. Could she pull it off? If he did turn loose of the reins, was she brave enough to take them?

"I don't know about that, darlin'. I think he's been waiting for you to show an interest in coming home. He knew how far he'd get by forcing the issue. You're too much like me to be bullied." Her mother looked as tired as Juliette felt. "Remember what Grandma Hattie used to say? 'Man plans and God laughs.' " She sighed and yawned. "I'm wrung plum out. You think it over, and we'll talk more later. I'm confident you'll make the right decision."

"Dang, Mama, that sounded suspiciously like a compliment." God, how she used to turn herself inside out for one of those, but they were no longer the hallmarks of her success. She found she had a newly acquired ability to see her parents as people, warts and all. Despite their faults, she loved them, and they loved her. For better or worse, she was home. It was up to her to choose what she made of it—platform or gilded cage.

Chapter Six

Beck dropped his keys into the cup holder beside the driver's seat and patted his full belly. He'd enjoyed an exceptional meal at Bistro Lisanne, a fantastic restaurant around the block from his home away from home. Red snapper, blackened and served on a bed of tender rice slathered by a flavorful sauce of stewed tomatoes and okra. Damn, that was good. He scolded himself for letting the food in Europe supplant the truly extraordinary low-country fare of his hometown.

He'd had a productive five days. Using his cover as an antique buyer, he'd scoped out the other businesses occupying the remainder of Rochambeau's building. A flea market offering space to small antique dealers looked especially promising. The store was dusty and down on its heels despite the stellar location. He'd spoken briefly to some of the stallholders and browsed for several hours among the bric-a-brac covered spaces. The most exciting aspect was its proximity to his target. Convenient and oh so enticing was the common wall the shop shared with Juliette's home on the upper floors.

Tonight was the night for an "unscheduled visit" to their sanctuary. Hopefully a connecting door, long unused and forgotten, joined the two spaces. The building had once been all one space, designed and built to house the biggest cash crop of the South—

cotton. Rochambeau, the oldest commercial resident of the structure, walled off their corner façade using slave-made brick two feet thick in places. The upper stories, however, were clad in a wooden exterior skin of ship-lap lined by plaster and lath. Very negligent on the part of one of the oldest families in Charleston. One could even say—arrogant. *Go ahead on, wave a juicy steak at wolves. Then dismiss the pack as a nuisance and see what happens.*

Small wonder they'd become a tempting prize for Hank Santos. The syndicate operated on muscle power, not brains. The past detailed their mindset quite plainly—three brute-force, armed attacks in the last thirty years. The first attempt was a bust from the get-go. The second one, twenty years back, landed Hank in Broad River Correctional. The last one, although the most successful take wise, put the Rochambeaus into panicky high alert and made his job much harder. Upgrading security systems and modernizing their surveillance was underway. He had to get in, get the prize, and get the hell out in the next couple of days, or resort to the path that churned his gut to a pulp—use his connection to Jules. This time his motives weren't altruistic, and hurting her again would be like chopping off his arm.

He started his car and rolled down the street, gliding quietly past people walking off their dinners or window shopping the quaint storefronts. At half-past ten on a weeknight, the town's busy commerce slowed to a stroll as it settled into bedtime. He made the turn onto Meeting Street and drove past Rochambeau, turning again onto Queen. The alley at the rear of the building was dark as pitch. During his recon earlier in the day, he'd spotted exterior cameras guarding the jewelry store and the silver tape of an old-school trip alarm on the antique mall's windows. Figuring an exterior alarm protected the shop's rear door, he chose the less appealing option, an old fire escape climbing to the second story level. He'd gone so far as to rattle the iron hard and was reasonably sure the structure would hold his weight. He'd be putting that to the test in the next few moments.

He pulled to a quiet halt past the edge of a streetlamp's pool of amber light. As he put on his gloves and zipped his black hoodie to cover his white shirt, he stayed alert for his bird dogs. Seth's boys had kept close tabs on his backside every time he'd stepped out of the house. He'd enjoyed playing hide and seek with them all day. The big redheaded guy needed to rethink his wardrobe. That puke green T-shirt and faded army logo stood out like a sore thumb in a navy town like Charleston. It wasn't Beck's first rodeo, and he'd ditched them for good in a hardware store's cavernous interior. The city bus he'd hopped back to downtown was a welcome break in the action. They'd pick him up again when he returned to his rooms, he was sure.

He tucked a slim penlight and leather-encased lockpicks into the hoodie's deep pocket. To ensure privacy, he popped the cover on the car's interior light and plucked out the tiny bulb. Slipping from the vehicle, he became a moving shadow in the alley's darkness.

He looked up into the skeleton-like bones of the fire escape. Familiar dread prickled his skin. He took a moment to inhale and regretted it immediately. The smell from the dumpster down the alley hung like a putrid warning in the air. The fish in his belly gave a rebellious, twisting roll. He swallowed hard and reached over his head for the ladder's lowest rung. The contraption creaked ominously but held stable as he kipped up to the second step. He gave a solid jump on the ladder and held his breath as the iron shuddered. A shower of rust peppered his head and shoulders. Exposure to the salty wind off the harbor locked the iron rollers tight to the frame.

This was the old-school B&E he *told* himself he loved, a light-footed and graceful Cary Grant-style stroll across the rooftops. He smiled as he recalled a moment long ago with Jules snuggled to his side watching another of the classic films she loved. He wondered if the incongruity of this situation would cause her to laugh along as he gave his interpretation of the fabled jewel thief from "To Catch a Thief." She'd be more likely to club him for putting himself in this position in the first place.

He shook the nervousness out of his hands and scoped out his distance from the ground. He forced a grin to relax his stiff jaw as he climbed the rungs and landed surefooted on the grill-covered top platform. It was dead quiet in the alley below. No sign of the oafish redhead or anyone else, save a skinny alley cat slinking away from the dumpster's overflowing contents. "Better pickings down the block, buddy," he said quietly. The cat's tail gave him the one-fingered salute as it prowled its way into the night. Beck's smile became genuine.

He quickly picked the door's lock and disabled the old-style magnetic sensor designed to trip an exterior alarm. He was frankly surprised they'd bothered to go that far. He slipped past the door and flashed his light around the crowded space. In the far corner, he found a dangling rope handle attached to an antiquated pulldown staircase leading to his goal—the third floor.

A long hour later, Beck clicked off his light and rocked back on his heels. "Well, damn and blast. Guess that was too much to hope for," he whispered disgustedly. His skin crawled with sweaty dirt and spider webs. Mouse crap and the moldy scraps of chewed-up receipts covered his clothing. The wall blocking him from his target might as well have been concrete. He couldn't very well bust out a saw and cut an access hole, now could he? He moved to the highest ceiling area and stood to stretch. His back popped and cracked like an old man who should have stayed on the ground floor in his wheelchair.

Frustration rocked him, and he tossed the nearest box of confetti into the darkness at the end of the room. A loud crack and the sound of breaking glass froze him to the rough planked floor. Moonlight cut a jagged shape into the pitch darkness. The silence on the stories below allowed him to take a relieved breath. "How 'bout that for providence?" he asked the emptiness. His excursion wouldn't be fruitless after all.

The box's impact had broken a thin board covering the pane of a grimy window so caked in collected dirt that it blocked the remaining light. Beck helped it along by thumping the frame hard. The entire casement came free in his hand, and he blew out a breath in relief as he lowered it to the floor without losing other noisy fragments. He crouched, silently listening for interest from the ground level—only his friend the cat singing to his ladylove.

He peered down into the alley and got the familiar wave of lightheadedness. Besting his fear of heights was the reason he'd started climbing in the first place. "Do what scares the hell out of you, and you'll be its master." His whispered mantra brought him the calm he needed. He breathed deeply and channeled his inner tomcat.

The opening was barely large enough for his head and shoulders to squeeze through. Once managed, he hoisted his hips up and turned. The edge of the roof an easy reach above his head. Taking regular calming breaths, he pulled up onto the tarred surface. The gentle incline rose above him like the open arms of an alpine meadow. He hummed the title song from another familiar movie as he climbed to the peak. The gummy soles of his climbing shoes were silent on the roof. The remnants of the sun's warmth clung to its expanse.

At the top, he took a moment to appreciate the panorama. To the west and north, the broad expanse of the city sparkled in the darkness. Below him, whimsical amber streetlamps defined Meeting Street as it plowed through the central business district. To the southeast, gigantic container ships formed pools of light in the dark sweep of the Atlantic. They looked like islands sprinkled across the water by the hand of God. "Damn, Arty, you would have loved this view," he whispered to the heavens. The memory of his little brother and the kid's puppy-like enthusiasm revived the aching guilt tangled around their time on Charleston's familiar streets. He rubbed at his chest and breathed in the briny air to alleviate the pain. It didn't work.

His gaze was inextricably drawn farther away from the beauty, to the hard-scrabble section of town. In that darker area lay the cramped clapboard pillbox where he'd grown up. His home bittersweet home. The place he'd learned his craft and buried two of the people he loved the most. He clenched his jaw and reminded himself to stay focused. Keep the ghosts at bay. Get the job done.

The gable delineating the Rochambeau attic space lay catty-corner across the building. Plumbing vents, clustered at the halfway point, offered a well of shadow. He slipped into their sparse cover and scanned the buildings across the street. The businesses and apartments above them were all quiet. There were no other late-night lingerers or midnight roof walkers in sight. Sure would be shitty karma to get popped this early in his recon mission.

He crept across the patched tar surface and peered around the gable's framed edge. To his right was a wide fan window that allowed ventilation to Rochambeau's third floor. He prayed it wouldn't take much effort to get it open. The problem was, of course, he'd be exposed to the street as he worked. He checked his watch—coming up on midnight. He'd hunker down in the shadow alongside the sheltering wall and give the locals a chance to get comfy in their beds. Beck braced his climbing shoes on the roof, leaned back, and settled in to wait.

****

In the quiet attic, Juliette carefully set the glass back in the condensation ring on the dusty highboy beside her. She wriggled to an old desk lamp and ran her hand up the cord until she could flick the thumb switch to click on the light. Remnants of fringe clung to the ruffled edges of the fluted silk shade. The square marble base and diamond-patterned carnival-glass globe of the center section testified to its age. It had probably graced some elegant relative's vanity table. Like the rest of the debris in her parents' attic, the lamp was relegated to history and disuse.

Since her first escape to the top floor of the building, she hadn't been able to resist the draw of happier memories. Every night after the house settled down, she mixed a tasty drink of lemony sweet tea and bourbon in an ice-filled glass and climbed the narrow stairs to her old hideout. She'd moved around some boxes and made space to pull the old couch out from under the eaves, giving herself comfortable headroom. She ignored the dust motes that flew up with each brush against the fabric. If she started cleaning now, her mother would get curious, and her haven in the rafters would be lost to more nosey questions than she cared to handle.

Roland had made himself scarce, but to where? And was he planning some other display of stupidity? She'd been unsuccessful at convincing her father to press charges; he stubbornly refused to subject the business to another episode of bad publicity. *So much for being in charge.*

Then there was the replica necklace. She'd gotten the opportunity to take a close look at the copy, and it was good—really good. Chet had a future in the art forgery business if he ever wanted a career change. The work he'd produced would have fooled her entirely if not for the heads-up. Even the white stones were expertly recut to match the original diamonds that totaled over twenty-five carats. It was an astounding work of art. For now, as far as the staff was concerned, the original was in Chet's hands for repair, and he made sure the door to his office was locked to all comers while he worked.

The days were so hectic she'd had no chance to start her appraisal on Marie Antoinette's infamous gift. Chet promised her she'd be able to begin the evaluation as soon as they could get the store up and running again. If luck were on their side, that would be next week with a grand reopening scheduled to include the Smithsonian/birthday party. She'd about talked herself blue in the face trying to get her mother to back off that piece of craziness—no such luck.

She glanced at the open window and took a sip of her icy drink. She sighed in pleasure as she rolled the cold misty glass across her forehead. The headache she'd been fighting all day abated slightly. The breeze carried the earthy scent of night-blooming jasmine. The plants thrived in flower boxes clinging to the sills of every window below her.

She sat back on the couch and pulled her keepsake box onto the cushion beside her. She'd been slowly rereading the letters she and Beck exchanged back in the day. Parsing out the joy and pain. Five years in college and ten on her own was more like half a lifetime. She barely recognized the girl who'd written the sweet longing notes to the boy she was convinced she'd loved. One of the bitterest pills she ever had to swallow was when he returned them. The package of them showed up wrapped in her favorite scarf and tied to the front door handle the morning he left. A note scrawled on the back of a receipt from Eggsperience Diner was attached. *To help you remember things I'll never forget. B*

So dramatic. But she was glad now that he'd done it. They'd helped her find perspective as she recovered from the gaping wound caused by his leaving.

Their secret summer romance had played right into her overactive and inexperienced imagination. The buzz of longing and awakening desire was a heady brew that turned them into satellites of one another. She was the girl unnecessary to everyone except Becket Ford, and he was the boy unloved by everyone but Juliette Rochambeau. They filled each other's cup in a frenzy of stolen days. Together they explored every aspect of their bodies and minds in an unfurling world of sensual delight. How those searing experiences turned out to be so one-sided was unfathomable. She'd forced herself to bury the hurt under a layer of calloused independence and moved on.

Seeing him again brought the scar alive with a sizzling jolt. Like a lightning strike to dry tinder, the heat licked her. And foolishly, she relished the burn. Christ, had she learned nothing since high school graduation? How many times had he contacted her in the years since? A big fat zero. That *should* be plain enough. Yet every time the blasted store phone rang, she jumped and hoped and called herself a fool.

She dropped the letters back into the box and fingered the bracelet. The links were cold against her skin. The shells, however, retained the soft warmth of the beaches where they were found. A dichotomy, like her life. Southern girl living in the north. Fiercely independent yet needing to belong. Afraid she was wrong about the choices her independence demanded. Choices that kept her alone.

She stood and paced to the window. "Pff," she said

and blew out a self-disgusted breath. "Go back to England, Becket. There's nothing for you here." The remains of her sweet tea and bourbon washed the sour taste of disappointment from her throat as she pushed on the upper portion of the window to lever it closed. She turned back to the couch and dropped the bracelet into the box. The lid closed with a decisive snap. "I can't move forward by looking back, now can I?"

****

Becket rose from his hidden perch beside the gable. He flattened out against the wall and edged forward beside his objective. He tested the edge of the trim on the frame for stability; plummeting to the street below wasn't the way he wanted the night to end. A missed handhold or a dicey grip, and that's precisely what would happen. He regretted lacking the foresight to bring his harness and a coil of rope.

He leaned out around the edge and went stock still. The window he planned to jimmy was standing wide open, and a soft glow of light spilled into the darkness. Stunned, he held his breath and listened. The soft rustle of paper and the brush of footsteps reached him. Not at all what he expected. He readjusted his hold and silently slipped to the edge of the casement. The gummy soles of his climbing shoes clung to the roof as they would to a rock wall. His black hood shadowed his face from the moonlight as he chanced a lingering peek into the light.

There she was. Pale blonde hair, a halo of silver and gold awash in the lamplight. The silhouette of her face shown through the fall of color. His breath stalled in his chest. She picked up her glass and rolled the surface across her forehead. Her eyes closed in pleasure, and he swallowed hard as a droplet rolled down her cheek to land on the curve of one breast. Now was not the time to remember the taste of her skin. That didn't stop the tightening in his groin.

Fascination pinned him in place, and he ignored the need for cover. He tracked her movements as she opened a box on the cushion beside her and withdrew a packet of envelopes. His breath stuck as he recognized the bright scarf covering them *and* the ribbon holding them together. She'd worn the ribbon, she said, because Shakespeare's Juliet used to do the same. He'd tucked it into his pocket after their first kiss. When he left Charleston, he'd seen returning the letters as a heartfelt gesture straight out of the classic romances she loved so much. The hero protected his lady's reputation by returning any evidence of indiscretion. They'd been *very* indiscreet that summer. His nostrils flared as he remembered swallowing her cries when she came apart beneath him. The paint on the window frame flaked and crumbled in the clench of his fingers.

He was a hair's breadth away from swinging through the window when she returned the letters to the box and lifted out the charm bracelet. He held his breath as she turned the silver links in the light and ran a gentle finger over the surface of the shells. She sighed, a desolate and lonely release of air. Then with a soft curse, she stood and moved toward the window.

Surprised out of his perch, he had to scramble back into cover. His whole body attuned to her as she leaned on the windowsill.

Her voice was as clear as if she spoke in his ear. "Go back to England, Becket. There's nothing for you here."

Each syllable was like a cut with a poignant wealth of pain attached. He tightened his grip on the gable edge to stop himself from launching through the window and pulling her into his arms. Showing her how much he regretted leaving her behind. Confess that, in doing so, he'd lost part of his soul.

And he knew, in that instant, he'd be a fool to even consider spending any time with her. Keeping his emotions out of the mix would be impossible. His feelings would show like a candle flame every time he looked at her. Even if he managed to get the necklace and slip away unseen, she'd still pull him under. He'd either have to go back to England and suffer the consequences or find a way to stop Jules from hating him when who he really was came out. Neither of those choices held promise in the real world, and both ended with him hurt or dead. His head hung in defeat.

Rock—meet hard place.

Chapter Seven

Becket startled awake and peered at his phone. He scrubbed a hand over his face as he answered. "Just gimme a minute. Christ, man, it's still dark here." Fucking five a.m. and Yosef was freaking out in the middle of goddamn Piccadilly Circus. He sat up and shook his head. The stubborn cobwebs of a short restless night stuck to his brain like, well...cobwebs. "Okay, start over. You went to her apartment, and what now?"

"Yes, but that's not the point—*I give up*. I can't find Renée anywhere. The job she pretends to show up for hasn't seen her in days. The last time her chums on the corner spied her was the day before yesterday. I called every mate I know of, and no one's seen her. Someone searched her apartment, and none too carefully, either. That disreputable piece of crap she drives is in the car park, hasn't been on the road lately. Two tires are flat. This isn't good, Becket. She promised she wouldn't take off, and she's ditched us. She's gone."

Fucking Renée. The only predictable thing about her was her unpredictability. Sometimes she'd take a flyer and disappear for days. Generally, she could be trusted *not* to be dangerously harmful—recent examples to the contrary. Hopefully, that was the case here, but Yosef wasn't a guy who panicked for the hell of it.

He blew out a long, frustrated breath. "What about Renée's boyfriend, no word there either? You can usually find him at the Dram and Thistle. You try that?" Where else? Did he need to go as far as checking hospitals? Police?

"Of course I checked with the boyfriend. Said they'd had a blowup, and she told him to go stuff himself. He wasn't interested in helping me look." Yosef paused and lit another cigarette. "What if something's happened to her? What if Singh—?"

"Fuck, man, don't even go there. Besides, I've only been here for a week. He's got no cause to doubt me." Unless, of course, Seth was whispering in his ear. An icy chill brought him upright. He would have loved to blame the AC. Unfortunately, the sensation usually warned of trouble headed his way. "I'll call and smooth his rumpled feathers. Invent some bullshit or—"

Yosef coughed. "Bullshit? You mean…bluff? You don't have a plan? At all? Beck, the clock is ticking, my friend."

"I *had* a plan, but I…it won't work." Charming her out of her panties and then her inheritance was up in flames now. Besides, it'd left a day-old-puke taste in his mouth. "Don't worry, I've got a plan B. Stop freaking out and find Renée."

No reason to sweat yet; he had another week before the Smithsonian stepped into the picture. Sure, seeing Jules had thrown him off his game, but he was already back in action, wasn't he? He needed more than smoke and mirrors to offer Singh. "Look, Yosef, I got this end. Keep looking and stay in touch. Eyes open and be safe. Check the hospitals and find out if they've seen her. Yeah?"

He winced as Yosef swore a streak of Farsi.

"I've got an awful feeling about this, Beck. I'll keep turning over rocks till I find the brat. I'll call you later." The phone went silent in his hand. Yosef wasn't the only one with a lousy feeling.

****

Fanish Singh tightened the belt of his silk robe; the luxurious silver fabric glinted in the light of the fire gently crackling in the hearth. The flame's colors played across her face. She was a pretty picture except for the bruise marring her cheek and the swollen look of the skin around her eyes. He didn't mind the puffy lips, though; he'd enjoyed the extra cushion as he slipped between them. Of course, the straps that fixed her chin in place and tilted her head back to keep her mouth open were an added benefit. *One couldn't have any biting incidents, now could one?*

He ran a soft finger over the puffy flesh, and she flinched away. He smiled down at her and caught her tear on his fingertip. He rubbed the salty fluid across her tongue, and her whimper rewarded him. His hand caressed her darkening cheekbone. She'd been an amusing distraction for a few hours. He'd come back for more of Ms. Greenleaf after he attended to some business. Yes, she would provide diverting entertainment for him later on.

"You rest now, my dove. I'll have my man see to your comfort."

She whimpered again, and he laughed. He pressed a button on the wall, and the door opened. His servant's stoic face appeared through the crack.

"Give our guest some help sleeping, Jasper. You can take her down then, and be sure she's prepared for me when I return this evening. Good man."

The dog-faced man bowed and held the door for his employer.

Fanish smiled to himself as he climbed the stairs to his private quarters. Having Ms. Greenleaf as his guest would be an added incentive to remind Mr. Ford of his level of interest in the smooth completion of their transaction. According to his informant, Ford's attachment to the chit would better ensure his cooperation. He was a man who'd go to great lengths to protect the friends he'd acquired. The exploitation of such character flaws required as much skill as the thief himself employed. And he was an expert at recognizing the vulnerabilities of his targets. Renée Greenleaf was one of those critical liabilities.

He stepped into his opulent bathroom and started the water running in his spacious shower. He let the hot, prickling power of the stream massage away the remnants of entertaining his guest. The spray poured over the breadth of his sleekly toned body, cascading over the planes of his pecs. It enhanced the artful greens and grays of the great python tattooed up the length of his thigh, around his waist, and up over his shoulder blade. The snake's head curled over his collar bone and rested on his chest just above the flat brown disc of one nipple. His badge of honor as it were, bestowed on the eldest son of his father's family since the beginning. He flexed his pec and rolled the defined muscles of his abs. The snake appeared to undulate against him, a subtle reminder that the quest for the stone hadn't begun with him. Restoring it was a sacred duty three centuries old, beginning in ancient Golkonda.

In that time, they'd purchased, stolen, and traded

countless stones. All proved to be false pretenders. Immense power and everlasting honor were promised the generation who succeeded in restoring the gem to Ganesha's sacred throne. He hungered to claim that glory.

With a twist of his wrist, the pounding water stopped, and he reached for a towel from the warming rack. The plush fibers absorbed the dampness from his skin in a single pass. He stepped to the mirror and brushed the cloth over the surface. The man looking back at him bore the chiseled jaw and widely spaced black eyes of his country's elite families. His aristocracy was there for anyone to see. That he held sway from a posh home in London instead of the throne to which he was entitled was as if he were a royal in exile. And like those hapless expatriates, he was no less confident of his place in the hierarchy of history. His family took the road less traveled—less accepted— didn't make them less deserving of a return to their rightful place.

He lathered his face and scraped a straight razor across the angles and valleys of his skin. He rinsed the blade and the soap from his face. Floating in the mist behind him, he imagined the image of his father. "Step by step," he said to the apparition, "I will see the return of our name to greatness. Inch by inch, I will claw my way back to our rightful place. I swear."

A smile, cunning and determined, slid onto his lips. The stepping-stones on that journey weren't always easy to manage. Experience proved those in his employ should never become too comfortable in their nests. They needed to remember he was always watching.

He strolled to his bedside and picked up the phone.

Perhaps Mr. Santos could be useful, after all.

He cleared his throat and waited a moment for the call to connect.

"Good evening, Mr. Santos." He waited for Seth to recognize his voice.

"Well, hey there, old buddy. Hold on for a minute, will ya? The bar is hoppin'. Let me get to my office." Music in the background faded, as though he was moving away from a crowded club scene. A door closed, and Seth's surroundings went quiet. "That's better. Now, what can I do you for?" Seth's false cheerfulness reinforced Fanish's delight at catching him off guard. "Great take, huh? I put one of my best guys on the shipment. I hope you were satisfied."

"Precisely why I'm calling. The weight was as advertised, though the quality was less so. Not unexpected when one considers the source."

The man was a fool if he thought the jewelry he'd sent would pass as merchandise from a storied firm like Rochambeau. Santos had cherry-picked the best for himself. Fanish couldn't really blame him. He would have done the same were he in Seth's shoes.

"Whoa now. No sir-ee, I wouldn't do that to you. We're just beginning a relationship here, building trust an' all. That wouldn't be good business."

"I'm glad you understand. That would be a grave error on your part, as I'm sure you know." He waited a breath for the threat to sink in. "I'll be reducing the amount of your payout to reflect the deficit."

"What, now? Reducing by how much?" Seth's register inched up with each word.

"I believe sixty percent should cover it." Fanish laughed to himself. This oaf was straight out of an

American cinema characterization of a hillbilly huckster.

"That's total bullshit, Singh. The goods are on the up and up. If I'd known you was gonna treat me this way, I woulda kept the whole fuckin' take and let you pound sand."

His tone was cold and matter of fact. "Again, Mr. Santos, that would have been a critical error in judgement, for it would ensure my retribution." He found that a quiet threat carried more menace that a shouted epithet. "The result would be, shall we say, a painful parting of our ways."

Seth cleared his throat and shifted his tactics. "Why you gotta be like that, man? You sound like you're the Godfather or somethin', all threatenin' and the like."

"How astute of you." He let the implication hang. He preferred to keep dealings with his associates in Miami to a minimum. "Let me speak plainly. If you'd like to make up the difference in the shortfall, there is a job you can do that would be helpful."

"Oh, yeah? What you got in mind?" It appeared Santos's bravado was as fluid as his accounting practices.

"As you know, I've sent Becket Ford to do the job you failed to do."

"Yeah, I ran into him the other day. He's pumped to be your go-to guy. Wish you'd called me before making that move. I think your eggs are in the wrong basket. Beck was a fuck up and an entitled little shit back in the day. Don't look to me like much has changed since then."

"His reputation is solid, but then again, so was yours. We know how that turned out, don't we?" Fanish let that linger for a moment. "At the moment, Ford is playing his plans close to the vest. I'd like you to keep an eye on him and report back to me daily."

"Simple enough." Seth agreed too quickly, which meant he was already watching his stepbrother. "Anything else?"

Fanish's finger tapped impatiently against the receiver. Explaining the basics was so tedious. "For now, I don't want you to get in his way. I may call on you to have a more active role should the need arise—an insurance policy, if you will."

"Yeah, sure. Like what in particular? A couple of things come to mind. How about somethin' that would suit us both?"

"I'll get back to you on that as the situation develops, Mr. Santos. In the meantime, earn back my trust and your commission."

Chapter Eight

Beck had had a busy morning after the panicky phone call from Yosef. He quickly located the company hired to upgrade the system at Rochambeau, Inc. Even less trouble got him an appointment to discuss installing an alarm system in his "new retail store downtown." The salesman was only too happy to brag about the latest installation for their biggest client. While in the company's office, he'd helped himself to a blank order form left unattended on the receptionist's desk, and a couple of business cards from the handy display.

The local electronics store provided a decent set of gear for circuit testing and rerouting, as well as a compact Wi-Fi jammer/router. He bought a fast laptop, an all-in-one copier, and a small laminator to manufacture a convincing ID badge. Simple really.

Across the street from the jewelry store, he relaxed into his seat. The sedan's ordinary appearance and tinted windows provided a secluded vantage point. Stevens Security's lead installer was shaking hands with Edward Rochambeau while his crew loaded up the last of their equipment. The Stevens van pulled away. In short order, Juliette and her mother followed them down the street. Hopefully, they'd be gone the whole day. Not that he'd need it.

He'd bluff his way in, get a look at the system layout in the guise of verifying the installer's work. His goal—locate the Wi-Fi router and plant the devices to disrupt the system's ability to sound an alarm via the internet and key the video loop. Find the phone panels and patch in remote access to disable them if required. Most importantly, plot his route down from the attic. He figured, if all went well on the night of his job, he'd need no more than a few minutes in the confines of Rochambeau, Inc. Stevens Security was using a system about as predictable as the tides in Charleston Bay. Seamless integration should be as easy as the flip of a switch.

He waited twenty minutes, texting back and forth with Yosef. Renée had vanished, and they agreed on the gut-clenching conclusion. Her disappearance wasn't by choice.

Becket flipped down the mirror over his steering wheel and fingered the Band-Aid on his cheek. The simplest way to keep people from remembering your face was to hand them a distraction to look at. He shaped the brim of the old River Dogs ball cap he'd found in a thrift store and scrubbed the mud off the crown onto his jeans. The smudges resembled those on his zippered windbreaker well enough to pass for part of his newly acquired uniform. He adjusted the I.D. badge clipped to his chest and stepped out of his car.

Laptop case weighing down his shoulder and clipboard in hand, he strode across the street and took the steps up to the entry two at a time. The heavy glass door swung open smoothly. Inside the store was pandemonium. The air was filled with the pounding of hammers and the shrill scream of power drills. Juliette's father and a plump man were deep in conversation at the center of the maelstrom.

Beck stepped up to them and offered his newly minted business card to Edward. "Mr. Rochambeau, I'm Chip Stevens. My uncle asked me to come by and check to make sure all the work was to your satisfaction."

Edward hesitated for a beat, then took the card and pumped his hand. "Yes, your crew left a few minutes ago. Far as I know, the new system is up and running. Why? Is there a problem?" He glanced nervously at the round man beside him.

"No, sir." Beck gave him a reassuring grin. "No problem. The crew is new to us, and we want to double-check their work's up to snuff. Y'all have had enough trouble. I'm sure you don't want any surprises." As he spoke, he spotted the bubble-shaped domes of ceiling cameras in the corners of the showroom and their buddies covering a stripe down the center. Motion sensor cubes, their red eyes blinking, sat like silent sentries in between—overkill for a space of this size. The security company was making a tidy profit on the job. In the back of the showroom stood the hulking vault door. Beck swallowed a laugh. *Fancy seeing you again, sweet thing.*

The barrel-chested man stuck out his hand. "Charles Foreman, sales manager. I can show you the control panels. Is that okay, Mr. Edward?"

Edward glanced around, seemingly distracted by all the movement. "Yes, yes. That's fine. Careful of the walls, though. The paint is wet. Charles, please make sure he gets what he needs. I'm goin' back upstairs to make some calls."

"Of course, sir." They were quiet as the older man wove his way through the workers and opened an ornate gate beside the vault. The grinding of an old-fashioned winch kicked into gear as he closed the door.

"Huh. Private elevator?" Beck asked. "You don't see those very often."

Charles continued to watch the door long after the gate closed. "Indeed. It's part of the history around here. His mother had it installed in the twenties." He cleared his throat and motioned Beck to follow him into the inner workings of the store.

As they walked, Becket paused to examine the safe nestled in an alcove off the showroom and visible from the retail area. Painted a sleek black and decorated by scrolls and golden flourishes, the behemoth was a substantial remnant of times bygone. He hitched a thumb at the vault door. "Let me guess. That monstrosity is older than the elevator." He didn't have to fake his delight.

Charles raised a disapproving eyebrow. "Correct, and like the elevator, it continues to serve us very well."

Beck suppressed a smile as Charles motioned him to follow.

"Shall we?" He punched in the code on the keypad newly installed by Stevens Security.

"You want me to help you change the installer code?" Beck asked. Charles nodded, and Beck smoothly reprogramed the panel to let Charles input his numbers. Fortunately for Beck, the man was too short to shield his entry. Beck gave him a mild smile while advising him to change the code regularly.

They pushed through a door in the back wall, and the glitzy glamor of the retail space ended abruptly. A well-lit, utilitarian, beige hallway led the way to Rochambeau's inner sanctum. Charles paused and indicated the workshop to one side. "The shop." He flicked his wrist. "It's locked at the end of each day." A stretch of windowpanes allowed a view of the narrow room. Eight jeweler's benches lined the far wall. Each bench sprouted a pole stand holding two small motors that dangled from cables and ended in silver handpieces. Beck was reminded uncomfortably of the dental appointment he'd missed by signing on for this crazy job.

The compact workstations, though bristling with hand tools, were ruthlessly well organized. Each bench housed a small bi-valve torch and contained a central metal-lined drawer.

"All work, completed or not, is moved to the walk-in safe nightly." Charles nodded to a gray steel door at the end of the room. "Same goes for the precious metal, the diamond melee stock, and the colored stones. Our lead jeweler handles all of that. His office and workbench are through there." He pointed to a doorway across the hall.

Beck noted the omnipresent dome cameras covering each area. Not much went unnoticed in this place. Unsurprising considering the amount of money in expensive replacement parts they must go through daily. Tiny gold and platinum findings were ripe pickings for sticky-fingered employees.

The whole area was neat and orderly. On close inspection, Beck noticed the walls carried a fine sifting of residue from years of polishing dust. He bet a finger swept over the surface would leave a noticeable streak. *Note to self—don't touch the walls.*

"Wow," he said, "this is so cool. I've never been behind the scenes in a manufacturing jewelry store.

There's a lot more equipment than I expected there'd be." His curiosity wasn't entirely fake. Hunks of machinery he couldn't begin to identify cluttered one wall. "What's that?" He indicated a tall plexiglass tank on a stand. Gloves extended into the interior like a hospital incubator.

"Sandblaster," Charles clipped. "Beyond the door beside it is the polishing room and casting facility. All of those vent to the outside."

"Right, I'll need to check the sensors were installed properly on that stuff." Beck made a show of consulting the work order on his clipboard. "For now, though, what I need to check are the system integration panels. Where are they?"

Charles moved past the shop, and they came to an intersecting hall. He indicated the turn to the right. "Store manager's office. Happily, vacant for the moment."

Beck took note of his pleased tone. Had they fingered Seth's inside man? Interesting.

They turned left. "The panels are back here, next to Mr. Rochambeau's office." He stopped at a narrow louvered closet beside the owner's door. "Space is tight; no room for us both. Do you need me to stick with you?"

"Nope. I'm sure you've got your hands full. I'll be running checks on the video system and inspecting the wiring harnesses. This new Wi-Fi-based system makes my job a lot easier." He patted the laptop case dangling from his shoulder. "Won't take me longer than an hour. I'll shout when I'm ready to check those sensors." He dropped the case to the floor. "Thanks for the tour. Be sure to tell the owner we're glad he chose our company to do the job. Sorry what happened made the work necessary."

"I'll do that. Call when you're ready." Charles turned to leave. "We hope to be operational by the weekend."

"No problem." Beck turned back to the glorified closet. Overhead, a florescent light came on when he flicked the wall switch. A server rack covered one wall. The newest addition's shiny sticker advertised the Stevens Security logo. Beck stashed the small Wi-Fi jammer behind the server box. Next, he opened his laptop and booted up the program Yosef had sent him earlier. In short order, he'd cracked the server's firewall and was riding shotgun alongside the original signal.

Experimentally, he toggled control back and forth between his laptop and the Stevens facility. Seamless. They'd never know he was there even when he cut them out. When the moment came, Yosef would take external control of the system. Only the sleepy-eyed guy in the Stevens office would be able to detect the flicker as they looped the video surveillance to replay a quiet store environment. Beck bet the low man on the totem pole wouldn't notice the blip.

The old-school exterior alarms he was prepared to bypass by gaining access through Juliette's attic hideaway. He doubted that equipment more sophisticated than a wall-mounted keypad guarded the rear stairway leading from the residence to the store. If so, he'd deal with them as before—pop the cover, bypass the wiring, and pick the lock. Easy peasy.

Cracking the safe was a foregone conclusion. Fortunately, the family believed in the preservation of history and the perception of safety a three-ton block of steel gave the customers. As luck would have it, Bernie Greenleaf's crew made him cut his teeth on an exact duplicate when he first got to London.

He'd spend a good chunk of his allotted time finessing the hulking relic. The large central handle and pair of combination dials were his focus. Precise movements, a delicate touch, and a sensitive receiver attached to an earbud would get him in without a glitch.

The plan settled, he packed up his laptop and retraced his steps. He doubted Charles would follow him up to the roof vents to "check the sensors," so he had the rest of the afternoon free.

****

Juliette sighed and settled back in the bistro chair. She'd forgotten what a day of Evie Rochambeau-style shopping required. Her feet hurt, and she was cranky—being dragged around by her personal southern hurricane had that effect. The street-side café where they'd stopped for a late lunch was paradise compared to spending an excruciating couple of hours fending off a very determined dress designer. She'd finally put her foot down and refused the pile of pea-green chiffon the designer attempted to foist on her. They'd compromised on a beautiful, soft, rose-colored, beaded gown for the Smithsonian presentation. The torture, however, wasn't over.

"Thanks for giving me today, sugar plum." Evie smiled, sipped her white wine, and consulted her notepad. Pen in hand, she ticked off the list of their accomplishments. The dress was covered, hair and nail appointments made for the morning of the reception. Carpet samples assessed and installation confirmed for work in the showroom. Suppliers promised they would finish the acres of glass in the wall displays the day after tomorrow. The showcases requiring complete replacement were ordered and guaranteed to be on-site shortly. "I hate we'll have to make do with replacements, but I've been tryin' to get your daddy to let me redecorate the showroom. So in a way, the robbery goosed his backside into lettin' me have my way."

Next on the list—caterers to finalize the menu for the party/reception. "How do you feel about crab puffs? Too cliché? What about angels on horseback? They're your daddy's favorite. Then we can do prosciutto-wrapped asparagus and assorted cheeses. What do you think?" She continued to make notes in her neat hand.

Juliette shook her head and sucked down the dregs of her wine. "I don't *think* anything, and don't pretend like my opinion actually counts here. You already know what you want, so you can handle that on your own." She was sooo over playing chauffeur and package schlepper for the day.

Evie squinted at her. "True. But it *would* be nice if you'd have some input. I mean, seriously, Lettie—"

Juliette rolled her eyes. "Please, don't call me that."

"—the only opinion you've had all day, besides the dress, was on the case lighting. All that technical falderal is a mystery to me. So, see? I needed you." Evie dropped her pen and combed through her purse, drawing out a package of…cigarettes?

Juliette froze, dumbfounded. Her mother wasn't a smoker! She had never been. As Evie searched for a lighter, a tan hand clutching a flashy gold lighter appeared over Juliette's shoulder.

She jumped, and his warm palm pushed her back into her seat.

"Good afternoon. May I get that for you?"

The voice was warm syrup, and she closed her eyes. Jeez, this could *not* be happening. The spit dried up in her mouth. She was seventeen again and terrified her parents wouldn't approve of the boy she loved. She forced herself to look up and grimaced at the dimpled grin Beck flashed Evie Rochambeau. Her mind went blank. She didn't know whether to introduce him or get up and run.

Evie blushed and smiled coyly. "Why, yes, you may. Thank you." She raised her brows at her daughter as if to say, "I still got it." She allowed him to light her cigarette and blew a blue cloud in Juliette's direction.

Beck's smile broadened as he stepped fully into Juliette's line of sight. "I don't mean to interrupt. I noticed you lovely ladies from across the street and wanted to pop over and say hello. I hope you don't mind."

Evie recovered first and extended her hand. "Have we met?"

"No, ma'am, we haven't. I'm an old friend of your daughter's."

"Really?" Evie thumped Juliette with her toe, and she jumped for the second time.

Christ on a cracker, dammit. He was trying to push his way in. Now wasn't the time to get tongue-tied. "Sorry, Mama. This is Becket Ford. Beck, my mother, Evangeline Rochambeau." The heat of a blush crept into her cheeks. "Beck and I knew each other in high school." She frowned and drew a bead on Beck. "What are you doing here?"

"Goodness, Lettie." Evie's eyebrows rose higher. "My daughter's apparently left her manners up north. Won't you join us, Mr. Ford?"

She smoothly indicated the other chair at their table, and Becket smirked at Juliette. As he sat, his knee brushed hers, and she scooted away.

Evie leaned forward eagerly. Her palm cradled her chin as she balanced on her elbow. "High school, you say? Can't say as I remember you. When did you leave Piedmont? Lettie loved her days there, such a good school."

"Beck and I weren't at the same school, Mama. Actually, we met at the beach before I left for USC."

Met, loved, and lost—all in six short months. Her gaze remained fixed on his. The intense gray of his eyes glinted mischievously, and she sat on her hand to keep from whacking him. Her gaze flicked to his mouth, and the corner lifted in a hint of a knowing smile—the smug bastard.

"Becket went to public school. North Charleston. Isn't that right, Beck?" The slums. *Take that, hotshot.*

He canted his head, blandly accepting her judgment. "Yes. I wasn't fortunate enough to have Lettie's—"

Her glass thumped the table. "What *is* it with everybody calling me that?"

"—advantages." He shifted his scrutiny to Evie. "I'm only here for a short time. I'm glad some of my old friends are still in town."

Juliette swallowed back a retort. Friend?

"Really?" Evie looked from Juliette to Becket and back again. "Where do you call home these days?"

"England, ma'am. I have an antique business in

London. I've come over to collect a piece of art for a client."

"London, you say? Well. My, my. You're a long way from home, aren't you?"

Juliette took a shaky drink of her water and signaled the waiter. "What will you have, Beck? Tea, or how about some wine? The Chablis is quite good. Huh, Mama?"

"Yummy, and I'll have another. Our home is all over hell's half acre right now, but we'd love for you to join us for dinner while you're in town." Her toe bumped Juliette harder. "I'm sure if my daughter ever comes to her senses, she'd invite you herself."

Juliette rubbed her shin and kept her face carefully blank. "Mama, I'm sure Beck is busy. Leave the man alone." A polite conversation at her parents' dinner table was more than she wanted to endure, especially under the astute matchmaking eye of Evie Rochambeau.

Beck chuckled when she glared at her mother. Under the table, his knee found hers once again. "I'd love to, ma'am, if you're sure it's no bother." He smiled wickedly at Juliette. "Since I've run into you, Lett...ah, Juliette, would you join me for a drink tonight? We can reminisce about our school days, revisit some old haunts. Remember Lisanne's? We can catch up over some of those she-crab cakes you used to love."

Juliette just stared at him. *Pushy devil.* How incredibly convenient to be able to box up what they'd had and forget. She'd never acquired the ability to wipe away the years between the wound and the healing. He'd sliced her once. Why in the world would she continue to pick at the scab? If he thought he'd reinsert himself in her life, he had another think a-comin'. Feigning calm, she said, "It's off Bay and Commerce now. I'm sure you can find it."

Evie made an exasperated noise. "For cryin' out loud, Lettie, this good-lookin' boy just asked you out." She grinned at Juliette's obvious discomfort.

"I can't. I've got work to do at the store. Daddy needs—"

"Gracious, you don't have to work your fingers to the bone. We can manage." Evie patted her hand. "Daddy and I will be fine as frog's hair. Go. Have a night out, have some fun."

Becket's smile turned victorious, and he bumped her knee. Again. "Yeah, Lettie. Come out with me. It'll be an adventure. You remember, just like the old days."

She frowned at him. "Sure. Fun. Just like old times." She pressed her palm to her stomach. It didn't help settle a regrettable flutter of interest.

His smile became brittle. "Great, then. I'll pick you up at, shall we say, eight?" He extended a hand to Evie. "A pleasure finally meeting you, Miss Evangeline, or is it Evie? I can see where Juliette gets her best attributes." All suave European manners, the insufferable jackass kissed Evie's knuckles, and the woman simpered like a girl. Juliette about gagged. *Sure, fall for his prince charming act and see where it gets you.*

Chapter Nine

Juliette left the bistro and beat feet back to the store—after she made sure Becket and her mother parted ways. She figured the less time he had to ingratiate himself, the better her chances were of avoiding an awkward family dinner with him grinning across the table at her.

Charles waved at her and swept his hand out in a grand gesture. "What do you think?"

"It's coming along. Great work, everyone."

Heads popped up from all corners.

"If anyone is hungry, I'll order in supper for you."

Tired cheers rose from the ten or so staff and workers around the showroom.

"Hope y'all like pizza," she sang as she quickly crossed the room and headed for her father's office.

Charles showed her the newly installed keypad entry to the back offices and the shop. He punched in the code, and the lock disengaged.

"Fancy," she said and patted his shoulder. "I should be able to remember that." 1818, the year the company was founded. A date they could all stand to remember.

As she passed Chet's door, she paused and knocked. Ancient history now, but the last time she'd interrupted him as he worked, he'd been deep in concentration setting a stone. She'd come bursting in, eager to share some news or other, and he jumped in surprise. His razor-sharp engraving tool scored the surface of a thousand-dollar emerald. The same stroke jammed the tool's point deep into his knuckle. To his credit, he hadn't screamed or thrown a tool at her; he'd merely dropped the work and asked her to get the first-aid kit. After the bleeding slowed down, he'd let her put on the double Band-Aid. Some lessons she learned the hard way.

The sound of his lock turning preceded his frowning face peeking through the crack. His frown melted, and he pulled the door open. "Hey, piglet. I was hopin' you'd be back before I left."

She laughed. He'd hung the nickname on her when she was a kid whose hands were usually black from "helping" the polishers clean up their filters. She preferred piglet to the god-awful Lettie anyway.

He turned back to his bench and settled into his chair.

She stepped up behind him and took in the array of paraphernalia on his bench. The glittering, historic necklace twinkled from its nest under his work light. His shoulders relaxed, and he turned to her.

"I was hoping you'd started on that," she said. "How bad is the damage?"

"Coulda been worse, and nothing I can't fix." He peered at her through the magnifying lenses of his headgear, turning his eyes into oversized, comic googly eyes. He raised the gray plastic frame and blinked at her, returning them to their original merry blue color and size.

She stepped to his elbow and peeked over his shoulder. A shallow iron bowl filled with shiny black pitch held the Rochambeau necklace in its sticky grip. Chet was old school. No fancy plastic resins came near his bench. He said he preferred the smell of burning pine tar to melting Tupperware. The large center stone was half out of the solid gold cup that cradled its back.

"When can I have the ruby? I want to get started."

"I'll finish in, say, ten minutes or so. I've about got the prongs lifted. We only lost three out of the twenty so far. The diamond halo is tight to the center stone, but I shouldn't have to pull more than four diamonds to fix them." He dropped his lenses back into place. "Then there's the damage to the links to deal with as well. I'd rather not use the laser; the repair would be too obvious. Fortunately, because of the work I did on the copy, the solder color will be a good match to the wire color."

She nodded, pleased she'd be able to start right away. She needed to get her mind off Roland's disappearing act. And off Becket Ford with his annoyingly insistent habit of showing up when least expected. Twice was two times too many.

"I only need the center for now." She brushed her fingertip across the antique-oval red stone. "The copy, by the way, is astounding work, Chet. Incredible. If the two ever get confused, I'd be hard-pressed to pick out the original."

"No sweat. Some of the silk shows the lead glass filling. Close inspection would pick it up. Using a scope—no problem. Overall, the heat-treatment brought the color up to match the original extremely well. Like I said, I started with pink sapphire, so most tests will be positive for ruby. You want a quick way to pick which necklace is the original?" He grinned like a kid at a magic show. "Looky here, and I'll show you." He lifted the cloth and rotated the pitch bowl, bringing the clasp of the necklace into easy reach. "There's a tell. See this link second from the end on the right-hand side? Look close at the jump ring." He pointed to the elongated rectangular ring that connected the last two chain links.

She pulled down the bench light. The spring-loaded arm gave a complaining creak as she moved the fixture closer to the necklace. "What's that? An incomplete joint?" A thin line of darkness marred the wire surface, leaving a tiny split in the polished metal.

"Good eye, piglet. It wasn't apparent before the bastards jerked it around. It's not bad enough to fix, so I'm leavin' it alone. The point is, my piece is perfect, including that one spot. Run your nail across it, and you'll feel it."

She followed his instructions, and sure enough, she felt a hitch in the smooth flow of the gold. "Again, good to know. I'll be sure to call it out as an identifier in the appraisal of the overall piece. Anything else I should know? Hidden signatures? Maker's marks other than those on the clasp?"

"Not that I found. Between your daddy and me, we've been over every square millimeter of this piece." He returned the orientation of the jewelry and was ready to resume removing the stone.

Juliette flicked his lenses back down over his eyes and kissed his cheek. "I'll be in Daddy's office setting up my equipment. Can you bring me the ruby when you get it out?"

He nodded and was back to work before she made it out the door.

****

Hours of exhaustive testing and retesting left Juliette baffled. A pounding headache made her findings much harder to swallow. What she'd discovered couldn't be right. No way. The center stone was a ruby. Period. It had to be a ruby. They'd always *assumed* it to be a ruby. Yet according to her lab equipment—it wasn't. Nor was it garnet, or spinel, or rubellite, or any other obscure red gemstone. The weight was wrong for a stone of its size, the specific gravity was off, and the refractive index was—way the hell and gone from where it should be. Then what about that troubling inclusion buried deep in the stone's belly? She struggled to find a way to dispute her findings. That would mean...

"Occam's razor," Juliette murmured into the silent office. She couldn't deny her test results. She'd eliminated all possibilities and was left with the only conclusion available—no matter how improbable. The stone wasn't ruby. It was...nope. She couldn't bring herself to commit. It couldn't be. "Diamond," she whispered, and her hands began to tremble.

She pushed herself back and wrapped the stone in a crisp velum stone paper, then tucked the packet in her pocket. What was she missing? She'd ask Chet to review her findings, and he'd help her see where she'd gone off track. He wasn't a gemologist, although his years in the business held a treasure trove of accumulated knowledge.

She left her father's office and retraced her steps to Chet's door. The workspace was locked tight. She stomped a frustrated foot on the cold tile. A glance at her watch showed it was after seven. And there she was, acting like a spoiled kid. The man had gone home—like a sane human.

She stopped at the entrance to the showroom and punched in the code, pleased she had enough remaining brain cells to remember the numbers. The room was quiet on the other side. She was the only crazy person left on the ground floor. Stepping to the elevator, she slipped her key into the control panel and punched the down button to summon the car. The old machine clunked and clanked its way to her, and she bounced on her toes while waiting out the return trip up to the residence. Was it slower than it used to be? As a kid, she'd fancied the lift as her ride up an imaginary launch tower to her handmade rocket ship. She smiled, recalling the scolding Grandma Hattie used to give her for abusing her privileges.

She stepped out of the car and into the hall. Light spilled from the living room, and she prayed her daddy was up for the news she was about to drop in his lap. He sat under a reading lamp in his favorite chair. A curl of cherrywood-scented smoke spiraled from his pipe toward the ceiling of the quiet room.

"Hey, Daddy. A pipe. Honestly? Mama will have a fit, you know."

"She'll get over it," he grumbled. "Besides, it's the only vice I've got left."

She dropped a kiss on his cheek. "Where is she, anyway?"

"She's got one of those infernal dating shows on in the bedroom. I can't stand all that fake carryin' on, so we struck a deal—I don't watch, and she doesn't make me feel guilty." He smiled up at her. "What you doin' so long downstairs?"

"I've started the appraisal."

His pipe stem wavered in his mouth as though he chewed a thorny problem. "Oh? You decided not to wait till Chet finished?"

She frowned at him; he knew the only reason she'd agreed to do the damn appraisal in the first place was if she could run her examination on the loose stone. Had he forgotten?

She studied him carefully. "Uh—yeah. He pulled the stone earlier this afternoon. I have to say, it's not going the way I expected."

He took off his glasses and laid his book on his knee. "What do you mean? Is there a problem with the stone?" His face was blank composure. The same expression he got when her mother caught him in a half truth. Her suspicion-meter pegged the red line.

"Not exactly. Let's just say my test results are very different than I thought they'd be." She sat down on the coffee table in front of him and rested her elbows on her knees. Leaning forward, she looked him in the eye. "You know why that would be?"

He blinked and shifted uncomfortably.

Her guts knotted. "You know, don't you?" Her pulse rate picked up; Occam was right after all.

He glanced around the room as if he expected someone to jump from a corner. A jolt of sympathy punched into her chest.

"I don't know what you mean. You tell me, is it ruby or...not?" His gaze flickered to hers and then away again. She was reminded of a cornered dog, afraid the prize he'd just dislodged belonged to someone bigger and meaner. His hands came up in a helpless gesture.

Holy crap. "Not a ruby. You know it's not. I ran

the damn tests four times and always the same. The results were so crazy I was sure I'd lost my freakin' mind. Why, in the name of God, didn't you shout it from the housetops?"

She had her answer before she stopped speaking—the ever-present, ever-scheming Roland. Her father was afraid the stone would be too much of a temptation for his greedy brother, and he wasn't confident he could defend against him. The effect of Roland's betrayal made her head spin.

"You've known this for a year, I'd say. Along about when you commissioned the copy."

His head bobbed in acknowledgment. He pushed his glasses up into his hair and rubbed his eyes. "How could a stone like that go unnoticed, unrecognized for centuries? It was just too hard to believe. I was afraid I didn't have it in me to protect it, let alone give the piece the justice it deserves."

"That's not the case now, though, Daddy. The world needs to know." Jesus, she could kill Roland for turning her strong, assertive father into this tentative, indecisive copy of the man she knew. This time she didn't resist the urge to envelop him in a hug.

"It does? Are you sure we shouldn't just keep this between ourselves?"

"Absolutely not. We've got a miracle of nature in our hands." Time to lighten the atmosphere. She shook his shoulders. "Now what shall we call it?" Sarcastic humor had always been the route she used to smooth uncomfortably emotional moments. She released him and tapped her chin, pretending to search for a name. "How about 'Antoinette's Nipple'?"

"Don't talk like that in your mama's house, young

lady." His mouth twitched as he pretended to be scandalized. "If we're gonna holler, let's do it right. It's the largest and most exquisite red diamond in the history of the known universe, isn't it? What else would we call it?" His voice took on the sonorous cadence of a preacher with a proclamation. He stood and raised a finger toward the sky. "It shall be known as—the Rochambeau Red. Our name will forever be emblazoned beside the Hope and the Star of India in the annals of gemological history." His face creased into relieved joy as he shook his declaration at Heaven.

Juliette slapped her hands over her mouth and squealed through muffling fingers. "Holy sheep shit, we're famous!" She jumped to her feet and bounced up and down. Her reputation in the business world would be stellar. The woman who identified the rarest, most extraordinarily valuable gemstone in history. The Rochambeau Red. Her mind spun with the possibilities.

He waved her down off the cliff. "Shhh! Quiet down. I don't want your mother to hear. She'll have a coronary."

Her hands landed in his. "She needs to know. Daddy, you can't keep news like this from her. The stone is worth..." She blew out a long, bubbling breath. "I don't even know. The largest red diamond to hit the market was a third this stone's size. It went for thirty-nine million, and that was years ago. I...I can't even..." She began to hyperventilate, and her head got as light as a helium-filled balloon. Her knees went to jelly.

He grabbed her as she wobbled. "Keep it together, sugar." Taking her arm, he pushed her down onto the couch and hustled to the bar.

A short glass of bourbon landed in her hand. She

took a couple of slugs and coughed out the burn that streaked down her throat. "I couldn't believe it. The readings were all screwy, and then I put it in the scope. I expected to find silk or clusters of garnet, and I spotted—"

"Oh, thank God." His words dripped relieved excitement. "I was afraid I'd stepped over the edge. You found it. You found the included diamond crystal. Honey, I 'bout dirtied my long johns when I spotted it." A huge grin split his face, and he clasped his hands like a choir boy about to belt out a high-octane hallelujah. Pride glowed back at her. "It's tough to see, practically invisible. I knew, if it was there, you'd find it. In all the years we've had that rock, I bet it's been under a scope dozens of times, and we never thought to question our preconceptions." The fierce joy on his face wiped away ten years of aging. He did a spritely jig, and she laughed at his antics.

She wrapped her arm through his and joined him for an impromptu reel. "I know. It's like a tiny skyscraper in a lake." She planted a sloppy smooch on his cheek. "This is like Christmas times a gazillion." They grasped each other's arms and danced in a circle. "We hit the lifetime lottery *and* the Irish Sweepstakes. Rochambeau, Inc. just became the most famous company in the world." She slid to a stop. "Oh, my God, Daddy…we gotta call someone. Like GIA, Carlsbad. The Smithsonian. The Wall Street Journal and…then the world."

His grin faded. "We're not calling anyone. Not till I decide what to do."

"Excuse me, decide what exactly? We blast the news on every network on the planet and put all those other stones to shame. That's what we do."

He cleared his throat and tapped out his pipe. "I hate to toss water on this bonfire you've got goin', but I'm thinking about sellin' it. I talked to your boss, and he thinks after the Smithsonian exhibit he can find a solid buyer. We need the cash, honey."

Was she hearing him correctly—sell the Rochambeau necklace? He had to be nuts. "Daddy, no. You can't do that. The necklace is part of the family— part of our history—my history." She began to pace. "I get you're worried about the business after Roland and all. We'll come up with a plan. Mama's right. Think about stepping back till you feel better, or consider retirement if that's appealing. Just don't be hasty. Heck, you could turn the place over to me. I'll run it. You don't have to be concerned." *Wait.* Yup, she'd done it again, offered herself up on the altar of their family legacy. Was she crazy to think it wasn't such a horrific choice after all?

His eyes widened. "Sugar, you say that now, but I don't want you to feel forced into taking on this dinosaur of a business." He took her hand as she passed him. "You have your own life, your career. You've worked damn hard. I'm proud, so proud of what you've accomplished. I'd be honored to have you here, but don't you see—selling the necklace would keep this store in the black for decades. Especially now. How can I *not* consider turning loose of it?"

She went from high on headlines to apoplexy in zero point three seconds. Flabbergasted, she dropped to the couch. "You sure as hell can't sell it, not now. This discovery is going to create a worldwide frenzy in the industry. Imagine the exposure we'll get from the press.

Not to mention our bottom line." She gulped down a couple more swallows of brown liquor and prepared to argue her point.

Evie's voice echoed down the hall. "Lettie? Tick tock, honey. You've got a date in half an hour."

Getting her mother involved in her argument was sorely tempting. Did she have the energy at the moment? Absolutely not. The adrenaline rush of the discovery had taken the starch right out of her.

Edward sat beside her, and she dropped her head against his shoulder. "Oh, man, I forgot all about Becket," she mumbled, and her father stiffened.

"Becket? Becket Ford?" He frowned at her. "There's a name I haven't heard in a coon's age. He's that boy from high school, right?"

She winced and nodded. "*Not* my idea. Mama sorta twisted my arm," she whispered to him. Hell, she had more important things to worry about now, like talking her father out of making the worst mistake of his career. Sell the stone? No way in Hades she'd willingly agree to such foolishness.

"Well, you don't have to go, and that's final. The boy was bad news years ago, and he's probably bad news today." His volume rose to carry its message down the hall. "Your mama should know better than to pair you up with the likes of him."

Juliette reeled back. Did he know about Beck? "I haven't seen him since then, Daddy, and that was a long time ago. What have you got against him, anyway? I didn't think you knew him."

"I don't know the boy, but—against him? Well, let's see; I know you spent months mooning over somebody. That whole last summer, you were either dancin' on air or cryin' yourself to sleep, and by the time you left for college, you were like the walking wounded. If he's the one responsible for that, it'd be enough for me take him on a one way trip to the swamp."

Her chest constricted. If her father bothered to notice what a tragic lump she'd been that last summer, it sure didn't feel like it at the time. "I was just a kid. I got over it." She waved away his concern.

Becket was like a troublesome gopher who continued to pop up and screw with her plans, her obligations. This had to stop before he somehow managed to tumble every last barrier she had.

Perhaps she should teach him a lesson about messing with her. "I just got an idea." The last thing he'd suspect was that she'd put him to work clearing up a problem simmering in the worried edges of her brain. She drummed her fingers on her lips and smiled slyly as her thought took form. "I *could* use him to do a little reconnoitering."

He frowned suspiciously. "What's that busy mind of yours chewing over now?"

"Aren't you curious where your loving brother is hiding and what he knows? As much as I'd like to believe he was the mastermind of the robbery, you and I both know it's unlikely. He's probably off licking his wounds at his favorite haunt, and I'm not dumb enough to go traipsing into the lion's den alone. So while I'm out with Becket and his impressive muscles, I'll pay the place a visit. See if I can get a feel for whether Roland knows about the stone. If he does, then we'd best get our prize discovery the hell out of here before they try again."

Yes, Becket could be her bodyguard on a stroll through the darker side of Charleston. Before Edward could voice an opinion, she reached into her pocket and retrieved the diamond in its rectangular stone paper.

Her father held up his hand. "Now, Lettie, simmer down. You've got a vengeful look in your eye. Don't go gettin' foolish."

"Who? Me?" She tossed him the stone. "Put this back in the safe for me. I've got a date."

Chapter Ten

She forced herself to concentrate and purposely took her time dressing, chiding herself over the shiny fuchsia butterflies flapping around in her belly. She shouldn't be nervous—or excited. This date was a mission, and Becket was a tool to get the job done. That's right, a means to an end. Find Roland, taunt him, and get him to spill his guts bragging about his superior intelligence. With luck, he'd be drunk enough to shoot his mouth off before throwing punches. She could pretend contrition. Play the regretful niece and apologize for her actions. And kiss his feet. The butterflies wilted into a sickly, tarnished green. She briskly pulled a brush through her hair and ruled out kissing any part of his skanky ass. Ruthlessly, she pushed concerns about using Beck into place and stepped into her sandals.

Fifteen minutes later, those lousy insects fluttered back to life as she carefully climbed down the stairs and opened the private door at street level. And there he was. Wow. Soft leather jacket, collar turned up to highlight his square jaw. Hair tousled just so. The guy had grown into the quintessential description of her ideal man. This couldn't—shouldn't—be happening to her, not now of all times. She had work to do. A store to run. A world to rock. Becket Ford wasn't allowed to be any part of that.

Yet there he stood, hands shoved deep into his pockets, and looking unsure of himself. Just as he had on their very first date.

To make sure those butterflies wouldn't take flight and launch her across the threshold, she hesitated before she stepped out. "Hi," she said, gaze glued to her toes, afraid he'd catch a glimpse of her nerves. "Sorry I kept you waiting."

"Hi, yourself." He stepped up and kissed her cheek, a gentle brush of lips against her skin that left a trail of heat behind. "I wasn't sure you'd come—period."

"Oh." She jumped despite herself. *Stay cool, remain calm.* "Yeah, well, Mama practically pushed me down the stairs. So the choice wasn't exactly mine." *That's right. Remind him he'd trapped her into this soiree, and she got to choose how it played out.*

Hurt flashed across his face. "Oh, okay, then." He dipped his chin and peered up at her through his lashes. His killer smile snapped into place. "Come on, Jules, you gotta admit, that was pretty funny. I mean, considering how hard you used to work to keep me from meeting her back in the day."

She laughed despite herself and slugged his shoulder. Her hand stung. Man, he was as solid as a rock. "Can we go now? I'm your indentured companion for the evening. No need to head down memory lane right out of the gate." She took two steps past him, then turned back. "And I did not. You were like a master magician, making opportunities disappear. Why is that? Huh?"

He reached out and took her hand. The warmth and strength of his grip weakened her knees. "You were always too good for me, Jules. That hasn't changed, far

118

as I can tell."

Not. So. Fast. She stared down at his hand till he put it back in his pocket. Better. She couldn't breathe when he touched her. She searched around for an escape route. A late-model sedan sat at the curb. "This you?" She'd expected his beat-up old motorcycle. Lordy, how they used to tear up the back roads. Was that disappointment twinging her gut?

He scoffed. "Yup, I'm all about low profile these days." His chuckle rumbled down her spine as he opened her door. "Kidding. I left my Maserati home. Salty air doesn't do the paint any favors."

She rolled her eyes. "Maserati. Yeah, right." She quickly tucked the skirt of her lavender sundress around her knees as she slipped into the passenger's seat. As if *that* would protect her. God, she was acting like an idiot on her first date with the quarterback of the football team.

He dropped into the seat behind the wheel and closed the door. His scent surrounded her. *Focus—hold your breath.* Eventually, she'd have to have air—or pass out. *Heck of an idea—feign a good ol'-fashioned fainting spell.*

Frustrated by her lack of good sense, she took a shallow breath. It came charged with the seductive touches of spice that would forever be Becket's. Unable to resist another sample, she filled her lungs and got a heady rush of remembered kisses in theater balconies. Desperate for footing on the steep slope of lingering attachment, she stabbed at the window button. She didn't give a good god*damn* how crazy she looked hanging out the opening.

Amused by her actions, he snorted a laugh and

pulled her back in. "What the hell are you doin'? I just took a shower; it can't be that bad." He made a show of sniffing his armpit.

"Stop it," she said and covered her eyes in embarrassment. What the hell was she doing tip-toeing through the past instead of dealing with the present? Like the enormous honkin' diamond upstairs. "Can we just go?" She flapped her hand to hurry him away from the curb. "I've got a lot to do tomorrow. I can't be out all night."

"Hmph. Okay, then. As long as you give me a minute to do this." He moved lightning-quick and captured her lips. The kiss wasn't sweet or sentimental. The heat and thorough contact pushed her head against the seat as he sampled her mouth. Too shocked to move at first, she found herself following him when he pulled back. His lips were luscious and firm. Fully capable of driving her from lukewarm to rolling boil instantly. She felt the upturn of his knowing smile, and she scrambled for her good sense. This was *not* how the night was going to go. She wouldn't let it.

Her stiff palm landed against his chest and pushed him back. "Just drive, Becket. I didn't come out here to stir up the mud." Or get lost in the way they used to be. *Focus.*

He leaned against her pressure. "I'm pretty stirred up at the moment." He let his smile bloom millimeters from her mouth. His gray eyes darkened as he studied her face. A flash of regret wiped away the heat. "I'm so sorry I hurt you, Juliette. I truly am."

She stiffened. "I got over it." Her chin lifted, stubborn and self-protective.

"Keep telling yourself that." He eased away and

settled back behind the wheel. He scrubbed a hand over his clean-shaven face. "I don't blame you for making me prove it."

"I don't want you to *prove* anything. There's no need, okay?" This was a stupid idea and dangerous to boot. She reached for the door handle, and he clicked the lock button. She jiggled the lever and bumped the frame with her shoulder. "Open this door right now, Becket Ford."

"Nope. You're mine, all mine, for the night—"

"Evening. And I've changed my mind."

"—so stop trying to run off. One drink won't kill you." He started the car and flipped on the turn signal.

Damn the man. She jerked the seatbelt strap into place. This was the game he used to play all the time, smoothly refusing to fight and leaving her to choose how far she wanted to take the argument. If she continued to spit and scratch, she'd be the only one affected. She made a frustrated noise and crossed her arms over her chest. She didn't have to see his face to know his devilish grin had made an appearance. *Criminy.* She needed to get this night back under control. If she let him set the pace or dictate the agenda—she'd be on her back before the ice melted in her glass.

He pulled away from the curb and prepared to turn at the corner. Juliette cleared her throat and got herself back on track. "Wait. Hold up a second. You want to make up for being an asshat? Fine. You can start by doing me a favor." *Be my bodyguard.*

"Oh, yeah? What's the favor?" His voice was suspicious as he smoothly completed the turn.

"Take me someplace I'd be crazy to go on my

own."

Beck winced. "I'm gonna regret this, aren't I?"

****

Longfellow's had changed a lot. The clip joint had classed up its act considerably since Beck had last been inside his stepfather's former bordello. The floors were no longer tacky with spilled booze and grasping despair. Now a deep pile carpet covered the entryway, and the hardwoods smelled freshly waxed. All in all, if he didn't know better, he'd mistake it for an upscale bar ready to serve the city's wealthier clientele. Despite the classy veneer, the place stank of his stepbrother, and the Santos Syndicate was the rotten core.

Beck pulled back a chair for her. "You plan on telling me what the hell we're doin' here?" He scanned the bar area and came up empty of the one person he didn't want within fifty feet of Juliette Rochambeau.

"Research," she said and picked up a drink menu. He gave her a narrow-eyed glare as she pretended to peruse the offerings while peering over the top at the patrons around the bar.

"You don't need a microscope to find the slime in this place. You know this used to be a front for a whorehouse, right? Probably still is." His stomach did a roll at the idea of explaining his knowledge.

"What have you got against working girls, Beck? I would think, now that you're all cultured and stuff, you'd have a more cosmopolitan view of commerce. A girl's got a right to make a living however she can." She folded the menu and gave him a bland smile.

"I've got no problem with the act or the exchange, as long as it's fair and voluntary. The girls who used to be the stock and trade here weren't putting themselves through college, Jules." His knee started a nervous jiggle. He forced it to stop. Might as well piss her off and improve their chances of getting the hell out of here without tipping off the management. "Business bad up there in New York City? You planning a change of career? I'm surprised. The way I remember it, you enjoy sex too much to charge for it."

That jerked her straight. She glared at him. "I do enjoy it, you pompous ass. And I've learned to tell the difference between making love and fucking. You taught me that. So thanks for the reminder." She signaled a server and frowned at the girl's barely covered nipples as she leaned over the table. "Gin martini, dry and very dirty, three olives." She raised an eyebrow at him. "Beck?"

Point to Jules, their score was even. *Christ.* "Beer, tall, cold, and blonde," he said, and the waitress wobbled off on impossibly high heels. He ran a finger under his collar. "Glad I served my purpose, then." Did Jules have to be so…happy to be rid of him? "What's the reason for this walk on the wild side? You want to, what, rub my face in my past? Point out all the reasons we would never have worked?"

"Don't flatter yourself, Becket. And I haven't quite figured out how to go about the why-we're-here part."

Their drinks arrived, and he handed the girl a twenty.

Juliette sipped thoughtfully from her glass. "Okay, look. If I tell you, will you keep it to yourself, not bring it up when Mama drags you to dinner? 'Cause trust me, she won't be happy about this."

He squeezed the lime sticking out of the neck of his beer bottle and pushed the frayed green rind down into the pale brew. He considered the foam intently while he stalled for time. This whole excursion was about the robbery or the turncoat. Knowing where her mind was at would be handy. "I promise not to tip her off that you're playing detective." He grinned when she jolted. He'd nailed her intent. "I'm warning you now; we're not doing anything crazier than have this drink. No snooping in back rooms or asking questions of sleazeballs. We clear, Nancy Drew?"

A triumphant smile peeked out from behind the rim of her glass. "Crystal. Let me give you some background. I came down from the city to appraise the family's necklace before lending it to the Smithsonian. I'm sure you've figured that out."

She dropped her voice, and he nodded.

"What you don't know—what nobody except the senior staff knows—is that we believe the robbery was a setup. Staged to cover other thefts from our business."

He remained quiet and controlled his breathing.

"It's an open secret Longfellow's runs under-the-table gambling, has for years. My uncle hangs out here like a regular. I found out through one of the jewelers that he spends big and loses even bigger at the poker tables in the basement. Sounds to me like Roland got in deeper than he could handle." She dusted her palms together. "Presto change-o—markers paid."

Beck's brows reached for his hairline; he was amazed she'd worked that out. "So leave it for the cops. Charge him with conspiracy to commit a crime. Don't put yourself in the middle of a situation where you're liable to get hurt. The necklace isn't worth that. Not to your folks and not to the damn Smithsonian." He couldn't feature the Rochambeaus condoning this in any way.

"Yeah, I know that's true. Or it was till today. Beck, I…"

A thunderous blast overrode her as a door slammed open beside the bar. A man with graying temples in his black hair stumbled out. Blood coated his face and shirt. Behind him, Seth came into view with one hand fisted in the man's collar and the other gripping the guy's belt. He didn't slow his forward momentum as he frog-marched the poor slob across the bar and out the door to the parking lot.

If it were possible to drop behind an invisible screen, Beck would have jerked them both into its cover. Instead, he grabbed her purse, slapped it against her chest, and hoisted her out of her seat. Places to hide were scarce; the only option was a tall potted palm to one side of the entry door. He ignored her angry sputter, hustled her around the ornate pot and into the dicey obscurity of its shadow.

She jerked her arm out of his grip and pushed on his chest. "That was my uncle! I told you he'd be he—"

Beck pushed her back and jammed his lips over hers, swallowing her words. "Quiet," he whispered furiously against her mouth and pressed her into the shadow. He prayed Seth hadn't spotted them huddled like clay pigeons in the middle of his bar room. "You are *not* getting mixed up in your uncle's shit," he hissed. "Seth Santos is a shark, a man-eater. We're getting out of here before he sees us. Got that, Nancy?"

Her eyes grew round, and she nodded. "But h-how do you…"

"Shh," he mouthed.

Seth blew back through the door, headed for the

bar. Beck wasted no time. He slipped an arm around her waist, swung them both past the palm and out the door. He didn't slow down till they were on the street. He checked both directions and powered them toward the car.

Juliette stumbled and pointed; a whimpering sound spilled out of her. On the pavement beside their car, Roland lay face down. She shook off Beck's grip and crouched over the man.

"Oh, God. Roland, are you okay?"

She touched his shoulder, and he moaned.

"Uncle Roland, answer me."

He rolled to his side and clutched his face. A bloody streak swept across his jaw, and the shape of bone underneath wasn't right. She reached out a shaky hand. He flinched, rolling away with a mewl of pain. The sound was so pathetic it could have come from a dying animal. Her terrified eyes looked up at Beck.

He swore roundly. "Help me get him into the car. If we leave him here, they're liable to finish the job."

He yanked the back door open, and together they shoved Roland into the opening. He landed like a wet gunny sack on the seat.

Glaring at Juliette, Beck slammed the door behind him and jerked the front door open. "Get in the damn car," he said through clenched teeth. "We'll drop his ass at the ER, then I'm taking you home."

"W-we should call the police, shouldn't we? That man could have killed…" She slapped a hand over her mouth and glanced back toward the club. Tears brimmed her lashes, and all color leached from her face.

Beck's rigid stance softened. This was Jules, his

Jules. She wasn't some hard-bitten chick from the projects who understood the wages of fucking with a guy like Seth—or like himself. In the final analysis, he was a barely painted-over version of his stepbrother. "Trust me, that's a bad idea. Just get in the car, and I'll take care of it."

He pressed on her shoulder, and she folded into the seat. Movement in the club's entry grabbed his attention. He didn't need a genius to tell him who that might be. Beck slipped into the driver's seat, stabbed the start button, and slapped the car into gear. The tires made a satisfying screech on the pavement as they streaked away.

Long hours later, they were back in the car and pulling into traffic headed away from Roper Saint Francis Hospital's ER. Beck was silent. The picture Singh had shown him in London kept crashing into his mind—the one that finally convinced him to take on this crazy-ass job. She was just as fragile and frightened now as she had been in the grainy photo.

At the hospital, she'd pushed aside her suspicions about her uncle and treated the guy as if she cared. She'd handled his admission, waited out the results of the X-rays and CAT scan, and made sure Roland was taken care of before she agreed to leave. Now her head rested against the window glass, her delicate face pale and exhausted.

He cleared his throat and spoke softly into the quiet broken only by the sound of traffic around them. "I never got to feed you tonight. Want to stop for a bite? Or you want me to take you home?"

"No." She closed her eyes and sighed tiredly.

"Not hungry?" He flicked the turn signal and

changed lanes. "Home it is, then." His mouth turned down in disappointment. He'd never been able to give this girl what she needed. Not back then and not now.

"No. I don't want to go home. Not now, anyway." She pushed her hands into her hair and righted herself in the seat. "I'll have to tell my folks about Roland. They need to know, but I can't deal with it tonight." She turned toward him, and a glimmer of hope rose in his chest. "Where are you staying? Could we go there?"

"Uh, sure." He paused, surprised. "If that's what you want. I can even scrounge up the stuff for an omelet." He *could* give her a small gift—a quiet place to hold back the tide. Foolish, but he was grateful to provide such simple comfort. God knew she'd done much more than that for him when they were kids. He prayed she wouldn't hate him quite so much when all this was over. "Just don't you be getting any ideas, young lady. I'm not *that* kind of guy, you know?"

She laughed outright. "Since when?"

He laughed with her. Yeah, he was precisely *that* kind of guy.

Chapter Eleven

Juliette hung back to take in the small front porch on Beck's house. She'd expected modern, stripped-back efficiency, not this quaint bungalow with a brick walkway and draping bougainvillea. In the moonlight, it was romantic and tropical, like a honeymoon cottage. She wanted to take off her shoes and sit a spell beneath the hot pink blossoms.

What a night. Not at all the way she'd thought it would be. She'd only wanted to gain some ground on the whirlwind. So many eventualities and problems crowded her brain she'd been a heartbeat away from dumping them all in Beck's lap. Talking to him about her father, the store, Roland, *the stone,* and all the insane happenings since coming back to Charleston seemed like the most natural thing in the world. Then again, holding back was the smart move. When, for crying out loud, had she started thinking of him as being on her side? She didn't really know this version of Becket Ford.

"This is nice, Becket. How did you find it?"

"A friend of a friend." He entered the security code and slipped in his key. "Come in. It's a bachelor pad right now, so you'll have to forgive me if there's clutter." He walked a few steps ahead of her and flicked on a light beside a deep loveseat. The place came alive in warm sunset hues against sand-colored walls.

She breathed out in pleasure. "So lovely. You're lucky to have such friends." She slipped off her shoes and padded across the kitchen to the french doors. "Oh, sweet, a private patio. I miss lounging outside in the evenings up north. I have a balcony that's twenty stories up and exactly like all the others." She spotted a comfortable pair of Adirondack chairs and a small table. An excellent place to sit and put some distance between her and decisions she wasn't fully prepared to make. "Can we sit outside?"

"Sure. You want some wine while I see to the omelet?"

She picked up a nervous note in his voice and smiled to herself. The balance of power was shifting. Surprise, surprise, and she liked it.

To test the waters, she ran her hands through her hair and shook the mass down her back. "I'm not very hungry. I can wait." She glanced at him over her shoulder and smiled secretly when he swallowed. The temptation to tease him warmed her blood. Too bad she hadn't worn a sweater, she would have peeled it off for effect.

She unlocked the doors and pushed them wide. Warm damp air filled the small room with notes of jasmine-laced honeysuckle. She drew in deeply and exhaled the tension she'd been dragging around like an anchor. The patio brick was warm against her bare feet as she walked to the chairs. A three-wicked candle and lighter lay in a tray on the iron table. She struck the flames and let them banish the shadows into the low-growing azaleas edging the patio.

Behind her, the fridge opened and closed, followed by the clink of glasses. Then Beck's warmth was at her back as he set the wine on the table. She moved into him just enough that his arm brushed hers as he leaned past, and she registered the subtle contact of his hand at her waist. His touch echoed along the length of her spine, and she shivered.

"Cold?" His deep voice was beside her ear, and his breath stirred the edges of her hair.

"Not really." She turned just enough to kiss his cheek.

"What was that for?" He leaned back slightly and peered down at her, his face confused. His hair was a rumpled mess as if he'd run nervous hands through the thick strands.

"Saying thanks for tonight. I'm glad you were with me." She let her gaze slide from his eyes down to his mouth. *Just for a while, wouldn't it be nice to step out of the tornado?*

His tongue darted out nervously, and then he frowned. "You're jerkin' my chain, right? You've been ticked off at me all night."

"Have not," she argued teasingly. "Well, some of it. You can be very bossy, you know. Do this, do that. Don't poke the lowlifes, grab his feet, watch his head. Very bossy."

She grinned at him, and he answered with the wide smile she loved so much. It took years away from a face that could be very serious.

"Well," he said, "you clearly needed my direction." He gazed down at her, and his attention drifted to her mouth. "Apparently, you lack experience choosing appropriate date-night locations *or* the correct manner by which one loads semiconscious bodies into cars. Someone needed to take charge."

Her lips tingled with anticipation. "Listen to you. You sounded very English just then."

His teasing smile faded, and he moved away. "That surprises you? It's been years." He splashed wine into both glasses and handed one to her. Gone was the warm humor of a moment ago.

She felt the loss as if the barriers between them had solidified. "Why is that, Beck? I never did understand. You didn't even look back the day you left, and you stayed gone. Not even a note to let me know you were okay." She took a sip of wine to wash away the bitter hurt coating her words.

He settled into one of the chairs and shrugged with a resigned shake of his head. "Too many ghosts here, I guess. Too many losses."

She'd thought…it didn't matter what she'd thought. "Hmm. I remember. Your little brother, then your mom." She sat and drew her knees up to her chin, tucking the skirt of her dress around her shins.

"And you." He swirled his wine. "You had a whole shiny world ahead of you. A bright future waiting for you. I didn't see a place where I'd fit." He sounded resolute and a touch sad.

"Then you didn't look hard enough." She cleared her throat of the pressure building there. "I would have done whatever you asked to keep what we had." She didn't want to fight with him, not tonight. Not about what they couldn't change.

He rocked forward and focused those startling eyes on her. "That was it exactly, Jules. I was afraid you'd do just that. I had enough on my conscience; taking you down that road would have killed us both."

"What?" She sat up straight. Not this again. "Oh,

for cryin' out loud, Beck. Don't you dare throw my family at me. How much money we had in the stupid bank never mattered. We're hardly high and mighty, you know. So scratch that off the list of reasons you dumped me." Fighting wasn't off the table after all. Dammit, she hated when he said stuff like that.

"Oh, stop fussin'. You know it's true," he said over the rim of his glass.

She catapulted to her feet. "Is not! You got scared."

He was suddenly in front of her and gripping her chin between his fingers. "Is so." He swallowed her next barrage in a smacking kiss. "I always did love pissin' you off, you know?" He kissed her again. His lips moved against hers with a hungry finesse that robbed her ability to do more than hang on. His hand slipped from her chin along her jaw and into her hair. Fingers tangled in the strands, and he pulled her to him.

Her breasts pushed into him. Her nipples hardened into jutting knots of sensation against the hard slabs of his chest. Her palms slipped up the firm contours of his biceps to spear into the thick hair at his collar. She begged for air when he released her mouth only to sigh when his other hand flattened against the small of her back. The length of him pressed firmly against her lower abdomen.

She whimpered out a curse as he kissed his way down her neck. He strung together a gentle trail of nips and soothed them with the wet of his tongue. Gooseflesh rose to attention all over her body. He ran a finger beneath the strap of her sundress, and it slipped from her shoulder easily. She would have shrugged it off completely if she'd been able to muster the coordination to make her body obey. He kissed the exposed skin and retraced his path to her mouth.

"God, Beck," she whispered as he took her lips. Pent up discontent evaporated in the heat. This kiss was different yet again. Focused and determined. Drugging and demanding. His hands ran up her rib cage and found the softness at the undersides of her breasts.

"Yes. Touch me. I've missed your hands," she mewed, afraid she'd cry out if he stopped. She needn't have worried. Cold air brushed her skin as he released the buttons at her chest. The rough-textured pressure of his thumb raked across a tip. He stroked it in synchrony with the swipe of his tongue in her eager mouth.

Juliette levitated to her toes. Her hands took on a mind of their own. She gathered fistfuls of his shirt, desperate to expose his skin to her touch. He took the hint and allowed her to pull the fabric over his head and toss it to the bricks beneath them.

He was gloriously warm to her fingers. She broke their kiss and watched as her hands mapped a path across his hard chest and the ridges of his abs. His tan skin quivered in the wake of her fingertips, and she smiled, remembering how ticklish he was.

"Don't even think about it," he said roughly and flattened her hand against his stomach, then brought her palm to his mouth.

"So bossy," she whispered and murmured a curse when he bit the soft flesh below her thumb.

"That's right. Let's take this inside. I want to touch the rest of you, and I don't want to share you with the neighbors."

A happy, girlish giggle billowed out of her when he pulled her toward the doors. "I thought you weren't that kind of guy." She tripped along behind him down the short hall until he pushed her back against the doorway to the bedroom.

"I lied." His voice was dark, rich chocolate over shards of glassy praline. Her mouth watered with the hunger to taste him.

They studied each other in the dim light. The silvery gray of his eyes darkened like storm clouds. His face became harsh lines and fierce arched brows. A flicker of apprehension made her shiver. She didn't *really* know this man whose touch was so familiar. What she felt wasn't fear. It was—like the pause at the top of a rollercoaster—breathless excitement.

She wanted to gorge herself on it.

He kissed her again, dragging her bottom lip away with his teeth. "Now take off your dress."

Her fingers shook as she undid the remaining buttons to her waist and shrugged off the wide straps. The skillful construction eliminated the need for a bra, and she cupped her breasts in offering. Becket's hands covered hers as he accepted her gift. They moaned in unison as he took one nipple into his hot mouth. Her back arched into his heat as a jolt of electricity lit up her core.

She slipped her hands away and reached for the snap at his waist. The heat of his skin warmed her fingers as she sprang the closure. "Mmm," she hummed when her fingers brushed the velvet tip of his erection. "Commando. I'd forgotten."

He allowed her nipple to slide free with a pop. Reflected light gleamed on the pebbled tip. His lips quirked up. "When the occasion calls for it. So have a care with the zipper." He pushed himself harder against her fingers. His eyes closed, and he groaned a dark, hungry sound.

She slipped her palm down his length, protecting him. His breath caught. Air sawed through his open mouth as her other hand inched the zipper along its track. He sprang free into her palms. Juliette gripped him experimentally, enclosed his circumference, and stroked him tip to root and back again. Her thumb spread the collected moisture she found at the peak. He quivered as he rocked into her grasp. Encouraged, she repeated her stroke, and he moaned an enticing rumble that made her increase her grip.

"Stop, or this is gonna get messy." He took her wrists in one hand and raised them above her head. His other tweaked her nipple. "I want you out of this dress and on my bed. Then I'll help you remember everything else you've forgotten."

"There you go again. Always telling me what to do." She laughed as he pushed her back onto the bed.

****

He loved the noises she made as he nibbled the soft flesh of her inner thigh. Her skin was like silk and honey. Her scent was fresh and warm, laden with the wet promise of pleasure long buried. He nibbled the crease of her leg as it joined the valley at her center. She whimpered out a curse, and her hips rose to greet his mouth. She was smooth and hairless, a hot surprise. He loved her surprises. "I remember golden curls and…" he murmured and lavished attention on the skin above her cleft. Beck paused to investigate a small tattoo. "This is new. A seashell?" A permanent souvenir he recognized as a moment of homesick longing. He nibbled around it, and she shivered. "Please tell me a woman did this."

She covered the ink with her fingers. "No. A big hairy guy named Figaro. He was very...thorough. Jealous?" Her lips quirked up when he growled. "God, I love that sound. It used to mean you were mad. Are you mad now, Beck?"

His nimble fingers spread her wide, exposing her to his gaze. His tongue traced the contours of her folds. She squeaked when he buried his mouth on her center and sucked her into his mouth on a long deep draw. He moved with ruthless intent, swirling and raking her bud before answering her. "Completely insane"—another luscious circuit of the swollen knot of sensation that made her arch off the bed—"to think I'd ever get over you."

Her breath left her, and her fingers tunneled into his hair, holding him in place. Her hips rose and fell. Together they chased her sweet spot.

He pushed her thighs wide open, never leaving his focused onslaught. His fingers took the place of his mouth on her center, and his tongue swept her opening. She coated his senses in the remembered flavor of summer. He let the memories gloss his heart. His Jules. His.

The first delicate flutter of orgasm began, and he returned his lips to her center. He lapped her with the flat of his tongue and pushed a thick finger into her tight channel. She writhed and called out his name. "Come. Come for me, Jules." His words rumbled against her swollen flesh. He pumped in a second finger, curving it to strum her G-spot. She stiffened and cried out. Joining his advance and retreat movements, she drew him deeper as she pursued her pleasure. He followed every step of her journey until she slowly relaxed into bonelessness.

She purred out a single word. "More."

He kissed his way back up her body, wiping moist cheeks as he went. He wanted her bathed in their mingled fragrance. He wanted her to remember how they burned for each other. Levering up on his forearms, he took in the satisfied, wistful smile coloring her lips. Her hair spread around her like a cloud of spun gold. She'd ripened like a peach on the tree while he languished on the other side of the Atlantic. She was at the peak of her womanhood, no longer the knobby-kneed girl that handed him her virginity like a tightly wrapped present. This was the waking dream he believed would never come true.

He gave himself a silent pat on the back for having the forethought to place a condom on the nightstand. He wasn't about to stop and have a health discussion at this moment. He'd never been harder in his life. Every muscle in his body strung tight, every beat of his rampaging heart focused on the woman beneath him. His fingers trembled as he sheathed himself.

"Now, Becket. I want you deep in me." Her voice was refined desire, and she reached for him, guiding him to her welcoming entrance. "Hurry, Beck. I've waited long enough."

They were pieces of a puzzle, a thousand moving parts jostling toward the completion of an undisclosed picture. Holding himself back was no longer an option. She was his, and he would find a way to make this right.

He slipped his hands beneath her knees and hoisted them over his taut shoulders. He forced himself to slow, rocking and retreating to slick his tip and ease his entry.

"No more waiting. Not for either of us." And drove home.

Chapter Twelve

Becket stood, coffee cup in hand, staring blankly at the vacant patio. The morning light was beginning to return to the bright azaleas. Rising doubts crept along with it. Behind him, the quiet was telling. Jules slept like the dead, one hand beneath the pillow and the other under her cheek. When he slipped away, she was peaceful and sated, like a cat with a belly full of cream. Good, she needed to replenish the energy they'd expended last night. And he needed the time to figure out what the hell his next move would be. He smiled sadly into his cup.

Christ, last night. Her taste, her essence was burned into him. The sound of her cries as she came was the stuff of his fantasies—the ones he'd banished to the rubbish heap of impossible hopes. Strangely enough, time—always his enemy in the past—was now an ally. Dreams had a way of dissipating in the light of day. Memories would fade, and senses would fog with distance. He would be okay. Eventually. They would both be fine. Just—fine. *Stop dreaming.*

He slugged back the scalding black coffee and didn't notice the burn. He'd been so stupid, never should have caved to the impulse. Jules was so much more than he'd expected. He was an idiot to try and convince himself he'd be able to make love to her and walk away. If he'd just kept his hands to himself and the rest of him tucked safely behind his zipper, the damage would have been manageable. Now *feelings* were involved. Now her pain would blossom into genuine hatred, and a piece of him would wither and die. He'd known it the second she breathed out his name as he entered her. And he'd kept pumping away—trying to drive back the fear. Foolish. Insane. Careless. Unforgivable.

He pushed open the doors and heaved the cup against the brick wall. The shards exploded into a shower of white and disappeared into the bushes. He could relate. The metaphor was perfect.

He felt more than heard the front door open behind him. He spun on bare feet, expecting Seth or one of his goons. Instead, a sunglass-wearing Yosef stuck his head through the opening.

"I was hoping you'd be up." His friend gave him a sheepish smile. "I thought you could use some backup. So I brought reinforcements." He stepped in and extended a hand back out the door. A long-fingered, delicate hand slipped into his palm, and he guided Pashmina Mirin through the door.

"Wh-what the hell are you doing here?" Beck glanced nervously down the hall. Thankfully, no eavesdroppers.

Yosef caught the movement and pointed at him. "Ha. Knew you couldn't leave well enough alone. My 'girlfriend' and I came to visit. Isn't that nice?"

"He doesn't seem glad to see us, Yoyo." Pashi's smooth, round tones spoke of a posh boarding school education. They were as far from the truth as she was from the slums of Mumbai. She dropped her flashy leather bag beside the loveseat and relaxed against the arm. "Be a dear and get your 'sweetheart' a cuppa, won't you, darling? I'm dry as dust." She smiled sweetly at Yosef.

"Absolutely not." Beck growled and grabbed her bag off the floor. "Don't care why you came or how you got here. Y'all need to leave. Now."

Her laugh tinkled. "Y'all? Listen to you, darling." Her slanted eyes reminded him of a cat stalking its meal. "Come now, Becket, don't be rude," she said through pursed lips. "Our mutual friend sent me to hurry you along. He wanted me to bring you a reminder." She reached for her bag and pulled out her phone. Her red, lacquered fingernail casually tapped an icon and scrolled through several screens. "Let me see, where did I put it? Ahh, there it is." She grimaced as she thrust the screen toward him. "I believe you've been looking for this."

He snatched the phone from her. Renée. The picture showed her face half obscured by limp, greasy hair. One eye stared into the camera; the white was bloodshot, the pupil dilated and glassy. The skin beneath marred by a bruise the color of eggplant. Her lip carried a gaping split, and brown saliva crusted one corner. His hand began to shake, and the grip he had on the phone threatened to crush the screen.

Pashi tugged the phone from his grasp. "I took that yesterday at Singh's," she said quietly. "He roughed her up and doped her, but she's alive."

His nostrils flared, and he swallowed hard to force the coffee back in its place. "What were you doing there? Booty call?"

"Hardly." She dropped the phone on the cushion behind her. "He wants me to take charge of the necklace for him." She glanced at Yosef and smiled fondly. "Yoyo and I have come to help you complete your assignment."

Yosef held up innocent palms. "I just happened to be on the same flight, actually. I knew you could use the help." His eyes widened, and he cleared his throat. He nodded down the hall.

Beck turned. Jules leaned against the hallway wall, her face an ashen mask above the T-shirt Beck had worn last night.

"Assignment?" Her voice was just above a whisper.

"Uh-oh." Pashi sniggered. "Somebody's in trouble," she sang.

Beck wanted to strangle the amusement out of her. He was well and truly screwed now. He took a step toward Jules, and she put out a hand to stop him.

Her wide blue eyes filled with hurt. "Me? Am I the assignment?" Her chin jerked into the air. "Or…no. I'm the means to an end." She took a step back and then another. "How stupid of me; I should have known. Thanks for clearing it up for me." She spun on her heel and sprinted for the bedroom.

She was fast. Beck was faster. He snagged her around the middle before she could get a foot through the door. She got in a solid elbow shot to his ribs as he wrapped himself around her. Flailing heels threatened to cripple him, and all that hair blinded him as they struggled for control. She whipped her head back and rattled his jaw with the force of a sledgehammer.

The blow made him gnash his tongue. "Ow! Fuck! Stop it, Jules. You're gonna get hurt."

She only struggled harder. He finally got her hands

in one fist and jerked her feet off the ground. It didn't stop her from hooking a foot behind his knee, bringing them both down. He flipped them over and blanketed his weight on top of her.

"Get off me, you lying motherfucker," she wheezed. "I…I can't breathe."

He wasn't falling for it; the girl was slippery as an eel. "No. I'm not lettin' go till you listen to me. I can explain."

She was a quivering mass of pissed-off alley cat. Her butt pushed up into his groin, and he grinned. Good thing she couldn't see his face.

"I swear I'll tell you the whole story. You've got to promise to listen, no more wrasslin'."

She relaxed a fraction, and Beck peered down at her cautiously.

"Are you done now? 'Cause you made me take a hunk out of my tongue."

"Good. Too bad you didn't bite it clean off. Woulda kept you from tellin' more lies." Tears coated the ragged edges of her words, and she bucked beneath him. "Get off me, Becket."

He rolled to the side and kept one hand pressed to her back as he scrambled to his feet.

She pushed him away and stood up on her own. "I want my clothes." She stomped her foot and swiped a fist across her eyes. He stepped aside, and she swept past him like a beauty queen. She tried to slam the door. His forearm blocked it.

"Get out," she shouted. "I can't even look at you."

"Tough. I'm not going anywhere."

She huffed. "Fine then, suit yourself." She whipped his shirt over her head and threw it at him. She spread her arms for a split second. "Take a picture. It's the last damn chance you'll *ever* get to see me like this." And she flipped him off for good measure before stepping into her dress. Her fingers shuddered so hard she swore and settled for the buttons easiest to manage.

"Need some help?" He was poking the bear, and he couldn't help himself. He'd never fully appreciated the degree of her spunky pride or her hard head.

"Touch me, and I swear you'll draw back a bloody stump." She wrangled the last button and ran shaky hands through the mass of tangled gold spilling over her shoulder. She gave him an angry shove and pushed past him. "Get out of my way."

He was right behind her as she reached the living room. He grabbed her elbow and spun her around. "You're not leaving till you listen to me, Jules. You'd best accept that."

"You plan on addin' kidnapping to your crimes? The only way I'll hear what you have to say is if you force me."

She grabbed for her purse, and Yosef snatched the bag out of her reach. She glared at him and planted her hands on her hips.

"Relax, would ya? I haven't done anything yet, so quit throwin' a hissy fit." Beck stepped around her and pointed to the couch. "Sit."

It wasn't a request. She had to listen to him, and he had to decide how to confess his sins. He scowled up at the spectators. Pashi and Yosef appeared to be enjoying his discomfort immensely.

He growled in frustration. "These too-curious-for-their-own-good idiots are friends from London. Yosef, Pashi, give us a minute, will you?" He gestured to the

145

patio doors. "Go enjoy the sunshine, and I'll try to make this quick."

Pashi snorted in disbelief and sauntered toward the door. She quirked her finger at Yosef. "Come, darling. Becket thinks he can talk his way out of this." She shook her head with an amused, condescending smile. Casting Beck a commiserative glance, Yosef followed her out.

Juliette sat primly on the sofa. "Who the hell are they? Your cohorts in crime?"

"My friends, yes." He sat on the low coffee table facing her and leaned forward, hands gripped between his knees. "You have to understand why I'm here. Are you ready to listen?"

"Seriously? I was born at night, Beck—just not last night." Her arms clamped over her chest. "Sure. I can't wait to hear how you planned to use me. Go for it. Tell me all the reasons that's okay. All the ways you'll laugh behind my back as you walk away. Again." A muscle ticked in her jaw.

He hung his head and flexed his hands. God, some master of the wily con he was. Why couldn't he find a slick, easy way to tell her, or a shortcut that would get his ass out of this mess? Maybe an appeal to her conscience would work. Drowning men grasped at any straw they could get their hands on, right? "You remember how we used to hide out downtown watching old movies and pretend it was normal to avoid everyone who might have an opinion on us being together? You thought we were ducking your family—that mine was less likely to disapprove of us, right?"

"So? You were the one who was embarrassed by our differences, not me. You treated our money like some cultural divide. I never did."

"Yeah. True, but it's not the only reason." He held his breath and jumped in with both feet. "I didn't want you to meet my kin because my people are thieves, Jules. All of them. My stepfather was Hank Santos. Does that name ring a bell?"

Her gaze snapped to his. Santos, she remembered him. How could she not? The old man had made a career of armed robbery and drug smuggling. His favorite hobby was harassing a particular downtown jeweler. "The bastard died in jail. He got his just deserts considering all the pain he caused. You're his son. Big surprise. You're just like him."

"No, I'm not. I'm his *stepson,* and it hurts you'd think that. It does. Christ, Jules. I left Charleston—I left you—so I wouldn't turn into him. I didn't have any other choice. My family, they're like a disease you can only cure by lopping off your arm. I went to Europe to change." He blanched when she huffed her disbelief. "Yeah, well, the best-laid plans and all that. What's important here is that I left to *protect* you. Hank got interested in our relationship. Started making noise about using you to get to your father. Then after my brother—" He stopped, his words catching in his throat. *Fuck it.* He'd promised her the whole sordid story.

She sighed and sat back. "I remember. You felt responsible."

He took it for softening. "I *was* responsible. Arty was just a kid. A kid who followed me around like I was some kind of superhero. I couldn't stand the idea of him becoming fodder for the federal pen. If I'd grown a backbone sooner, he'd be alive for a come-to-Jesus shaking. But that wasn't the way it went down. He dogged my heels until he was such a distraction that I flubbed a simple lift."

Confusion wrinkled her brow.

"Pickpocket." He wiggled his fingers. "Anyway, one of the cops recognized me and chased us. Arty was quick and had staying power. He hung with every twist and turn I made as we got the hell out of there.

"When we finally got clear, we were down on the battery. He was so jazzed at getting away he jumped up on the seawall. He lost his balance, and I tried to jerk him back." Drying seaweed had coated the wall's rough surface with slime. His brother's eyes had gone wide in surprise and then terror. His thin arms had windmilled as he fought gravity, and he pitched backward into thin air. "All I managed to grab was the edge of his jacket." The slick fabric had slid through his desperate fingers. Arty's slight body made a sickening sound as it hit the rocks and heaving water below.

If he had to put a finger on the moment his life irrevocably changed, that was it. His world had imploded in a split second. Arthur's death and Beck's failure to protect him had brought about a cascade of events that determined his life for the next decade and a half. He was no longer the heir apparent, the darling of Hank's eye. And his mother, already sick, had taken a nosedive into depression. In the space of six months, he'd seen her buried too.

He gathered himself. He had her attention—now he could make her understand. "I finally got it. If I wanted to become more than they'd taught me to be, I had to leave, and Mom left me the way out—a ticket to England. She had a friend who offered to help me. But it didn't work out the way I hoped. He was this wonderful old-timey grifter. Tough guy with a big heart. I know this sounds like a cop-out, but we spoke the same language." Another excuse? Probably.

"So you kept on stealing for a living. What? Couldn't you use your brain to make a buck? Like, find a real job? Earn a living like the other ninety-nine percent of the world?" She tsked her disapproval.

He shrugged. "I could have. I tried to. The straight and narrow was so—boring. I lasted two months and damn near starved. Would have if not for Bernie and his daughter, Renée. Then we got a rhythm, and the money began to flow. Once I figured out I could do what I was good at and not hurt anyone—I was all in. The penny-ante stuff got left behind pretty quickly."

Her brow wrinkled in a hard, disbelieving scowl. "That's what you tell yourself so you can sleep at night, Becket. Victimless crime doesn't exist."

"I'll grant you that. There *are* different classes of victims, though, and I don't pretend to be Robin Hood. The people I relieve of their money can afford to lighten their pockets. The difference between the Santos family band and me is I don't suck my living out of the poor to make a buck." Enough of making his case. "You want to know the real reason I do what I do? Fine. I steal because it's all I know, and I'm fucking great at it. Full stop. No excuses. It's a thrill like nothing else, and I've never been caught. Not even close. I take pride in choosing my marks for the maximum return on investment balanced against the risk to my crew and to me. I treat the people who work for me fairly and never leave a man behind to take the fall. You can look down your nose all you want, Juliette. It's who I am."

Her lips flattened into a hard line. "Pride goeth before a fall, they say. Cut to the chase—the necklace. Your stepdad tried and failed. Then you and Seth. Or were you flying solo on this last attempt?" She narrowed her eyes and clenched her jaw.

"No, I wasn't even here. Seth fucked that up all by himself."

"Either way, you're not a saint." She tsked her disbelief. "I bet it's no coincidence we're both in Charleston at the same time."

Her rigid spine showed him how well his attempt to get her to understand was working. He'd hoped for empathy and got self-righteous indignation and betrayal.

"Don't make the mistake of painting me the same color as Seth, Jules. And no, it's no coincidence." He stood suddenly and stalked away, the muscles in his forearms and calves rigid. "I never wanted to involve you in what I do. I came because of a screwup that happened in London. The girl I mentioned, Renée, got in deep to a man who'd as soon kill her as look at her. I owe her father." He shrugged. "So I said I'd stand good her debt. The man wasn't satisfied with how quickly I could get it done. The necklace is the price of her freedom. Now it's my price as well." He picked up Pashi's phone and woke it up. The picture of Renée filled the screen, and his stomach rolled at the sad remnant of her once beautiful face. "See for yourself." He tossed the phone to the cushion beside Juliette. "He grabbed her off the street two days ago. Needed to give me the incentive to get the job done."

She blew out her annoyance and picked up the phone. Her startled gulp as she took in the grisly picture was a hopeful sign.

He prayed the shock value would have the same effect it had had on him. Jules considered herself a tough and worldly city girl who could handle most situations. Just the opposite was true. She had a warped and entitled sense of reality. Christ, her folks had sheltered her from the grittier side of her hometown. Learning to avoid muggers to get across the city wasn't at all the same as being confronted by Singh's remorseless disregard for suffering.

A quiver developed in her pursed lips. "My God, Beck. Nobody deserves…" Her eyes had taken on a haunted quality. Good. She needed to get the whole picture—to know the consequences. "This man, the one who'd do this, what's his name?"

"Fanish Singh. He *will* kill her, Jules. He'll kill us both if I can't bring him what he wants."

****

Juliette's blood pounded in her ears. She managed to lay the phone gently on the cushion beside her. She was in an untenable position and overloaded by a mix of emotions and conflicts. He had no idea what she'd discovered about the stone. How could he believe she'd stand by and let him steal from her? Just hand it to him like it didn't matter. Thank God, she hadn't revealed the whopping details of her appraisal, or that its value had multiplied from a million or so to a virtually incalculable number. She didn't want to be the type of person who'd hang a price tag on a person's life. Even a thief's life.

Dammit to hell. She was tempted, though.

She tried to stop the numbers from rolling through her brain. Relentlessly, they came anyway. The Hope diamond—three hundred fifty million dollars, or approximately seven-point-seven million for every one of its forty-five-plus carats. The Rochambeau Red, at just over twenty carats—could be worth five times that, if not more. It was so rare, so one of a kind, it couldn't be fairly valued by anyone's scale. Trying to do so would be like calculating the worth of one of the pyramids.

She rocked forward and spat a dispirited laugh into her palms. She was screwed if she relented or callously selfish if she didn't. Assuming she could believe Beck at all, and that was asking a lot at this point. She tracked his pacing across the kitchen and back. Tension strung his neck and shoulders tight. His movements played well to convince her of his regret and pain at finding himself and his friend in danger. If—that was the question. He'd already admitted to being a con and a thief. Did she dare trust him? Rationally, no. Emotionally—she wasn't so sure.

Last night had been the culmination of better than a decade of loss. The rejuvenation of a dream she'd left tucked in that box in the attic. She wanted to believe him. However, like sharp stones, hard-learned lessons hurt every time she was stupid enough to ignore them. Her eyes stung, and she slumped in defeated acceptance. The happily ever after moment, so inevitable last night, wouldn't be happening for her and Becket Ford. She needed to accept that.

Decision made, she pushed to her feet. "Are you keeping me prisoner, or can I go home now?"

He stopped mid-step, crossed his arms, and glowered at her. "You know that's not my style. If I meant to keep you here, you'd be tied to a chair like my

152

friend Renée," he growled.

Her chin came up, and she pinned him with an unrelenting stare. "Prove it. Let me go home. But, Beck, know this—I will not hand over my legacy to you or anyone else. You can try and take it. If you're as good as you say, I can't stop you anyway."

"Oh, I can come up with one really good way to stop me—you can call the cops, and I'll never make it out of the country. Why should I trust you? Unrequited love?"

She snorted. "Yeah, that ship sailed a couple of hours ago. Let's call it curiosity. You say you want to be different—you want to be more than the petty thief they made you. Well, I say—prove it. *Be* that guy. The one who does the right thing even if it's hard. The one who deserves better from me than hatred and pity."

He straightened at that. She'd scored a direct hit to his soft spot—integrity.

"What are you suggesting, Jules, a contest? Your defenses against my skill?" His mouth quirked up in an arrogant half smile, and damned if it didn't make her thighs tighten with need. He was just so—cocky. Not wanted. Not devastatingly absorbing. Not the man or the lover she'd used as a basis for comparison against all others.

She walked toward him and plucked her purse off the small kitchen island. She pushed back her shoulders and cocked her head. She refused to let him see she was afraid he'd call her bluff. "Wanna bet?" She stuck out her hand.

He sighed as if she were foolish to test him. "You'll lose. How are you going to feel then? First, think about that."

She shrugged and shook her hand at him impatiently. Beck's grasp was strong as he pulled her against his chest. Her breath whooshed out in surprise, and she pushed back, only gaining a sliver of space. He grinned down at her.

Her eyes narrowed. "If you win—I'll be pissed, and I won't stop hunting for you till I put you in prison. How about that?"

"Deal," he said and kissed her hard.

She struggled for a tick of the clock, then gave back as good as she got. Two could play at the game of seduction. She had a card or two she hadn't laid down.

He released her as suddenly as he'd grabbed her. "Go. Get out of here before I change my mind and tie you to the bed instead." His breath was rough against her face.

She wiped his kiss from her lips with the back of her hand and tucked her bag under one arm. As she pulled open the door to the street, she turned to him. "Come and get it, Becket." She tossed the challenge at him like a gauntlet and stepped into the sun. "I dare you."

Chapter Thirteen

Fanish ran his thumb across the photo. His father's face was so young and carefree in it. The background showed a vague outline of a temple in silhouette against an impossibly blue sky. Golkonda. An ethereal land filled with magic and spirits and gods in human form. Rationally, he knew the reality of the dirt-poor existence the people experienced. That didn't stop him from fantasizing about the existential rebirth of it as a seat of power. His power.

A soft knock interrupted Singh's ruminations. "Come," he said and slipped the picture of his father back into the drawer. "What is it, Jasper?"

"You wanted to be advised when the girl woke, sir." Jasper's truncated body bent slightly at the waist. "She is clean and ready for you at your convenience."

Fanish waved the news away. "My interest in her has—flagged—shall we say." His time in the company of Miss Greenleaf had begun in such a promising way. Her complete capitulation left her too much like a broken toy. He'd wait to toss her to the dust bin until it served a higher purpose.

"As you say, sir. She's quite docile this morning."

Jasper's affected accent always made Fanish smile. The ugly pug of a man tried so hard to assume the cultured tones of his betters. The gutter still managed to leak into his speech. He really should give the girl to his lackey as a perk for his diligent attention to detail.

"You may take her some food. Keep her company if you like."

Jasper's smile was as grotesque as the man himself. "Of course, sir. I'll keep her entertained. Will there be anything else?"

"Not for the moment. Be ready, though. We may be traveling soon." His fingers drummed on the rich mahogany surface of his desk.

"America, sir?"

Singh sighed. "Possibly." He shooed Jasper away and opened his laptop. Santos owed him an update.

He lit a long narrow cigar and rocked back in his comfy leather chair. A few keystrokes and his laptop displayed the feed from Santos's phone. "Are you on-site at Ford's accommodation?"

Seth rolled his eyes. "Yes, boss. Right where you told me to be. We been watchin' the place for half an hour."

The view on the laptop swiveled to the carriage house. They watched as two new players strolled up to the door and disappeared into the house.

"See that?" Seth asked. "Doubtful those were tourists, Mr. Singh. They yours?"

"Correct, although only the woman is on my payroll. She likely brought along an assistant." That was troublesome. Not terribly concerning. Pashi had her instructions, and she'd proven reliable in the past. Besides, once she had the necklace in her hands, she'd be much wealthier than the monetary value of the jewel. She might even prove to be a long-term asset in his dynasty.

Seth's face filled the entire screen. "Hey, boss

man." One eye twitched as he glanced over his shoulder. He pulled back and flashed the view of the back seat of his vehicle. "Before you rip me a new one, I gotta ask. How was I supposed to know you wanted ol' Roland, here? You don't tell me nothin'."

"Anticipating my needs is part of your job, Mr. Santos." A muscle jumped in Fanish's jaw. "Are you so dense that you couldn't see the wisdom of holding on to a possible piece of leverage? The uncle may be useful. Since you've yet to determine how Ford plans to accomplish his mission, we need as many cards as possible to win this game." Honestly, working long distance had its disadvantages—dealing with morons was one of them.

"I'm just sayin', I had him. Fuck, I kicked his ass and tossed him out the door of my bar. If I'd *known*, I woulda held on to his raggedy butt and wouldn't a had to drag him out of the hospital."

"Enough!" Fanish's palm slapped the desk. "You're walking a thin line over there. Prove yourself more capable and less like Ford's mentally incompetent brother." The urge to reach through the screen and snap the man's neck like a pencil made his fingers itch.

"All right, all right. Chill, man, 's all good. Calm down. Told you we'd collect the trash. See?" Seth grinned into the frame and jutted his phone toward the back seat.

Their prisoner sat slumped in the back seat of the SUV, pressed between the hulking shoulders of Seth's two thugs. Roland whimpered and bucked to straighten his shoulders. The thugs only leaned harder against him. Fanish took another moment to enjoy the misery displayed on his pinched face.

Roland begged through teeth locked together by his wired jaw. "Seth, please. It wasn't about you. Juliette showed up at your bar out of the blue. It's not like I told her where I'd be, so she was looking for me. She would have brought the police if she had any concrete evidence on you."

Seth craned his neck around and scowled at Roland. "You better pray that's the case, asswipe. You've caused enough problems. I don't need the cops sniffin' around to boot."

He straightened behind the wheel and turned his camera back to watching Beck's house. "Well now," Seth mumbled, "what we got here? If it ain't the tasty Miss Juliette Rochambeau, in the flesh." Seth moved the phone's camera to take in the scene. "She's got her phone glued to her ear. We're only a couple blocks from her store. She sure as shit ain't callin' a cab." He swiveled in his seat, and the image blurred for a moment. "Reese, you follow her. Text me regular, you hear?" He handed the other man a small object. "Junior, get up alongside Beck's ride and stick that under his bumper. Don't get caught."

The men peeled away from Roland and slipped out of the SUV. One crossed the street and dropped in behind the striding Juliette. The other, a hulk in camo, slid across the street and behind Beck's car.

Seth repositioned the phone into the mount on the dash. He grinned at Singh. "Thought it would be handy to know where my boy is in case he gets slippery."

"Indeed. You're showing promise, Mr. Santos."

"Just anticipating your needs, Mr. Singh." He sounded pleased with himself. "We should move down the block and see if the cops come a-knockin'. If not, then I guess we're still in play. Hard to believe Beck convinced her to hand it off in trade for some puddin' an' pie, that's for damn sure."

Roland's voice was a raspy grate through his teeth. "She's too much of a daddy's girl to do that." He was the picture of defeat as he laid his head back on the seat.

Seth snorted his disgust at the quivering man behind him. "Well, she just walked away after meeting his crew, and Beck ain't stupid. No way that woulda happened if she wasn't willing to deal."

Roland moaned out his fear. "I'm not popular right now, I know. How about I go to Edward?" He struggled upright in the seat. "He'd come apart at the seams if Juliette was in league with Ford."

"Fuck, you're mule stupid," Seth snapped. "We *want* Beck to do the job *for* us."

"Yes," said Fanish, "and to that end, I believe it's time to put the trash to work for us. Mr. Ford needs another inducement to hurry our job along. Flushing him out of his burrow will be quite sufficient." *Oh, this is rich fun.* "Since Roland has proved so problematic, I'd like you to bring a permanent end to his dealings with you. I will, of course, cover your losses in exchange."

Eyebrows raised in surprise, Seth licked his lips in anticipation. "I get your drift, but just to be clear, this cheatin' asshole has reached his expiration date. Correct?"

It appeared Seth had learned to ask clarification before acting on his own. "Yes, yes. Use whatever method suits the situation best, Santos. Be sure to leave the evidence as close to Mr. Ford as possible, but not so publicly that it makes the job impossible." Ah, being the puppet master never failed to please.

"I get it. In plain sight but not propped up against his door."

Roland's terrified moan filled the car. He grabbed the door handle and rattled it furiously.

Seth laughed at his panic. "Child locks. Ain't they great?"

The remaining associate in the passenger's seat cleared his throat. "Not sure what you got in mind, but if you swing around this corner, there's an alley just past Ford's hidey-hole. It's quiet and has a straight shot to the next street over."

Seth reared back and chuckled. "Reuben, my man. Good idea. That could work. That could definitely work." He gave the man an affectionate punch to the arm and glanced into the rearview. "Sorry, Roland. Looks like we've come to the end of our time together. Can't say as I've enjoyed it much." He made a sharp left into an alley. Reuben jumped out and hurried around to the passenger's door. Roland scooted as far away from him as he could. He hissed out a painful curse as the armrest cut sharply into his side. He cowered in the seat as the door sprang open beside him. Seth grabbed his collar and jerked him out of sight.

A better camera angle on the phone would have allowed Singh to witness all the details. Still, the sounds from the transatlantic connection gave him a vivid account of the situation playing out in the dim alley. He imagined the stench and the panic. The sense of hopelessness Roland experienced as his knees hit the filthy pavement.

A muffled pistol report and a flash of light lit up

the glass at the side of the SUV, as the bullet exploded into its target.

"One less detail to track." Seth's matter-of-fact words echoed across the ocean.

Singh smiled and stumped out his cigar. According to Pashmina's report, Ford would be making his move on the stone tonight. Assuming his success, they would be in the air to pick up the stone shortly after completion. He rocked back in his chair and linked his fingers behind his head. All in all, the situation in South Carolina was developing quite well.

"Nicely done, Mr. Santos. Don't forget to keep an eye on Mr. Ford for me. I'll be in touch." He didn't wait for a preening reply before he closed the connection.

Loving the ability to keep his finger on multiple problems simultaneously, Singh lit another cigar and switched the connection on his laptop to the CCTV feed from the basement. Audio was the newest addition to his security. He settled back to watch Jasper enjoy his gift.

"I remember you. You—you shot me up." Renée's mouth sounded dry as sand. "Please, no more drugs. I'll be good, I promise." Her voice was reedy and pleading.

"Sweet girl," Jasper whispered and smoothed his fingertips over Renée's cheek. "My name's Jasper. I'll take care of you now."

She jerked her face away. Her hands fluttered ineffectually on the thin gown she wore. The chill of the basement cell caused her nipples to peak beneath the fabric.

Jasper licked his lips and shifted closer. "I must say, the master put you through the wringer, didn't he?"

He stroked her matted hair as he spoke reassuringly. "They say good lessons are those you live through."

He glanced up at the camera. Was that a smidgen of disapproval? Fanish chuckled. This was better than any program the telly had to offer. He caught another glance—this one from Ms. Greenleaf. Ooo, she was silently seething. Perhaps she wasn't a broken plaything after all.

"Stay away from me," Renée hissed. She slapped at his hand. "I'll fucking kill you if you touch me, you disgusting little prick."

Jasper's muscled arm snapped out, and his hand tangled in her hair. He jerked her face toward his. "Difficult to manage given your circumstances, wouldn't you say? So you might want to consider being nice to me."

Her blue eyes snapped open wide, and she cringed away as if she expected a blow.

"You were foolish to step out of line, Renée. I thought you were smarter than that. Very naïve of you."

"Like I care what you think. Let go of me." Her hands gripped his wrist ineffectually.

"It doesn't have to be like this between us."

He released his grip on her ratted hair, and she scuttled as far from him as the tattered mattress would allow. She flinched away from the stone wall behind her, and Fanish smiled, imagining the searing contact of the rough cold against the welts on her back.

"What does that mean? You've come to take his place, is that it?" A touch of anger leaked into her expression. "Am I your fuck toy now?" Her spirit held on.

Fanish shifted, his gaze glued to the mini-drama

playing out in his basement.

Jasper shrugged. "He's done with you now, and he said I'm to keep you company. That's good, right?"

Her shoulders slumped in resignation, and he raised his palms to appease her.

"Don't worry, I won't treat you the way he did." He held out a plush robe. "Look. See what I've brought you? I knew you'd be cold." Gently, he draped the soft fabric across the rigid foot of the steel cot that had been her only comfort during her captivity.

She grabbed the robe and gathered it to her chest. Her hands trembled into its folds as she watched Jasper suspiciously. "Sure. You only want to be my friend. Is that the way of it?" She struggled to her knees and pulled the robe onto her battered body. She jerked the belt into a cumbersome knot.

"Is that too big a leap for you?" Jasper reached out and gave a hard shake to one of the bars extending from ceiling to floor beside him. "I can at least make you more comfortable."

Fanish tapped the ash off his cigar. Did Jasper remember the animal cages from his days as sideshow mongrel? Had those cages seen the kind of degradation and death as this one?

"You want to comfort me?" she asked. "Then let me go. Please." Tears resumed their escape from her swollen eyes, catching in droplets on lashes stuck together into spikes. "He's a butcher," she whispered, "who loves to play with his food before he kills it. Please, I don't deserve to die because I was stupid, do I? I want to go home."

He shook his head and smiled indulgently. "I can't, darling girl. He'd kill us both if I did. Don't worry. It won't be long now. You'll see the end of this soon enough."

"One way or another, you mean." A disbelieving huff rattled out of her throat. "The sadistic bastard is waiting for Becket to do what he promised. Not much hope for me, then, is there?" She shrugged a delicate shoulder. "He's deserted me before. I wouldn't be so sure he won't do it again."

"I can't say what will happen, Renée. But yes, that's Ford's way, from what I've heard. What did you expect to do, set up an installment program? You can see where that got you."

Renée sniffed loudly and wiped her nose on the sleeve of the robe. "Story of my life, uh…Jasper." She pulled the collar snug around her neck. "Since you're my new keeper and all, could I have some food? I'm fair starving."

Jasper smiled broadly. "I'll attend to that right away, my darling girl. Soup will be the easiest with your lip split like it is." He rose to his full four-foot height. "Then how about some clothes? I've laundered the ones you were wearing personally."

A grateful smile blossomed on her face. This was going exceptionally well. Jasper's pet was learning to trust her new friend. A well-trained, well-placated animal was always easier to handle.

Chapter Fourteen

Juliette strode away from Becket like an out of control car careening down a steep grade. She palmed her phone and dialed. "Charles, would you contact anyone who isn't on-site and get them to the store? Set up a staff meeting for this afternoon."

Charles sputtered out a hurried agreement. "Is there a problem, Miss Juliette? Do I need to call in the extra security detail?"

"No. I'll reach out to them myself." She stopped at the first corner and battled to control her breathing. Every lungful of air sucked her closer to the edge of an emotional high dive.

Furious in general and Beck in particular, she jammed her phone back into her purse and stepped off the sidewalk. A blaring horn warned her out of its path, and she jumped back. *Christ Almighty, Jules, pay a-damn-ttention*. She glanced both ways and stepped carefully off the curb.

"Him and his sob story about his education as a big-time thief," she muttered. "As if I'd believe a second of it. Con. That's all it was—a con. Come home with me, Jules—make love with me, Jules—believe me, Jules." *The incredible brass balls of the man!*

She huffed out her disdain. Beck's two cohorts were the Middle Eastern version of Boris and Natasha. As perfect as if he'd found them in central casting under the heading "Spy on Vacation" and "Femme Fatal." And what the hell was with that woman's upper-crust accent? Who was she kiddin' anyway?

God, stuff like this didn't happen in real life—not in her real life. As if she was going to stand back and let him take the necklace. *Sure, Beck, it's all yours. Oh, and wrap it in my good sense while you're at it.* Puh-lease. Not happening. She'd stop him. She'd teach him to mess with her. Her breath caught in her throat, and she swallowed a lump the size of Charleston Bay.

Her steps hesitated as she rounded the last corner before the jewelry store. Scalding tears squeezed past her lids and spilled down her cheeks. She stomped her foot and dashed them away. He would not make her cry. She was tougher than that. Harder to crack than the naïve, small-town girl she used to be. She would *not* lie down and be his sucker.

"It'd serve him right if I put him in jail," she mumbled. Sour regret accompanied a vision of Becket behind bars. "Sonofabitch. Why, Beck? Was it all just a part of your plan? How come *I* have to be the one who finally jerks you straight?" Regret slumped her shoulders as she reached out for the door of the showroom. She had to find a way to make her point without the side effect of—destroying him.

The cool interior was a blessing to her overheated mind. At the main counter, Charles stood at attention like a kid fearing his first inspection at boot camp. "Miss Juliette. I've reached everybody, and they'll be here shortly. Just so you know, your mama's called for you a couple of times." He took in the wrinkled state of her sundress and disarrayed tangles clinging to her hair. "If I were you, I'd go up the back stairs."

"Thanks for the warning. I'll do that. How are we doin'?" She assessed the showroom. The wall displays were ready for glass. The new carpet was ready to lay, and the smell of fresh paint clung to the air. "Where do we stand on new merchandise? Have you gotten flak from our suppliers?"

"Nope, not a one. Roland made such a big stink about it I wanted to call them personally. Goods should start arriving this afternoon. If we're lucky, we'll be open for business right on schedule." He beamed, evidently proud of all he'd accomplished without Roland's interference.

"Good work, Charles. I don't know what we'd have done if not for you." She hugged him tightly. He was a gem with unparalleled attention to detail. That he was sometimes prissy and dour only made him more precious. She released him before she clouded up again. "I'm going to sneak upstairs and jump in the shower. Do me a favor, give it a minute, then call my mom and distract her. Will you?"

"You got it, Miss Juliette. It looks like you had quite a night." His eyes sparkled, and his eyebrows waggled.

"You have no idea," she threw over her shoulder as she crossed the retail space and punched in the code. Her steps were louder than she wanted as she ran up the stairs. At the top, she peeked out into the hall. The coast was clear for the moment, and she hurried to her bedroom, locking the door behind her. Not even a solid panel of wood would stop her mother from cornering her. She chided herself for reverting to the girl who used to hide away from moments of conflict and avoid the limelight at all costs. The veneer of brash and ballsy she'd worked so hard to cultivate was thinner than usual this morning.

She stripped off her dress and underwear, stepped into her bathroom, and cranked on the shower. The heat from the spray would go a long way toward soothing the ache building behind her eyes. She stood in front of her mirror and searched the face staring back at her. Her sky blue eyes showed the strain. Her lips retained the swollen puffiness brought on by his bruising kisses. And those weren't the only brands he'd left on her—a road map of reddish-purple smudges the size of nipping bites peppered across her breasts. The clear imprint of his fingers lingered on her hip. She should be angry that he'd marked her, left his signature. Her core tightened as she relived the mindless passion that brought them about. She should have remembered how absorbed he became. His total focus on her pleasure was so rare. A fact she'd only become aware of once she had a basis for comparison. It turned out not every lover was concerned about her enjoyment or cared if she got more than their company out of a night together.

She ghosted a hand over her breasts, circling each mark with a fingertip. Her nipples beaded in response, and a needy moan escaped her mouth. How could she wipe out the night they'd shared when he'd written it bold and unrepentant on her body?

Damn the man. She threw up her hands in frustration and stepped under the water. It was all part of Becket's fucking plan. Seduce her, make her a spongy pushover, and rob her blind. Yeah. That was exactly it, and she was the fool who waffled in indecision over whether to end it by calling the police. *Christ.*

She stifled an exasperated scream. Who was she fooling? She couldn't call the cops on him any more than she could walk away from her responsibilities to her parents. What she *could* do was see that he didn't have the chance to steal the necklace. Then sit back and see if he tried.

She quickly shampooed and conditioned her hair, scraped a razor over her legs, rinsed, and cranked off the water. She hurried through the rest of her bathing routine and was dressing when knocking erupted at her door.

The doorknob rattled. "Lettie, open this door." Evie's tone brooked no delay.

She closed her eyes and took a deep breath. She'd have to face her eventually. "I'll be out in a minute, Mama."

Evie harrumphed from the hall.

She wondered if it was possible to slow down the hail of questions headed her way by pleading starvation. "I could use some breakfast. Can you make me some of those eggs I love?"

Staccato footsteps retreated down the hall as Evie stalked away. "Kitchen. Ten minutes, young lady."

Juliette sighed in relief. She didn't bother drying her hair. A quick wet braid was all she could manage. She inspected the soft, mulberry-colored silk shirt she pulled over a cami and smoothed down her fawn-colored capris. The strappy heels she slipped into matched the shirt well enough. Despite her best efforts, she couldn't quiet the nerves vibrating beneath the surface of her skin. She'd have to be very careful about how she handled herself, or her mother would pick up on the vulnerable uncertainty of her wayward daughter.

Evie stood, hands on hips, as she entered the kitchen. On the bar, a fragrant plate of cheesy scrambled eggs and glistening buttered toast waited beside a cup of steaming coffee. Juliette wrapped her hands around the cup and breathed in the scent of freshly ground salvation.

"Well?" Evie demanded.

She flinched and focused on the hot brown liquid sloshing in her cup. *Be brave. Don't back down. No excuses.* "I spent the night with Becket Ford. Does that answer your question?"

Evie sputtered out a laugh. "Uh…yes. I thought I'd have to pry it out of you. The man's a charming scamp. I can certainly see the attraction."

"You can say that again," she said around a mouthful of eggs. "Too bad it's all smoke and mirrors, though." *Remain calm.* She forced her hands to get busy making a sandwich out of the toast and remaining eggs. "Guess what I found out this morning. Sort of a parting gift." She chased another bite with a gulp of coffee.

Evie made a wrap-it-up gesture.

"He's after the necklace, not me—how's that for a slap in the face?" If she kept her mouth full, she wouldn't reveal how devastating the knowledge was.

Evie gasped and clutched her pearls. "He…he's what?"

Swallowing was harder than expected. "A thief, Mama. My old boyfriend is Hank Santos's stepson. *The* Hank Santos. Daddy's nemesis. Guess the apple dropped straight through the branches and didn't roll when it landed."

"Sweet Jesus." Evie fanned herself with a dish

towel.

The next bite stuck in Juliette's throat, and she had to force it down. "I made him take me to Longfellow's and double as a bodyguard if Roland showed his face."

"Oh, for cryin' in the sink, Lettie. That place is a gussied-up dive. What were you thinking?" The towel became a missile lobbed at Juliette's head.

She slapped it away. "For starters, I figured I'd rub Roland's slimy face in it. It turned out he was in the middle of paying for screwing up with the owner."

Her mother covered her mouth to stifle a groan. "No." Her palm moved to her pearls. "So Chet was right?"

"Yup, he was right on point. It gets better. Wanna know who owns that bar?" She waited a beat. "Becket's stepbrother, that's who. When we got there, Seth Santos was hustling dear ol' Roland out the door. They broke his jaw and dumped him in the parking lot."

Evie tsked in sympathy.

"Beck and I took him to the hospital and left him. I probably should have called you right away, but I figured you didn't need to be upset in the middle of the night. Sorry."

Evie's hand left her pearls for her forehead. "Oh, good heavens, sugar. I'm glad you didn't call us. Daddy would have been beside himself. Sorry Roland was hurt, but he was lucky they didn't kill him. It sounds like he was even luckier you were on the lookout for him. He never knew when to quit, so he probably got what he deserved."

"According to Beck, Seth's a nasty character. Guess the whole bunch of them are. I'm not sure about Beck yet. I can tell you for sure, though, he's got his course set. And he intends to succeed."

"Seems to me he has more than one objective. Hate to break it to you, sugar, but you already gave up your half of the prize."

Juliette tsked. "I did. More than once, more fool me. But that's not the point." Now for the rest of it. "I challenged him." The admission brought a shiver of apprehension across her skin.

"You what?" Evie squeaked.

"I told him to come and get it."

Her mother grabbed the countertop. "Of all the damn fool antics, Lettie!"

Juliette waved off her concern. "It doesn't matter now. I have a plan—of a sort." She held her mother's gaze. "I'm going to let him take it."

****

Becket sat, head in hands. How the fuck was he supposed to do this? He was delusional if he thought he'd find a way to get her back after saying, "Oh, by the by, I've come to steal you blind." He'd managed to destroy every good memory and tender feeling she'd had for him just by being who he truly was.

She'd laid it out plainly enough. "Be that guy," she'd said, and he wished he could comply. He wished he could be the good guy. A lifetime of hard lessons proved he wasn't a fairy-tale hero. He wasn't the one who saved the day, rescued the damsel, protected the kingdom, and won his true love. The real world stood in direct opposition to changing himself into *that guy*. No matter how much he wanted it to be different, he suspected it was way too late for that.

"What the hell have you done?" Yosef's strangled voice jerked Beck to the here and now.

Beck straightened his spine and faced his friend. "The only thing I could do. I let her go." And she hadn't gone quietly. His lips quirked, remembering the challenge in her eyes as she laid down her "come and get it" glove.

"Well, that's just wonderfully—insane, isn't it?" Yosef flopped down in the chair opposite him. "She'll go straight to the coppers, and I, for one, have no interest in sticking around to meet the locals." He crossed his arms over his narrow chest and glared at Beck. "Thank God I didn't unpack."

"Couldn't exactly lock her in the closet, now could I?" He stood and paced. In the last few hours, so much crap had piled up in the corners the room had gotten smaller. Whatever he decided—to stay or to go—to steal or not to steal—he was the loser. The whole fiasco was a Shakespearian tale of woe. All he needed was a frickin' balcony and a vial of poison.

He paused his circuit of the room at the patio doors. The sunny area was empty. "Where's Pashi?" Great, two women had walked out on him in one day.

Yosef huffed and shifted in his seat. "She said shopping was in order and called a cab. I expect she wanted some privacy because she and Singh are having phone sex as we speak."

Beck huffed out a derisive laugh. "I don't get the connection. I never took Pashi for someone who'd do business with a bastard like that. She's certainly not in the dark about him." He had to find a way to gain some leverage in this shit show. Pashi could be the loose thread needed to shed some light on the guy's fixation on the necklace.

Yosef shrugged. "I asked her that question on the

plane. She said Singh's 'deeper' than she expected. I laughed, and she told me I should try it sometime. Told me to 'look for meaning in life beyond the immediate gratification of my left hand.' Honestly, Beck. How would changing hands make a difference?"

"I'd say she knows you pretty well." Beck shook his head at Yosef disgruntled expression. "Back to Singh, what else did she tell you?"

"Let's see. His family goes all the way back to the early sixteen hundreds. Closely connected to the throne in their ancestral home, Golkonda. He's the last in his line."

Beck's mouth dropped open. Golkonda was synonymous with the largest and most famous gems in history. The Hope Diamond, the Koh-I-Noor, and the Nassak had all come from the same region. Now this was getting interesting.

"She said he has this whopping big tattoo marking him as a member of a group dedicated to Ganesha. He wouldn't share many details. Apparently, it's *super* sexy." Yosef gagged. "Anyway, that confirms the dude is as woo-woo crazy as we suspected."

"All right, let's put this together." Beck ticked off his list on his fingers. "Historical connection to a geographic region known for huge fucking diamonds. So dedicated to cult or family that he permanently marked the proof on his body. Chasing a ruby as big as a pigeon's egg doesn't fit unless it has some significance connected to this cult or whatever." He rubbed his hands together. "Sounds to me like the stone is more than just an expensive rock. What if it's a relic? Could explain his single-minded approach and why he's dead set on the Rochambeau necklace."

"Exactly. So while the winsome Pashi was sleeping—snores like an adorable puppy by the way—I was researching the necklace's history. Specifically, for connections to our leading whacko." He wiggled his eyebrows. "The link to his family is sketchy, so bear with me. His people came to France shortly after the fall of the ruler of Golkonda. Our buddy's ancestor was this ambitious silk trader fresh out of Delhi anxious to expand his business sans the interference of the British East India Company. All of a sudden, he's a star in royal circles—the supplier to Marie Antoinette's court of glitz-hungry hedonists. We know the stone belonged to the queen. What if he used it to bribe his way into the high end of the market?"

"That fits with the story of how the necklace got into Rochambeau hands. Jules told me when we were kids that it was a gift from the queen to her pet, General Rochambeau, for keeping her lover safe during the Revolutionary War." God, that was forever ago. Time really was like a wheel. "Where did you dig up all this shit?"

Yosef preened. "I'm a freaking wizard with a keyboard, that's how."

"You're somethin' all right. This scenario plays, though." Beck scrubbed his hands over his face. Singh's focused effort to get his hands on the Rochambeau stone certainly smacked of more than simple greed. It wasn't a big leap to see him as a zealot hell-bent on its recovery, especially if a religious connection existed. What if the silk merchant had come by the ruby under less than honorable circumstances? Then the cult came on line to right a wrong to their deity. Was that even likely? He wondered if, on some

175

level, he and Singh had some things in common. They definitely shared a penchant for the drama of classic Hollywood. Regardless, Singh had a real flare for playing the moustache-twirling villain.

"I'm not sure it makes a difference for us." Yosef sighed and yawned while stretching his back. "Experience proves the more insight we have on a mark, the better our chance of success with the final score." He patted his pocket and frowned when his box of smokes revealed only a few left.

"Right or not, I say let's find a way to use it. He's on a mission. That's the best news I've had all day."

Yosef's eyebrows shot up. "Pardon me? As far as I can see, it makes him dangerous on more than one level."

"Precisely, Dr. Watson—more than one *exploitable* level. This isn't money-grubbing. He's got more to lose. Zealots don't have gray areas. They believe in righteous redemption or damnation, heavenly rewards or fire and brimstone. He's afraid to fail, and fear makes him vulnerable."

Chapter Fifteen

Juliette gathered her notes and waited for the staff to quiet down. She lifted her plastic glass of white wine. "If I didn't believe in miracles before today, all I'd need to convince me would be seeing all you've accomplished in the last week and a half." She swallowed down a knot of emotion and cleared her throat. "Family is a term often tossed around loosely in business. We've all worked for companies who use it to dismiss the need for thanks to those who work tirelessly toward accomplishing company goals. I want to assure you that each of you are an integral part of *this* family, and we're eternally grateful to have you." She saluted the upturned faces of her staff. "So before I start to blubber—here's to you. Thanks for standing by us and for coming in on such short notice. See Charles and Chet for your schedules starting Friday, and together we'll make this reopening a new beginning for Rochambeau, Inc."

Her cheeks flushed as the group of fifteen people applauded. She hadn't planned to come home to stay. But with each decision she made and every question she answered, the idea became more concrete. The way they'd seamlessly accepted her as the leader of the company bolstered her belief in her ability to succeed.

As the staff filed out, Charles handed everyone printed schedules, and Chet spoke to each of the men from the workshop. Within a few moments, the place had emptied, and her parents turned toward the elevator.

Her father paused before he stepped behind the swirling bronze decoration of the gated opening. "I'm so proud of you, sugar plum. I know it's not what you'd wanted, but damn, I'm glad you're staying." His focus flicked away for a moment and back to her. "You are staying, right?"

"Yes, Daddy, I'm staying. Don't worry. I got this." *Fake it till you make it.* The task she'd taken on was more than daunting. She laughed at herself. At some point between stepping back through the door to the showroom the first day and becoming embroiled in Becket's tangled intentions, her decision had solidified. They'd have to use dynamite to blast her out of Charleston now. She prayed Becket wouldn't light the fuse that blew her life to hell a second time. Thank heavens she'd kept her plan to herself.

A relieved smile painted her father's face as he and Evie disappeared into the elevator, and a warm glow bloomed in her chest. Finally, after all these years, was it possible he might approve of her choices? Of course, they were the same choices he'd been trying to get her to make for ten years. She pushed the niggling suspicion she was being manipulated back into its messy hole and turned toward the only people left in the store.

"Charles, thanks for pulling the staff together so quickly. In the next couple of weeks, I'd like to go over each member's productivity in case there are changes that need to happen."

He nodded, looking pained.

"Don't worry. I'm not canning anyone. I'm sure some changes will make for a smoother transition."

His face relaxed. "Whatever you want, Miss Juliette. I'm sure we could all use a refresher in training, etcetera. Would you like me to make some suggestions?"

"Yup, I would. Next week is soon enough. Go on home now and get some rest. Better yet, take your husband out to dinner. You've been here every waking hour since the robbery. I know he's missed you."

Charles blushed. "Danny understands. He's a good man. He'd have to be to put up with me for twenty years." The easy way he mentioned his spouse was endearing. The world had changed so much since she was a girl. People hadn't been as open back then.

She bent and pecked a kiss to the rosy apple of color on his cheek. "Get out of here." She patted his shoulder as he left.

She turned to Chet and Gabby. "I need to talk to you guys. Have you got plans for lunch?" She glanced at her watch. "More like dinner now. I guess time got away from me."

"A glass of wine sounds wonderful," Gabby said. "Shall we go to the Pelican? It's become our *lieu de secrets, non?*" She waggled her brows and grinned.

"Oh yeah, real cloak and dagger, that's us." Juliette composed a confident smile as she planned her next move. She spoke to Chet. "You finished the repair on the necklace, right?"

He nodded. "I reset the center stone this morning. Why? You want to inspect it?" His eyebrows rose in surprise at the question.

Juliette smirked; he wasn't used to anyone daring

to check his work.

She brushed away his concern. "No, I'm sure it's perfect. It's back in the vault, I assume."

He nodded again.

"And the copy?" She needed access to both pieces.

"Tucked away in the back of the top shelf." His mouth drew down in concern.

"I'll talk to you both at the Pelican. Order me a gin and tonic and a big ol' cheeseburger with sweet potato fries. I'll be right behind you. I need to do a couple of things first."

"Oh, man. Now what," Chet grumbled as Gabby hustled him out the door and keyed the lock behind them. Juliette grinned at their backs. They were so natural together. A sizzle of jealousy buzzed through her, and she brushed it off. She and Becket had lost the opportunity for effortless intimacy before it had a chance to start.

She spun on her heels and walked to the safe. The combination hadn't been changed in years—another item that needed addressing. The list of details was staggering. The tumblers sank silently into place, and she spun the spoked handle to open the massively heavy door. She put her back into stopping the smooth swing at the halfway point. Alongside the steel box, a wheeled cart used for loading and unloading the cases waited to be put to use.

Quickly, she glanced around the shop, halfway sure she'd see Becket dressed in his burglar getup lurking in a corner. She blew out a calming breath and plucked the box containing the original necklace from its designated place on the second shelf. The burgundy and gold of the cover glowed warm and reliable in the overhead lights.

She placed it gently on the cart and turned back to unload the top shelf until her hands touched the duplicate's box. Would this work? If not, they were all fools—her father for having the damn copy made, Becket for lifting it, and her for letting him.

Gently she placed the pretender beside its twin on the cart and reloaded the top shelf. She turned back to the matching boxes and brushed sweaty palms down her thighs. She cast a prayer into the empty store and unclasped the covers. The original's top moved with the silky smoothness of well-worn leather, and she paused, her bottom lip caught in her teeth. The box for the copy was only a couple of years old, much stiffer than the centuries-old version. Becket wouldn't miss a detail like that. She opened the second box and wiped her hands on her thighs again. On impulse, she plucked the copy from its nest and ran her thumbnail along the link Chet brought to her attention yesterday. The surface was smooth and unmarred by the treatment of Seth's thugs. Her lips tipped up confidently.

She whispered a sing-song taunt into the empty store. "I know something you don't know." Surprised at the weight of the necklace as she slipped the copy over her wrist, she laid her palm against its older sister. Carefully she scraped her nail along the telling link and caught the hitch on the surface. Chet was indeed a master at his craft. Only someone who knew the piece intimately would find the tiny defect. Gently she played her index finger along the length of the chain and across the graduated run of diamonds sweeping toward the center stone. She forced herself to breathe slowly.

Priceless—the term was a subjective construct before this. Now it was a reality.

Before she could change her mind about her plan, she slipped the antique from its bed in the older box and arranged the piece carefully in the new one. The copy found its home on the older cushion, and she closed both lids with a decisive click. She lifted the imposter to center-front in the safe and swung the thick door shut. The solid clang of metal on metal made her cringe, and she glanced around her again. Pins-and-needles-level nerves brought on a shiver as the door closed. She spun the exterior wheel to seal the safe. The spokes flashed, advertising her role as the newest guardian of Charleston's hidden riches.

She had to laugh at herself when she found she was hugging the red box to her chest like a fragile infant and hurried to the stairs. She ignored the jerky motion of her hand when she punched in the security code and rushed up the steps. At the top, a peek down the hall showed vacant territory between her and access to the attic. No one, especially Becket, knew about her stash of mementos. Until this was over, her childhood treasure trove would be her strongbox.

****

Incredulous, Yosef threw his hands in the air. "You have *got* to be winding me up." His tattered cigarette box offered up its last soldier. He tsked in disgust and pointed the black-and-gold wrapped butt at Becket. "Sure, just ring the psycho murderer and invite him to tea, why don't you?"

Beck's mouth twisted. "Yoyo" would have to stoop to American tobacco sooner than he'd like. "It's the only way that works. Unless, of course, you'd consider swallowing the goods. Because I highly doubt Pashi will consent to stuffing them up her lady-bits. It's not

182

like you can shove it in your pants and expect to get through customs, now is it?" The searches TSA put passengers through on commercial flights made transporting goods nigh on impossible. The shrill whistle of the metal detector wand would go off like a siren if it ran across a chunk of gold like the one in question.

"You've got that right, gov." Yosef sneered at the suggestion. "I'm not bloody volunteering to be your mule."

Beck laughed. "Yeah, no big surprise. If we're not hot now, we will be the minute they discover the necklace missing."

"Cocky beggar, aren't you?"

"Self-assured." Beck's jaw firmed. "That leaves only one option; I'll have to call Singh. Tell him the only way for the jewels to end up in his hands is to hop on his jet and come get them himself."

"This wouldn't be happening if you'd held on to your little friend. But nooo. You, in your infinite wisdom, let her go." He jabbed his cigarette at Beck again and slumped down on the couch. "You've still got the hots for princess white bread, chap. Admit that much." He tucked the foil end between his lips. "It chaps my arse that you've forgotten about the *other* girl involved here. What's to stop him from offing Renée to punish you?"

Beck glared at him. "Hold on, she got me into this, remember? He won't kill her. If he wants the necklace, he'll have to bring her to make the trade. Two birds—one stone, my friend."

"And then what? Everyone lives happily ever after? You and white bread, me and Pashi, Renée and whoever." He waved his hand dismissively. "You're dreaming."

"I know it's a long shot. And for it to work, I need both of them in the US. Besides, I want more out of this than clearing up a debt."

"Really. Like what, teaching Singh a lesson?" He deepened his voice, puffed out his chest, and hooked his thumbs in invisible suspenders. "Don't mess with Becket Ford, super thief. He's faster than a speeding cop car. He scales tall skyscrapers." He tossed the empty cigarette box at Beck's head. "And he's dumber than your average rock."

He batted it away. "Jesus, I didn't say I had it all figured out."

"Right, because doing some fancy sleight of hand with the necklace isn't just stupid—it's fantasy. The bastard has well-paid minions all over the world ready to hunt you down at the drop of a hat. If he puts a bounty on your head—or mine for that matter—we'll be dead before you can spit."

"I'm just trying to stack the odds in our favor, Yosef." Becket sighed heavily and surrendered to the weight of possible flaws in the bare bones of this latest strategy. "Ideally, I want Renée safe *and* Singh out of business completely. Don't care whether it's dead or shoved so deep into prison he never sees the light again. And then I want to find a place to put my feet up and just be normal. Start living. Stop looking over my shoulder, ya know?"

"Oh, bloody Christ. Are you talking about retirement?" Yosef closed his eyes and leaned back against the cushions. "You want this to be our last deal."

Beck shrugged noncommittally. "Yeah. Maybe. I guess." He walked to the french doors and leaned his forehead on the cool glass. Clouds obscured the sun, and he smelled rain in the air. Good, a moonless night lay ahead—all the better for his purpose. He chuckled at himself, taken aback at finding the prospect of getting out of his business more than a pipe dream. More than one of those dismissed aspirations. "I've got to make a change, and there's no time like the present. We can't keep going forever. The world is getting harder to crack than it used to be. We've had a great run, you and me. We've made a lot of money and wasted even more. I need to get out. If this is our last job together, we should go out with a blare of trumpets and a crash of cymbals."

Yosef cradled his head in his hands. "Yeah, well, it didn't turn out so great for Butch Cassidy and his buddy."

Beck grinned at his dramatic friend. "Jumping off cliffs is my specialty, Yoyo. It'll be fun. Watch and see."

Chapter Sixteen

Juliette dusted her hands and stood up. The light in the attic had dimmed in the last few minutes. She glanced out the fan window and noticed a few drops of rain on the glass. *Perfect.* She'd get drenched walking to the Pelican. What was she going to tell Gabby and Chet? She doubted they'd be happy about her plan. Too many variables could go wrong. Too many holes to call it a solid strategy.

Logically, tonight was the most likely choice for Beck to come for the necklace. If logic came into this insane cocktail at all. Who was to say she wouldn't miss him altogether? Conceivably, if her timing was off, he could get clean away. Being denied a confrontation wouldn't be as satisfying as catching him with his hand in her proverbial cookie jar. Camping out in the showroom wasn't a realistic option, nor was hiding cops in every corner. Although she was reluctant to accept it, envisioning him in jail caused a bone-deep pain.

Was she crazy to believe his story about the bad guy across the pond? No, she knew him well enough to gauge his reactions. Despite his claim that rescuing Renée was simply him keeping an old promise—he felt responsible for the girl. The same way he had for his little brother. Wishing he'd come back for any other reason was a pointless waste of heartbeats.

Sleeping with Beck wasn't just sex. If only it had been. She'd been blown away by the emotionally heated connection that exploded between them. She had no problem remembering the tenderness, the passion, or the desperate longing they shared. They'd rekindled a link impossible to ignore. Was it strong enough to surmount the avalanche of life-altering obstacles barreling down on them? Unless they lived through it together, they'd never know. And they couldn't do that from opposite sides of a jail cell.

She wanted to kick her stupid memory box and the confusion swirling around its contents right out the fucking window. "Dammit, Becket! Why isn't it ever simple between us?"

She waited for her temper to cool before crossing the attic to the stairs. At the bottom, the light's pull chain was rough against her palm as she jerked it. The closet blinked to uninterrupted darkness, and she paused to listen for movement in the hall beyond. The doorknob's glass ribbing was cool to her fingers as she quietly turned it and stepped into the hall.

"Want to tell me what you're doing in the attic?" Evie asked from the other side of the door.

Juliette leaped straight up and landed with a screech. "Christ Almighty, Mama. Give a girl a heart attack, why don't you." She slapped her hand on her chest to calm the muscle trying to beat its way out of its cage.

Evie's fingers drummed on her hips, and she squinted her eyes suspiciously. "I was just down in the showroom looking for you. I wanted to tell you what a good job you did at the meeting." She motioned her toward the kitchen. "Let's have a glass of sweet tea. I want to talk about the bombshell you dropped in my lap this morning."

Juliette summoned her backbone. "There's nothing to discuss. I've got it worked out. He won't win. Don't worry."

"Pfft," Evie huffed. "I'm glad you're so certain." She swept a hand toward the kitchen. "Humor me."

Juliette slumped like a kid headed to the principal's office. Gabby and Chet were waiting for her, so at least the grilling would be brief. A good ol' raking over the coals might help flesh out the bones of her plan.

Her mother grabbed two tumblers from the cabinet and jammed them under the ice dispenser. The motor groaned a load into each glass, and Juliette's stress level ratcheted up. Mama wasn't known for pulling punches.

Evie sloshed sweet tea into the glasses and plunked them down on the counter. "Tell me." Her glare was as hard as the cubes in the tumblers. The glass left a wet streak on the granite as she slid Juliette's into place.

"I switched the necklaces," Juliette blurted and cringed. So much for secrecy. For an instant, she considered telling Evie about the diamond and ruled it out. Her mother already thought she was nuts. That would confirm it. A ballistic Evie was not a pretty sight.

Evie rolled her eyes. "I know." She smirked when Juliette's mouth dropped open. Her self-satisfied smile said she was smarter than the average mother. "I bet Chet's hip-deep in this scheme."

Juliette shook her head. "All my idea, I'm afraid."

"I think it's a crazy idea. But nobody asked me." She snatched a napkin out of the chrome holder and wiped away a sniffle. "Back to your skulking around upstairs. I'd lay even money on your squirreling away the original and leaving the copy as the bait."

Juliette gulped her tea. When did Evie get to be a brilliant mastermind of the covert? "Of course I hid it. Guilty as charged, your honor." She shrugged helplessly. "I couldn't leave it in the safe, and I sure as heck don't want to sleep with it. The bank, where it should have been all along, is closed for the night."

"I see. I assume there's a reason you haven't called Harry Calhoon at CPD. He *is* your godfather, you know. He'd love to put another member of the Santos clan behind bars before he retires." She was being awfully reasonable about this insane idea.

Juliette frowned into her tea and avoided her mother's eyes. The condensation mimicked the sweat on her palms. She drew heart shapes in the dampness on the glass and quickly wiped away the evidence. "I know it's nuts, but I don't want to be the one who puts Beck in jail. Neither of us could stand that." She jumped when Evie's glass rattled down on the granite.

"Juliette Rochambeau," her mother cried. Disapproval pinched her mouth into a ragged line; her nails drummed out an agitated rhythm beside her glass. "Oh, for the love of God, don't tell me you think you're in love. Honey lamb, one tumble does not a relationship make."

Juliette reared back. "Who said anything about love! I've known Becket Ford forever. And yes, fifteen years ago, I thought he was all that and a bag of chips— the be-all and end-all. Then he left me behind and never looked back." She swallowed a mouthful of cold sweetness to kick the knot out of her throat. "Lessons learned and all that—I won't let him off the hook if he goes through with this." She paused for a moment.

189

Would the new, unprecedented intimacy between her and her parents help them understand? "After last night, I *need* to know if I'm important enough for him to find a way around his reason for coming back."

Evie's eyebrows formed a skeptical arch.

Damn, now she'd have to explain that as well. "Is that stupid?" The lump came back. "It is, isn't it?"

"Hmm. You *are* my daughter, after all." Evie's expression softened. "I've always harbored a soft spot for the bad boys, myself. Why do you think Becket's stepfather was always so dead set on knocking over Rochambeau from the beginning?" She blushed and made her own tracks in the condensation. "We had a little...thing for each other back in the dark ages. He didn't take it well when I chose security over, well..." She ducked and blushed harder.

Juliette barked out a laugh. *What? Mama has a past?* Funny, she'd never seen her as more than straight-laced. Even wilder—their paths were converging. "You're pulling my leg, right?" *The incongruity of it all.* "Huh, I guess we're more alike than I thought."

Evie shrugged her shoulders. "It's more'n likely genetic."

"Then you *can* understand. If Beck comes for the necklace, actually takes it from the store, I'll have my answers and no choice except to have him arrested. At least the real necklace will be safe. The problem, my problem, is he's motivated by more than money. His buyer is some big spooky guy from Europe, and Beck is scared of him. He's determined too. He believes he's the only one standing between the buyer and an old friend in trouble. He showed me a picture of what the guy did to his friend, and Mama, it wasn't pretty. She'd been beaten and possibly raped."

Her mother blew out a long breath. "How do you know Becket's not conning you, Lettie? He'd come by the tendency honest enough. His stepfather talked me onto my back and out of my panties before I could blink twice." She brushed away Juliette's startled choking. "Honey lamb, I can see you want to believe him. You're likely seein' him as a modern-day knight in shining armor, willing to risk it all for the sake of the girl in the tower. Let's get honest here. He could just as easily be a sleazeball in a pretty package lookin' for a fast payday."

"Jesus, don't you think I know that?" She jammed her fingers in her hair and ripped the hair tie out of her braid. The elastic band stung her wrist as she wrestled it into place. "That's the reason I'm taking a page out of Daddy's book and covering my bases. Beck is smart, too sharp not to spot police hiding in every corner. Staking out the showroom will be useless. The most likely point to catch him red-handed is when he tries to deliver his take to the buyer."

Evie appeared bewildered by her reasoning. *Welcome to my world.* Juliette had felt the same way when she was trying to make sense out of the readings she'd gotten during her appraisal.

She held up a hand to stay her mother's next question. "Remember me telling you his buyer is European? Well, he sent two people ahead to ensure no mistakes were made, so he's not working on the cheap. That means he'll be traveling in style. I doubt he'll fly commercial, and Charleston International's too public."

"Hold up now." Evie stopped her. "You think this

is gonna happen soon?"

"I'm not sure. I don't think he'll waste any time getting it done. That's why we have to be smart about this." Her heart was beating a thousand miles an hour. "There's only one other place with runways long enough for a private jet to land *and* janky enough to handle less-than-legal trade. That's Kinsey Exec. Can we talk Harry into setting a trap?"

"Ooo, James Bond style? Marvelous." Evie gave a gleeful shiver. "Oh, honey, you've got to let me be there." Nervous excitement practically vibrated from her.

"For cryin' out loud, Mama, this isn't a movie. Beck and his friends are pros. They're not going to say, 'Hey, we were just foolin'. Didn't mean to steal this, take it back.' I'm not sure how bad it could get. There could be real bullets and real blood. You don't need to be anywhere near that."

Evie jabbed her hands onto her hips. "If *I* can't be there 'cause it's too dangerous, then neither can *you*, young lady. I'm callin' Harry right now." She reached for the wall phone.

Juliette leaped and slapped her hand over the receiver. "No, Mama, you can't. I need to know what he'll do. I can't have him arrested for no reason. The only thing he's guilty of so far is twisting me up in knots."

Juliette swallowed hard under Evie's assessing glare. Mama getting her back up could be a formidable obstacle to her plan.

"Wanna guess what your father would say? Hmm? He'd say you're mad-dog crazy to wait. Dragging your feet is going to cost you more than just the jewels." Her slipper-clad foot stomped the hardwood. "No good ever came from believing the snake at your feet won't bite, honey."

"Mama, listen to…" Her argument was interrupted by the ringing of the phone under her hand. She growled in frustration. "Hello?"

A deep, scratchy voice filled her ear. "This is Chief Calhoon. I need to speak with Ed or Evie, please."

Juliette muffled the receiver against her chest. "What did you do, flash the bat signal?" She glared at her stubborn mother and handed over the phone. "It's Harry Calhoon."

Evie snatched the phone and took a breath before answering. "Goodness, Harry, we were just talking about you. How are you, and how's Betty?" Her voice was well-practiced calm as she smoothly stepped in front of the wall-mounted cradle as if Juliette planned to disconnect her.

Her desperate whisper filled the space between them. "Mama, please don't." Suddenly her future hung in the balance.

Evie listened intently, and her high color drained away. She reached out an open hand to Juliette. "Are you sure it's him?" Her fingers found Juliette's; her grip was iron-strong. Her eyes fell closed, and she tilted her face to the ceiling. "Of course. I'll get Edward, and we'll be down directly." Her voice caught on a sob. "Thank you for calling, Harry." The phone shook as she hooked the receiver gently back in its holder.

"What's happened?" Juliette's fingers laced through her mother's.

Evie's free hand covered her mouth for a moment. "It's Roland. They found him in an alley a couple of blocks from here. Harry said he'd been beaten and shot." Her voice was just above a whisper. "We've got to go identify his b-body."

"Oh, my God." She pulled her mother into her arms, and they rocked for a moment. Roland was an ass and a backstabber who'd taken advantage of his own brother. Nevertheless, he was family. A cold tremor rocketed up her spine. Becket popped into her mind. His house was three blocks from the store. Could he have—no, he wouldn't. Thief yes, killer no. At least he didn't use to be. Was he *that* desperate? If Renée was more than a friend, who knew what he'd do. He could be a very different person than she'd seen last night.

****

Becket leaned against a moldy brick wall in the passageway between buildings across the street from Rochambeau, Inc. and chastised himself for being on the scene this early. By doing so, he risked drawing unwanted attention. He was acting against every lesson he'd learned and couldn't stop himself. A persistent itch writhed between his shoulder blades. The kind that accompanied the crime scene tape roping off the alley near his rental. It'd be just his luck to get sucked into someone else's stupidity on the night of his last job.

He sloshed the to-go cup of soda he'd been nursing. The ice had long since diluted the syrupy sweetness into pop-flavored water. Weeping clouds above him brought the fresh scent of rain and early dusk. Soon it would be full dark—his time.

The wages of his twenty-ounce drink finally took their toll, and he stepped behind a dumpster to off-load the effects. As he rezipped his fly, he palmed his phone. Yosef's number was the first entry on speed dial. He glanced at the sky and breathed deeply. "It's time. Let's cut into their security feed. Tell me what you see."

Yosef grumbled about the appalling lack of good tobacco in Charleston, and Beck could hear him pushing clutter around on the table as he positioned the laptop.

"Okay, got it. The showroom and hallways are clear. The place is dark. It's early, man. You're not going in now, are you?"

Beck stepped to the entrance of the passage. "No, just getting ready. I had to backtrack around a cop set up at the alley down the block from us. Definitely a crime scene and there weren't any sirens last night. I can't figure why they'd keep it quiet. It makes me jumpy, that's all." Then again, he'd had a night that he'd never dreamed possible. Remembering their sweet heat made him adjust his jeans.

"Oh, yeah? I should take a stroll down there and see what I can find out."

"Good idea. No one's gotten a good look at you— you can play the worried tourist. Just to be safe, take my go bag and the laptops. Make sure there's nothing that can be traced to us. Set up at the coffee shop on the corner. It could be risky hanging at the house. I'm thinking it's a go for tonight, and we may have to split in a hurry."

"Got it. I'll text the details to Pashi. She won't be happy to leave her rags behind."

"Yeah, well, her boyfriend can replace them. She's the least of my worries." A blur of movement caught his attention. He glanced to his left.

Evie's silver Caddy turned the corner and sped past him. He didn't get a clear view of the three occupants, but if the family left as a group, then Jules was behind the wheel.

"Hold it," he said to Yosef. "They just left the house." He stared up at the façade of the store—all was quiet to the eye. A self-confident smile ghosted across his lips. He'd half expected her to hide out by the safe with her daddy's shotgun in hand. An early visit would shock the piss and vinegar right out of her. "Looks like we've been handed a gift."

"Don't be brash, Becket. It's practically broad daylight." His friend was out of breath as he collected what he'd need for the next phase of their night. "This bag is so damn heavy," Yosef grunted. The scratch of the zipper filled the phone. "Why is there a bottle of wine in here?"

Beck chuckled. "That, my friend, is very a fine Bordeaux. You never know when you'll need to endear a thirsty customs officer. Just wipe it down and leave it. If Pashi ignores your warning, she can use it to drown her sorrows on the way to jail or on the plane back to London."

Yosef huffed his disgust. "I'd spike it if I had any goodies with me. I can't believe she prefers that psychopath to me." He paused after complaining about being treated like a pack animal, and a door closed. "All right, I'm headed to the coffee shop. Bloody hell, it's spitting rain. I'll talk to the copper on the corner. Assuming he doesn't arrest me, you'll hear from me when I'm set up. Give me ten minutes."

Beck's waxy soda cup splash-landed in the empty dumpster as he slipped out of the alley and crossed the street. His nondescript jeans and hoodie blended well into the collapsible backpack over his shoulder. Dark clouds swirled above him. Phone to his ear, as though he was making a call, he slowly scouted the area. Unhurried, he rounded the building and paused to survey the sightlines.

Satisfied no thugs were lurking in the drizzly shadows, he entered the adjoining alleyway where the fire escape dangled an invitation to the upper floors. He blew out a breath to control the nerves tingling in his hands—the prospect of action was an adrenaline-fueled injection to his veins. It was always that way, like a dose that fed his addiction. He savored his final hit and pushed the tiny earbud into his ear. The bulk of the pack slipped firmly between his shoulder blades.

The ladder's wet rungs were rough against his palms as he climbed hand over hand to the landing. He leaned against the building under the narrow eve. It was shallow protection from the increasing patter of rain. While he counted down the last minutes till Yosef lit up his earpiece, he ran through the route to completion. Hold for Yosef's contact, slip back into the flea market, pull down the attic's trapdoor access stairs, shimmy through the window, and heave up to the roof. Cross the open territory and back in through Juliette's hideout. Hopefully, the storm would hold off until he slipped through the gable window, and he'd miss a good dowsing. Once inside—cross the attic, pass through the family level, and the stairway door. Hustle down the second stairs and punch in the code on the keypad. Check control of the eye in the sky. Finally, into the showroom and access the safe. Six years had passed since he last opened a steel box of its kind. Bernie, taskmaster and mentor, had pushed him into learning to crack a slew of different safe styles. His touch, his speed and proficiency, were so finely honed that he knew it would be like playing slap and tickle with an old girlfriend. He expected fifteen minutes tops, in and back out the way he came. Easy peasy.

Beck pulled his gloves from his hoodie pocket and worked his hands into the soft leather. He patted the other pocket that held his pick set, a penlight, and a small earbud wired to the miniature microphone he would use to detect the roll of tumblers. This caper was a bona fide classic—Bernie was probably laughing his ass off.

A quiet crackle sounded in his ear. Yosef cursed softly. "Shite tobacco and now bloody teabags. I can't wait to get home. All right, just a second, and I'll be back up and running." A moment later, he slurped in Beck's ear. "Okay, I'm in. No changes, and the pre-recording is running smoothly. You may proceed, m' lord."

He chuckled. "Thanks ever so, Jeeves. While you're drinking tea and chatting up the waitress, I've got business to attend to. Mind entertaining me with the scene down the street from the house?" He sucked in a fortifying breath and turned to remove the temporary fix on the magnetic alarm. Smoothly, he picked the lock on the door and retraced his steps to the third floor.

"Not much to tell. The bobby was very closed-mouthed. I gather some bloke met his end this morning, though I couldn't get a name. Shall I poke around in the police files? I'll have the time to crack into their data while you're waltzing around your girlfriend's house." Yosef's belief in his technical abilities wasn't unfounded.

Beck grunted as he clambered through the broken

window and looked up into the dark sky. "Don't get sidetracked. That's all I ask." The steadily increasing drizzle collecting on the old wood made the surface slick. He adjusted his grip on the roof edge and jumped, swinging his feet forward. The power of his legs propelled him up onto the asphalt and tar slope.

Beck paused in a crouch and wiped the rain from his eyes. The low cloud cover was working in his favor. He needed to hustle for the window before he left a trail of puddles delineating his path through the house. "I'm on the roof headed for the entry. Hack away, my friend."

"I won't fail you, oh, captain, my captain." Yosef's reference to the Whitman poem made Beck grin. He was always lording his level of education over Beck's lack thereof. What a strange miracle they were closer than brothers. He'd miss their daily interaction as much as he would the rush of the job.

He ran lightly up the slope of the roof and slipped down the other side. The rubber of his soles gave off falsetto murmurs on the grainy texture of the surface. He hesitated only a second before skirting the edge of the gable and pushing on the top of the window frame. It opened with a groaning squeak, and he slipped into the dusty, dry air of the attic. "I'm in," he whispered to Yosef.

"Excellent. And so am I. Blimey, a child could have cracked this. Or maybe I'm just that good." Yosef paused. "Quiet as a tomb below you."

"Right. Heading down the first set of stairs. Stay alert and out of my head. I need to concentrate."

"Touchy, touchy. Shall I order you a sandwich?"

Beck growled and pushed open the door to the

residence. As predicted, all was silent. Light-footed as a cat, he ran lightly down the last flight of steps to the showroom, punched in the code, and crossed to the safe. "Hello, my beauty. Let's get to know one another, shall we?" His leather-covered fingers stroked the glossy black paint and traced the intricate gold scrolls decorating the door. "You're a grand old girl, aren't you?" He patted the door lovingly and pulled out his version of a stethoscope. The earphone fit nicely in his unoccupied ear. "Okay, darlin', let me hear your heartbeat."

Yosef laughed. "That's rich. Safecracker porn."

"Shut it. And let's not compare fetishes, oh doll lover."

"Once. It was one bloody time, and I was very lonely. Don't judge me, you kleptolagnic ass," Yosef huffed.

"Ooo, big words. I admit to getting a touch worked up before a job. It's hardly sexual, at all." The distinct sound of retching reached him. "Now quiet while I pop this old lady's cherry." Ribbing his friend was as much fun as opening the safe.

He stuck the microphone to the safe door just above the combination dial and began his run on the Rochambeau necklace in earnest. A few deft movements later, and the primary tumblers clicked into place. He moved on to the second dial and repeated the process. The smaller dial required more finesse and stood a higher chance of causing a problem. This old girl was anxious to give up her goods. The final teeth engaged, and the spoked wheel on the front of the box spun smoothly to retract the bolts. "I'm in." Beck couldn't help patting himself on the back. "Three minutes and fourteen seconds. A personal best," he said with relish.

"Yes, yes, and you've been on site eleven minutes," Yosef muttered. "Hey, Becket, your girlfriend, does she have a large family?"

Beck ignored him and flicked on the powerful, slender penlight. Its bright beam swept over the safe's interior. Front and center was the rectangular red leather box he'd seen pictured in the newspaper story. "Pay dirt," he murmured. He resisted removing his gloves and caressing the supple-looking cover and bold medallion. For a moment, he envisioned standing beside Jules at the Smithsonian, sharing the happiness and pride at their part in providing the necklace for public viewing. He wished he didn't have to open the box and burst the fantasy's bubble of happy endings.

Beck pressed the tiny button, and the burnished brass clasp ticked open. His flashlight illuminated the glittering contents. "Damn." He took a long breath and blew out slowly. "Mmm, mm. Spectacular. You've got to—wait. What the fuck is that?" He trained the light on the center stone and twisted the lens cap to focus the light into a concentrated bolt of white. He rocked the penlight like an optometrist inspecting a retina. The spot played over the surface of the ruby, illuminating a billowing array of red and purple reflections. Each movement of the light caused a tiny rainbow to erupt near the stone's center. He closed his eyes in disbelief and reopened them, hoping he was wrong. There it was again.

An arch-shaped plume of refracted light. Absolutely not a *natural* inclusion for a stone of this type. Not an *untreated* ruby, that is. "Motherfucker.

Hold on. We've got a problem," he muttered. He patted his pocket and fished out the jeweler's eye loupe he always carried. "Son of a bitch," he ground out. *Come and get it.* The saucy challenge Jules had thrown as she left. No wonder a phalanx of cops wasn't surrounding him; the slick minx wasn't worried about losing the real deal. She'd left him a piece-of-crap copy instead.

"What? What's gone off?" Yosef's muffled voice sounded as if he was talking into his fist.

"Everything." Aghast, but impressed, Beck shook his head. "This isn't the original. She switched the fucking necklace." He almost laughed—almost. Now what? *Damn and blast it all. Think, Becket.* No time to toss the whole damn place; his deadline was perilously close. *Think like Jules.* Where would she stash a piece so precious? Somewhere unexpected, someplace as personal as the jewels staring at him from their nest. Somewhere obscure, yet easy to access. A place she'd keep her most precious treasures.

And then he smiled.

Chapter Seventeen

Juliette dropped her parents at the lobby entrance, then parked her mother's car in visitors' parking. She'd paid so many recent visits that Roper Saint Francis Hospital was way too familiar for comfort. She jogged through the rain and found them talking to Harry Calhoon. Decked out in full uniform, Harry was as traditional as cornpone and collard greens.

The lights of the lobby glinted off his shiny scalp as he swept Juliette into a giant hug. "Welcome home, honey. I'm glad to see you looking so well. Sorry the circumstances are so difficult." He patted her with a square palm and stepped back, resuming his professional demeanor. "I'd like to get this over as quickly as possible. Should be straightforward."

Her father spoke up. "I agree. Let's get downstairs. This is too public."

Harry blanched at Edward's formal tone.

Juliette's apologetic smile was sad. "Yes, Daddy's right. We know who it is. This is just a formality, right?"

Harry cleared his throat. "Absolutely. If you'll follow me, the medical examiner's office is in the basement. The elevators are this way."

He extended a hand toward the bank of gleaming bronze doors. With Harry in the lead, they stepped into an unoccupied car. He leaned around Evie and hit the

B1 button.

"I'm sorry about this, Ed. I know you haven't had an easy time since the robbery. I'm goin' to have to ask y'all to come down to the station and make statements. We can do that after if you wouldn't mind."

"Not your fault, Harry." Edward paused, closed his eyes for a moment, then shook himself up straight. "Evie said they found him this morning. Where was he?"

Harry pulled out his phone and consulted his screen. "Report says the location was an alley between Franklin and Logan, just off Broad Street. The body was reported at nine this morning by a college kid on his way to class."

Juliette flinched, and Harry nailed her with a hard look. *Oh, Christ.* She studied her feet. This could *not* be happening. Half a block from Becket's rental? The implications made her dizzy. Was he involved? No, not directly, because obviously, the patsy standing in her sandals had provided him the perfect personal alibi. No—Becket was not a killer. The same couldn't be said for his stepbrother. And Roland, the idiot, had been stupid enough to get between Seth Santos and his money once too often.

The numbers on the display panel ticked slowly downward. Every foot they dropped was like a brick in her gut. Eventually, the story would come out; she was only delaying the inevitable by keeping the details to herself. Seth was the one at fault in this. She was sure of it. He was the one who'd tossed Roland from the club and left him bloody in the street. He was the one who'd orchestrated the robbery and probably took part as well. While Beck came to accomplish the same goal, his methods weren't violent or destructive. She couldn't let a killer walk away if there was a connection. She needed to see Becket face-to-face and decide for herself if he knew about this. Was it merely a convenient coincidence? Had it happened—while he was screwing her brains out down the street? Her whole body itched to jerk a knot in his tail, and now she'd have to bide her time till they completed this gruesome task. She wanted to find him and face him with both barrels of her father's shotgun. In any case, he wouldn't go far till he'd finished the job. She suspected where he'd be tonight. Or he might be creeping around the store this very second. She clenched her jaw and kept her mouth shut.

The elevator dinged, and they stepped out into a corridor utterly devoid of personality—unless starkly lit, bland sterility was a style. Juliette shivered. "This is like a bad TV show." She envisioned rows of refrigerated drawers and sheet-draped bodies dangling toe tags. "I brought him to this very building yesterday."

A set of glass double doors etched with Charleston County Medical Examiner blocked their path. Her father stiffened at her side, and she took his hand. It was icy cold.

"You okay, Daddy?" She squeezed his fingers gently and wrapped her other hand around both for warmth.

He nodded and squared his shoulders. "You girls don't have to come in. Harry and I can do this alone." Unspent emotion scraped his voice raw.

"Whither thou goest, I will go," Evie quoted quietly and took his other hand.

Harry's gruff bass echoed in the empty hall. "There's a viewing room just through the doors to the right. Go in and have a seat. I'll make sure the ME is ready." He pushed open the doors, and the astringent smell of disinfectant and death engulfed them. Moving quickly, he opened a second door and motioned them forward. The viewing room was a narrow rectangle with clinical white walls. A flat-screen monitor hung on the wall like a picture in a lonely gallery. Several straight-backed chairs occupied the available floor space. Edward sat heavily on the center one.

"You won't have to go into the actual morgue. An image'll pop up on that screen." Harry indicated the monitor. "It's s'posed to make it easier on families. Don't 'magine it does."

"Thank you, Harry," Evie murmured.

He nodded curtly. "I'll be back in just a minute."

The door whispered closed behind him as Evie settled into the seat beside Edward. Juliette took up position behind them. Her hands rested steadily on shoulders thinner than she remembered. The silence was pervasive as if words would further desecrate the scene they were about to view. She closed her eyes and prayed what remained of her uncle wouldn't be a gruesome, disfigured lump of flesh. The whole situation was all too terrifyingly real. She swallowed hard. For some, Becket among them, bodies were most likely a common occurrence. The only body she'd ever seen was at Grandma Hattie's funeral. This horror show wouldn't be a respectful goodbye, nor would it be like those victims pictured in the whitewashed nightly news.

The monitor screen flickered, and all three of them stiffened.

"I caused this." Edward's whisper was barely audible.

Evie clutched his hand, and Juliette's grip tightened on his shoulder.

"He brought what happened on himself, Daddy." It sounded cruel—even to her ears. Roland Rochambeau was a sociopath consumed by his selfish cravings. He thought of no one past the tip of his nose unless it was with jealousy and avarice. She'd known it since age eight when he pushed her out of the workshop and disparaged her interest in the craft. His sarcastic voice rattled in her head. *Go. Be a pain in someone else's ass. Puff princesses like you should be painting their nails,* not *scrubbing polishing compound outta them.* Not even sobbing on her father's coattails had made a difference. The idea cemented in her young mind; if Daddy and Roland agreed, she'd never find a place in the fascinating world of glimmering gold and fire. She would only be allowed to watch from afar. She'd proved them both wrong.

The door handle turned, and Harry stepped in. His ruddy face was a cop's emotionless mask. "They're ready. It should only take a moment, and we'll be out of here." He stepped to the wall and pressed an intercom switch beneath the monitor. "Go ahead, Doc." The screen flared to life, and a collective gasp filled the room.

"My God. Oh, Edward." Evie's strangled voice spoke the words that had jammed up in Juliette's throat.

The image was glaring. The detail picked out in stark relief by harsh lighting. Roland's mouth was slack, and the color of the bruise she'd seen developing last night had degraded to charcoal and ink. His thin hair was coarse and sparse. Dull, like the waxy pallor of his skin. Juliette shivered as the word *lifeless* took on real meaning. She'd thought she was prepared to see him, but she wasn't ready for his stillness or disturbing lack of—presence. Even in unconsciousness, a living body retained some resonance of strength. Roland was empty. Absent.

"That's my brother." Edward cleared his throat, and his hands clenched into fists. "I want the person who did this to die by a needle in his vein. You understand me, Harry?" His voice quivered and escalated. "I want him found and slapped in jail till that happens. I don't care what you have to do or how you do it."

"We're on it, Ed." Harry pushed the power button on the monitor, and the death mask that had been her uncle faded to black. "I'll need a statement from each of you." His attention fastened on Juliette. "Y'all can choose now or in the morning."

"I don't want to drag this out." Edward stood on shaky legs. "How long before you release his body to us?" He was struggling to keep it together during the twisted end to his brother's story; Juliette witnessed the toll in every line on his face. He glanced at Evie for confirmation. "We'll need to call Culpepper's Mortuary and let them know." Now, on top of everything else, they had arrangements to make—a funeral to plan. Death wasn't the end for those left behind.

"Can't say for certain. It should be in the next couple of days. Monday for sure." Harry's cop-shell cracked as he held open the door. "This has been a shock, I know, Ed. Why don't I have one of the boys take you and Evie home, and you can come see me in the morning." His gaze swiveled back to Juliette. "Lettie, you were the last to see your uncle. Why don't you come back to the station with me?"

It was an order thinly disguised as a request, and she stiffened. *No point in delaying the inevitable.* She had to tell him what she knew and who she feared was involved, regardless of the outcome.

****

His clock had long since run out. Beck retraced his course, cursing himself for a fool every step of the way. If the goods weren't stashed where he hoped they were, he was screwed. He'd find himself playing dumb for Singh, and it would have to be an Oscar-winning performance. So, box tucked under his arm, he climbed the final set of steps back up to the top floor.

While he'd been in the store, the storm-born false twilight became the real deal. Driving sheets of rain beat against the fan window. He didn't risk flipping on the light dangling above his head or the antique lamp beside the old couch where she'd revealed her attachment to their past. He dropped to his knees and swept his arm under the frayed fabric covering the daybed. It reminded him uncomfortably of spider webs. Solid contact with a rectangular box had him sending up a note of gratitude to Bernie. "Know your mark," the old man told him over and over. And he prayed he knew Jules as well as he thought.

The cardboard whispered against the floorboards as he slipped it into the beam of his penlight. The multicolored flowers covering the skin had faded to soft hues. A lonely girl's box meant for keeping special secrets. He smiled as he remembered how shy she'd been the day he first met her. For all her reserve, she'd had the compassion to recognize a strange boy's pain and respond to it. Simultaneously the luckiest and the worst day of his life. His hand wandered spontaneously to his cheek, expecting the damage from Hank's beating to magically reappear. His skin held only the memory.

Cursing his scattered concentration, he pushed a gloved finger under the lid and pried off the cover. He'd expected the sparkle of the gems to gleam up at him. Instead, a familiar turquoise scarf was folded gently on the surface. The same one Jules had used to clean the blood from his lip the day she spotted him nursing his hurts on the beach. The stain clung—faintly visible on the delicate fabric. Longing, sharp and clean as a knife, jabbed him back into operation.

He shook his head to clear the memory and redirected his focus to reaching his objective. He flicked the fabric aside, and he caught a glimpse of burgundy leather. The breath he'd unwittingly held whooshed out. "Ahh...there you are, my beauty." A relieved grin split his face. "Thanks for the lesson, Bernie, old man." He plucked the box from its silky rest and popped the lid. An aurora borealis of light exploded into the shadows, and Beck paused in wonder. The copy was excellent. The real thing was spectacular. He ran an appreciative finger across the ruby and clapped the lid closed. His hand hesitated over the scarf. He told himself he was crazy to keep it. That he was a sentimental fool for needing a tangible souvenir. *So fucking what.* He stuffed it in his pocket. If this was the last time he'd be near her, it could be the only reminder he'd have left.

That being the case—he checked his watch, fifteen

minutes past deadline—a minute longer wouldn't hurt. He rummaged in his hoodie pocket for his lockpicks and pulled out a small pen and notepad. What should he say to the only woman he'd ever love?

Beck finished his note and loaded his take into the backpack. The pouring rain was unrelenting as he headed for the window. The sill was slick in his grip, and he paused to steady himself for his swing back to the roof. The pack bumped his butt with every hurried step. The stinging drops pelted his face as he maneuvered through his entrance back into the attic above the antique shop. His breath came easier once he hitched off his pack and passed through the door to the fire escape landing. He touched his ear and spoke over the drumming of the rain. "All's good. I'm out. I'll let you know where to pick me up."

The storm raged on like God had opened a spigot over Charleston. The only plus being the deluge was the temperature of a cooling shower, not England's icy equivalent. The sweatshirt hood did no more than deflect the rivulets out of his eyes. It didn't matter anymore; he was already soaked to the skin.

He shuddered to think about the smorgasbord of filth floating in the pond at the base of the ladder. When he reached the bottom rung, he launched as far from the deepest part as possible. His climbing shoes filled with the black water of the alley's backwash. At the end of the passageway, he stopped beside a gushing downspout, kicked them off, and rinsed the worst of the muck away from shoes and feet both. The downpour drowned out the *squish, squish* of his retreating footsteps.

He crossed the street, ducking from awnings to

doorways as he moved steadily away from Rochambeau, Inc. On the next street over, he waved down a reluctant cabbie and dropped gratefully into the passenger's seat.

The driver tsked in pity and stuffed a ragged towel through the sliding plastic partition between the seats. "Weather ain't fit for man nor beast, buddy. Where to?"

Beck used the cleanest corner of the cloth to sponge some of the water from his face. "Someplace dry what serves good Irish coffee. And don't spare the petrol." He let his thickest English accent loose, and the cabbie's eyebrows rose.

"You got it." The driver grinned over his shoulder. He had a tourist in tow. "My brother runs the best bar in Old Town, a couple of blocks from here. That suit you?"

"Absolutely." He shrugged out of his pack and lowered the bag between his knees. "Bugger me for a fool. I've not seen the likes of this rain since Turks and Caicos. And me without my brolly." He laid it on thick, bolstering his image. Another Bernie-ism *paint the picture.*

A few blocks later, they pulled to a stop beside a hole-in-the-wall bar. The covered walkway provided a few drenched tourists a view of the old slave market. Beck passed the cabbie the damp towel and his fare. "Thanks for stopping for me, mate."

The man pocketed the money and turned off the engine. Beck's senses went on alert.

"I could use a drink myself. You're the only business I've had in the last two hours. A day like this is useless as a huntin' dog gnawin' a ham bone."

"I do love your colloquial witticisms. So colorful."

Beck shouldered his pack and stepped onto the sidewalk. He hustled to the cover of the awning and surveyed the bar's peeling paint. Jittery neon splashed color onto pedestrians who had better sense than to accept the bar's offering of cold beer.

The cabbie brushed past him. "C'mon. I'll buy you that hot drink." He grabbed the door's rope handle and motioned Beck into the dark interior.

Much as he'd expected, the joint's bar top extended the length of the room. A bright collection of lighted brand signs provided the bulk of the illumination for a motley group of a dozen or so sleazy-looking patrons. The air hung heavy with the smell of old beer and years of accumulated tobacco smoke. He nodded to the barkeep and took a seat on the tall barstool closest to the door. His companion cozied up next to him and ordered for them both. Beck lowered his pack to his far side. No sense in giving the guy an easy target. "Thanks, mate," he mumbled.

"No problem. Name's Harley, by the way." He dug in his pocket for a pack of smokes and jammed one in the corner of his mouth. The butt flopped as he talked. "What brings you all the way across the pond?"

"Traveling's my passion. Have you ever been?" Best to turn the conversation back to his new friend.

Harley struck a match to his smoke and blew out a cloud. "Nah, never had the money. You said you were in the islands; that must not be an issue for you."

Beck smiled. The man was fishing and none too carefully. "Hardly. I hopped a ride with a bloke I know and slept on the beach for a couple of weeks. Just passing through town on my way north to meet up again before going home. His dad's got a job what flies him all over, so it didn't cost me a farthing to do some sightseeing." *Use as broad a brush as needed.*

"Always wanted to do that myself—throw every scrap I own onto my back and take off. The more kids I have, the better it sounds."

Beck caught the dash of Harley's eyes to someone behind him, and he tightened his grip on the thick cup that had just landed on the bar. The scent of cheap whiskey was rough in its steam. He took a sip, and the hot liquid scorched his tongue. "Fuck, that's hot." His accent slipped for a second, and he grimaced. He recovered quickly. "Fare took off a layer, it did." He took the opportunity to swivel slightly and get a glimpse of whoever had slipped up behind. Broad shoulders and an army T-shirt. *Oh, shit!*

"Boss's been looking for you, bro." The big goon who'd dogged his heels for the last week stepped out of the shadows and dropped a heavy-handed palm on the back of Beck's neck. His other hand reached for the pack. Beck reacted like a startled cat. Scalding coffee and alcohol launched into the thug's eyes as Beck crashed the heavy cup up against the man's lantern jaw. The guy dropped like a felled tree, and the patrons scattered away from the foray.

Beck jerked his pack's strap out of the dude's meaty paw and shoved a surprised Harley off his barstool. "Turned out the coffee was exactly what I needed. Thanks," he quipped and swung his pack over his shoulder. "Tell Seth to go fuck himself. Got to go—bro." He stepped over the downed man and rushed back out into the rain.

He hot-footed it to the next corner and stepped into a nearby convenience store. His phone case was slippery in his fist as he called Yosef. "How's it look?" he asked without preamble.

"Not good. Cops rolled up five minutes ago. Where are you?"

Beck gave him the address.

"I'm headed to the car." The sound of Yosef closing up shop filled the receiver. "See you in a few."

"One of Seth's boys just paid me a visit." Beck slipped farther into the store. Pretending to shop, he browsed the overpriced bags of snacks and racks of candy bars. At random, he picked a couple and moved back toward the coolers of soft drinks.

"Small wonder. I found out who wound up dead in your alley. Police chatter says it's one Roland Rochambeau."

Beck bobbled the can of soda in his hand. "Dynamite. Seth's cleaning house. Watch your back." Sheets of rain continued to wash the broad windows and fell in a waterfall off the roof covering twin gas pumps. A dark SUV rolled slowly past, and he stooped behind a pyramid of gallon jugs of electric-blue wiper fluid.

"You got it. Grab me some ciggies while you're at it, will you?"

Exasperated, Beck growled, "Oh, sure. I got nothin' else to do. It's not like a guy as big as a house didn't just try to grab me or anything."

"Don't be such a grandma. See you soon."

Chapter Eighteen

Fanish tapped impatient fingers on the knee of his pant leg. The wool was as soft and supple as the silk of his shirt—a perfect choice for traveling. Not the way he'd wanted to do this, but Ford's phone call had forced him into a box. If he wanted the necklace, he had to trade for the girl. Even Pashi, when he'd heard from her as well, confirmed that Ford wouldn't turn over the necklace unless Renée was alive and kicking.

His limo wound its silent way toward Farnborough Airport and his Hawker 800XP. Having his personal jet wasn't merely vanity. He traveled regularly across Europe and the Far East, although taking it across the Atlantic was a rare occurrence. The necessity of frequent refueling was annoying—once in Greenland and again in Newfoundland—before continuing anywhere in the US. The flight time was a pain as well. Unfortunately, he couldn't afford the loss of privacy to do it any other way. Eleven to twelve hours, his pilot had informed him; they'd be bucking a headwind the entire way. So by noon tomorrow at the latest, he would finally be hands-on with his goal.

He glanced across the limo at his passengers. Miss Greenleaf was docile; her head lolled against Jasper's rounded shoulder. The man looked positively replete. Fanish smiled to himself. Giving him the girl was a small boon for his most faithful employee. He really should remember to reward his underlings more often. It just never occurred to him; loyalty was his by right.

"Sir?"

Jasper's voice rumbled into the space between them, and the girl shifted. Fanish nodded for him to continue.

"If I might ask, sir, what do you plan to do about her once we reach our destination?"

He observed his servant for a moment. "Does it matter?"

The man's face soured.

"Surely, you know you can't keep her. She's a liability." His gaze on Jasper cooled. "Will that be a problem for you?"

Jasper lowered his gaze in acceptance. "Of course not, sir."

"Good." He nodded sharply. What was the saying—give them an inch, and they'll take a mile? Still, it pinged what remained of his conscience. "I'll have Denny take care of it if it makes you squeamish."

The small man straightened in his seat. "No, sir. She's my job. I'll do it."

Fanish nodded in satisfaction at the determined set of Jasper's jaw and smiled when the man's blunt fingers brushed the thin knife at his belt.

"I'll tell you when it's time. We need Ms. Greenleaf on the other end, but she is *not* coming back to England. Do you understand?"

Acquiescent, Jasper inclined his head. Fanish didn't miss the tightening of the man's fist against his stumpy leg. His servant's aspirations brought a derisive huff up his throat. The consequences for disobeying a direct order should be plain enough by now. Fanish sighed, exasperated. He'd have to keep a close eye on them until the job was over; apparently, his faithful dog had developed an attachment to his charge.

The limo pulled to a smooth stop beside the hanger at Farnborough, and the driver stepped briskly to the passenger's door. Fanish slid quickly across the leather seat and out into fuel-scented air. His jet was a magnificent, beautiful tool. The black-and-gold skin gleamed despite the overcast sky. Its whole fuselage strained forward, primed and ready. The steps lowered, and his pilot and copilot rushed down to assist their employer on board. He nodded acknowledgment to both men and ran lightly up the steps to the passenger cabin.

As he crossed the threshold, Jasper's voice carried through the din of the busy commuter airport. "Give us a hand, Denny. The girl's not well." A moment later, the cabin rocked slightly as the two pilots carried Renée into the main salon and buckled her into one of the tan leather seats. Her head rolled on her shoulders, and a breathy moan filled the compartment. Jasper's knowledge of sedatives was impressive. He claimed she wouldn't wake until they landed for refueling in Newfoundland. Fanish dismissed her presence and turned to the pale wooden door at the rear of the cabin.

"Let's get in the air as soon as possible, Denny. Jasper is in charge of her. If she becomes a problem in flight, toss her out, will you?"

Denny straightened and snapped a quick salute. "Of course, sir. We're approximately six hours out of Nuuk, and it may get bumpy. For your safety, please stay buckled in as much as possible."

Fanish acknowledged his update and strode

through the door. The hum of anticipation filled his belly. Awaiting the pushback of the jet climbing off the ground was one of his favorite experiences. The rush of power at his disposal brought him half hard. He imagined himself briefly as a celestial warrior sweeping from above to avenge a slight to his deity. Ganesh approved; he was sure.

****

Harry's phone went off like a clarion call. He excused himself to the side and left them huddled in a pitiful group in the lobby of the hospital. A moment later, he was back, and the thunder on his face brought her hopes to a screeching halt.

"That was the station." His face was an angry red under the bright lights. "There's been a call from your store. Chet came in to double-check the alarms and found the safe standing wide open." He paused before he issued the final blow. "He told the dispatcher your necklace is gone."

He kept up a running commentary as he rushed them toward the doors. Juliette caught little of it. She was too busy keeping herself from upchucking right there on the marble floor. Nor could she say for sure how they got back to the store. Once again, the place was lit up like Christmas, just as it had been that very first day.

Harry swept them into the showroom, and Evie, bless her heart, pulled off a swoon Scarlet O'Hara would have applauded. Juliette wanted to join her as she stared at the vacant space in the safe where the necklace box should have been—a gaping hole that matched the one in her chest. She didn't think he'd do it. Hadn't believed he'd have the gall to try it in broad daylight. Big surprise. The opportunistic bastard must have jumped at the chance when they'd rushed off to the hospital.

Harry's boys were clustered in front of the open safe. They gave their boss a quick rundown on the situation. No forced entry. None of the downstairs door alarms had tripped, and they were in the dark as to how the thief got his access.

So how had he…? A trickle of cold sweat slid down her spine. Surely not. *No! He didn't know. Couldn't have known.* Her hand landed on her forehead. "Harry," she spoke across the showroom, "was there any sign of entry down the stairs?"

Edward frowned and turned on his heel toward the private staircase. "Where the hell is the alarm company? They should be here to figure this out. What the hell am I paying them for anyway?" His grip on his phone was white-knuckled as he punched in the contact number for Stevens Security. "I want John Stevens. Right now." He paused, and then he shouted into the phone. "Why the hell aren't your people in my store, John? How come the twenty grand I just paid you didn't tell us there was a burglary in progress? Explain to me why it didn't blow the roof off this place."

Juliette flinched and followed him toward the stairs. She had a prickle of sympathy for the security guy.

"*What alarm?* My fucking alarm, jackass. Check your system, or do whatever the hell you have to do. Then get your butt down here and explain it to me—or return my goddamn money. You hear me?" He pounded in the code on the stair door panel, and an anemic beep signaled failure. He did it again, the same result, and he launched his phone at the door.

Harry's exasperated voice was loud behind him. "You're destroying evidence, you know." He snatched the phone off the floor and pushed Edward away from the panel.

"Let me get this straight," Edward snapped back. "You think a guy smart enough to sneak in here and crack my safe would suddenly get stupid and leave his prints behind?"

Definitely not. Juliette stepped forward. "Jeez, you guys. Can we cool off for a moment? Biting each other's heads off won't help." She placed a restraining hand on her father's arm. "Let me do that before you break somethin'." She tapped the numbers out, then caught Harry's eye. "Would you mind taking a gander upstairs for us?" The stress Edward had been under today was catching up with him.

Evie joined them, obviously on the same page with her daughter. "I'm sure we're just being paranoid." She turned to her husband. "But I'd feel better if he looked over the apartment, honey. Besides, I could use a glass of tea and some quiet. This afternoon has taken the starch right out of me."

"I'd be happy to," her godfather said and swept a hand up toward the residence. "Sargent Compton," he called over his shoulder, "you let me know when the Stevens Security boys get here."

A muffled, "Will do," came from behind the main counter as they trooped up the narrow staircase.

Juliette relaxed until Harry spoke quietly from behind her.

"We didn't get the chance to get to your statement. While your daddy rests, we should tend to that."

She nodded. The weight of what she'd set in motion by challenging Beck was like an anvil on her shoulders. Disappointment and betrayal churned her gut to acid. Bet he was laughing in his beer right now, congratulating himself on his win. And she'd have to spill the whole humiliating shebang, *including* sleeping with the enemy. She was the biggest fool who'd ever walked the planet. As far as she was concerned, Becket's fate was sealed.

First things first, while Harry was "ganderin'," she'd make sure her box of treasure was intact and then—let the chips fall where they may.

As the trio entered the living room, Juliette took the opportunity to slip into the hall closet and up to the attic. She breathed a sigh of relief—no flashing neon arrows pointing to suspicious wet footprints leading from the window. If this was how he got in, he was very good at what he did, which wasn't surprising. Beck wasn't a slouch. He'd always been more than he appeared to be. The tough kid who didn't care was really the beaten boy wading in a sea of guilt. The inventive boyfriend who found beautiful places to steal her breath away was actually the man protecting her from the *real* danger—his family. The lazy, devil-may-care rebel was really the plotting, analytical mastermind.

She was frankly terrified to open the can of worms that was her box of precious memories. What if he'd discovered her secret? He knew her well enough to know she'd do what she promised, or he wouldn't have let her go in the first place. The nature of his business would require at least a practical knowledge of the product. Knowing Beck, probably more than practical.

If he hadn't fallen for the copy, then their shared history might become a trail of breadcrumbs to his final goal. She racked her brain for a memory of ever telling him about her hideaway. Nothing. But he did know her exceptionally well. Knew she was *precisely* the type of girl who'd horde fond memories like old letters and charm bracelets. And where would that girl stash her souvenirs? Not in her panty drawer, that's for sure. Somewhere easy to get to yet secluded. She groaned and reached for her box of better days.

****

"I'm pulling into that rest stop," Yosef announced as they zipped past the blue-and-white highway sign. "I'm sick and tired of your wet-rat smell. What the hell did you do, roll around in the gutter?"

"I had an unavoidable encounter with an ankle-deep river of crap surrounding my landing zone." Beck shook his wet shoe and caught a whiff of garbage. "You need to suck it up till we make the turnoff to Summerville. It's a couple of miles ahead."

Yosef frowned and lowered all the windows. Damp air battered Beck's face; at least the rain had stopped.

"I'm just worried about Pashi, that's all. I left her a cryptic message. She didn't bother to call me back. If—make that when—princess white bread turns you in, Pashi's left hanging. You can bet Charleston's finest will make the house their first stop. They'll snap her up, and my plans to schmooze her into a bit of rough and tumble will go *poof*. Call me selfish, but she may never give me another chance, especially if she gets picked up."

"What the hell should we have done, huh? Stick around town till the cops cornered us, or sit sipping tea at the airport till Singh shows his ugly face? Besides, Seth's boys will be thick as fleas in Charleston. Summerville is a good place to lay low; he won't expect me to go there. We can kick back in the truck stop diner and wait them out."

"Hmph, I'd rather sleep in the car than put up with a bunch of sweaty lorry drivers all night, thank you very much." Yosef picked an ideal time to get prissy.

"Fine by me. I'd pick my own company over your whiney ass any day." Beck crossed his arms and glowered at his friend.

"Fine, then." Yosef punctuated his dissatisfaction by firing his ever-present cigarette butt out the window. "Someone's got to guard the take. Me—as usual." He jerked his head toward the back of the car. "Your bag, the one I *packed* for you, is in the trunk."

"Oh, for Christ's sake. You're acting like an old biddy. This is our exit, and the take stays with *me*," Beck snapped. He'd be damned before he let the necklace out of his sight.

A brightly lit sign, advertising the truck stop, towered above the trees. They slowed and turned up the off-ramp.

Yosef gave him an incredulous glare. "So what does that mean? All of a sudden you don't trust me?"

Beck tossed up frustrated hands. "Give me a break, Yosef. Of course I trust you. If shit goes south, I don't want you to get popped with the goods, that's all. At least I know the country. I have a clean passport and a driver's license if I need to split. Stop being so fucking pissy."

A parking lot filled by semi-tractor trailers slid into view, and they pulled into a dark corner out of sight of the road.

Yosef sighed and hung his head. "Sorry. Didn't mean to sound like your work wife. This is worst-case scenario for me." His friend worked his lips in and out. "You're breaking up the band, and I can see my shot with Pashi evaporating—if there ever was one. And before you say a disparaging word—yes, I know who and what she is. I know how she makes her money *and* the odds of her turning over a new leaf for me are slim to nonexistent. It doesn't stop me from becoming a pubescent bugger when I'm around her. I can't help it."

Beck dropped a conciliatory palm on Yosef's shoulder. "Yeah? That's going around, my friend." No one on earth understood more thoroughly than he did. Jules hadn't had to do more than set foot in Eggsperience, and he'd been a goner. What a fool. Had he sincerely believed pleading his case about Renée would cause a cataclysmic shift in her personality? Once a good girl—always a good girl. Their past and the heat between them didn't make a big enough difference. This was his last job, his coup de grace, and it didn't matter the slightest bit. He'd bested her, stolen from her, and blown her trust right out of the water. Love him? In some fevered daydream. Maybe. Build a life with him? Never.

He let out a breath that tasted distinctly like defeat. "Come on, buddy. I'll treat you to a good old-fashioned American experience—a gloriously greasy hot dog, all the way."

"All the way where?" Yosef pocketed the key fob and opened his door. Diesel fumes coated the warm damp air.

Beck laughed. "Southern comfort, Yoyo baby,

southern comfort."

Chapter Nineteen

Juliette touched the brittle cardboard of her strongbox, and her breath rushed out in relief. She closed her eyes and prayed for a break. "Come on, God. Work with me here. When I open this box, let it be just as I left it. All the hashing and rehashing paid off. The stone is safe. I wasn't stupid. I can move past my twisted-up feelings for a thief, and straight to the part where I watch his perp walk." A grim sense of conflicted satisfaction leaked into a clouded vision of Beck in an orange jumpsuit admitting his defeat. And guilt began to smother her conviction. Why did she have to be the one to punish the man? He made his choice, and she'd witnessed the act in real-time. *No going back from here.* The fox had done what foxes did—invaded her coop and stolen her precious eggs.

Expended adrenaline brought a shiver up her arms. Her skin itched as if ants were crawling under her sweater. She rubbed her arms vigorously to shake the sensation, and a memory snagged on the movement. Try as she might, the pictures flipped insistently through her brain. Beck sitting on a dune, shaggy, dirty hair in his face and his lip bleeding. He'd reminded her of a dog who'd gotten so used to whipping that he accepted it as part of his lot. Still tough, still able to fight back, but too tired and too despondent to lift a fist. On some level, he was still that whipped kid trying to right a wrong the only way he knew how. Not in the most socially acceptable way, of course. Then again, he'd only lived on the side of society whose precepts were need, greed, and avarice. He was still the rebel boy who refused to accept even *that* society's dictates.

"Oh, no. *Do not* start feeling sorry for him." She clung with a white-knuckled grip to the moral high ground. "Becket Ford left an empty fucking hole in your safe. That should prove plain enough where you rank in his world. He made his choice, and it wasn't you, Juliette. Get over it."

She jerked the box into the open, ripped off the lid, and threw it to the floor. For good measure, she kicked it across the narrow walkway. The impact dislodged a ragged pile of pillows, and they cascaded to the floor in a billow of dust and old cedar. The cloud poofed into her face and filled her nose. She tried to cough out the grit, yet every time she inhaled, she drew it deeper into her nose. Her eyes welled, her nose itched like fire, and she gave in to a series of wracking sneezes. One followed the next till her eyes streamed. To stem the flow, she snatched at the inside of the box to grab the scarf covering her secrets.

She stopped mid-scrabble—and patted the smooth texture of leather. "No. No. No."

She jerked back like she'd been stung and swiped at her streaming nose with the back of her hand. A tremor started in her arm and traveled down to her fingertips. Juliette forced one eye open. Staring back at her was the warm burgundy cover of the necklace's box. Just not the right box. Not the crisp new case, but the old timeworn cover. *Wait, what the ever-lovin' hell?* She shook her head in disbelief. She'd swapped the containers herself. This wasn't right—he took the copy and the old box from the safe.

I'm losing my damn mind. The emotional teeter-totter had to be getting the best of her. She'd simply screwed up and confused the two cases in a hasty attempt carry out her "plan." The alternative was unbelievable, inconceivable. Even if he spotted her ruse, he wouldn't have had an inkling of where she'd stash the original or the time to toss the entire house looking for it.

"Jesus, stop being such a coward!" All she had to do was open the case and rip off the Band-Aid. Then accept the facts of her tenuous relationship with a thief.

Her hand shook so violently she missed her target and tried again to spring the latch. The clasp's release was as sharp as a cocking gun in the silence of the attic. She flinched, knowing she had to look and dreading the final stroke that would slice him from her life forever.

A final breath—or a prayer—and she slowly lifted the lid.

Draped across the white silk nest was her charm bracelet. Beneath it, a note in Becket's bold scrawl.

Hide and seek was never your game, Jules.

I hope I get a chance to return your baubles to you.

The air in the attic thinned. Her attempts to latch on to a full breath sent her into a fit of hiccupping sobs. Her legs deserted her, and her backside landed with a muffled crash on the floorboards. Once again, she'd hoped for more than what she got. She should have known better. She was merely a convenient stepping stone on his chosen path.

Gone. The rarest of the rare and its pretender, the princess and the pauper. Just—gone. And it was her fault, her hubris that allowed it to happen.

How long she stayed in a crumpled heap was a mystery. Long enough to be grateful when strong hands hauled her up against a solid chest.

Harry's thick southern drawl rumbled into her ear. "What's all this sniveling about, honey? You got something to tell me?"

Her head bobbed against his starched cotton shirt. "Too late now," she blubbered. "I shoulda done it yesterday. I just didn't think…"

He fished out a white handkerchief and handed it over. "Blow." He studied her while she struggled to get her act together. "People always *think* they can figure their way out of a problem. Then they ask for help when they're in the thick of it. So why don't you start at the beginning and tell Uncle Harry what happened?"

She took in a calming breath and peered up at him through spikey lashes. "Uncle Harry or the chief of police?"

"Two sides of the same coin, honey." He patted her back, then pushed her to arm's length. "Toss up your story, and we'll see which side it lands on." He backed her up and pushed her down on the couch.

Where to start? At the beginning? Did she need to confess how much of a fool she'd been? How she'd allowed herself to be manipulated and set up for the most epic fail of her life? Yeah, she did. No choice now except to lay it all out there. The reason she came home. Their reconnection. The suspicion about Roland. The stone. Oh, God, the stone. Her daddy. The copy. Who she suspected for Roland's death. The challenge and Becket's betrayal. And finally, although she didn't fully understand it herself, an appeal.

"I know you'll think I've gone plum crazy, especially after…everything." She waved his hankie at the empty case and the note. "I mean, I am embarrassed. I *should* be furious at being the victim here. I just can't—locate the anger a rational person would feel. Considering the size of the loss he's treated me to, shouldn't I be chewed up by it?" How could she explain this stubborn ache to make sense of her convoluted emotions? "Dammit, Harry, it's just that Becket—he has his reasons for doing this, and I don't want to be responsible for him failing to save his friend." Traces of that old dream had stubborn thorns.

Her shoulders crept toward her ears as she admitted the last bit. "And then there's the huge part of me who doesn't want to be the one who locks him up. God, this is so screwed up."

He scrubbed his palms over his eyes and groaned. "Dumplin', short of y'all refusing to press charges and him returning both pieces—he'll do time when we catch him. There's no way around it. I *have* to alert the FBI, and they'll coordinate with Interpol or whoever."

"I know, I know. Then you'll sweep in like the cavalry and slap cuffs on the bad guys."

Harry nodded. "This happened, near as we can tell, an hour ago. It'll take them a while to get rolling. We'll get the word out across the state and set up around the airports."

"Yeah, I have some ideas about that." She sighed and stretched her arms above her.

"Figured you might." Harry patted her on the head as if she were still the good little girl she used to be and pushed her toward the stairs. "If we're lucky, we'll lay hands on him. While I'm doin' that, you need to come

231

clean to your folks."

The fatigue and worry she'd been carrying wasn't gone, but she was relieved to share it with someone besides the evil, little voice in her head. Her mama already knew. Her father would be furious. Hopefully he'd forgive her stupidity—eventually.

As for Becket—he wasn't reckless. He wouldn't stumble into a trap. Egotistical and overconfident worked in his favor.

****

Unable to find a comfortable position in the cramped back seat, Beck stretched his legs and groaned. He gathered the hood of his sweatshirt over his eyes and did his best to ignore the light leaking in from the god-awful blue-white arc lamps in the parking lot. He'd managed to drift off for a couple of brief moments. Then Jules came floating into his dreams, and he'd groaned back to wakefulness.

His stubborn idiot partner had traded places with him a few dark hours ago, claiming the car stank of rotten garbage. Yosef was currently playing guard dog by holding down a cracked vinyl booth in the coffee shop. More fool him because the coffee qualified as hazardous waste.

They'd gotten out of Charleston smooth and clean, and Seth's merry band of thugs had hundreds of places to search. This wide spot on a backwoods highway was in the middle of Seth's sandbox, so to speak. *If you've got to hide, do it in plain sight.* He pulled the fabric closer to his body and wriggled back into the seat. "Relax. If you can't sleep, let your mind float and dream of blondes and beaches." He practiced the breathing he used before a climb.

The drowsy haze before sleep crept toward the edges of his mind...

A cracking blow to the back glass jerked Beck to consciousness. Like prey hoping to avoid a predator, he froze in position. The hood dangled over his face, blocking his view of the intruder.

"Wakey, wakey, eggs and bakey." His visitor's taunt was low and oily with menace. No mistaking who'd come calling. "Look who fucked up now. Where's your brains, Beck? Lose 'em inside that sweet little rich bitch of yours?"

Beck raised his hands and slowly pulled himself upright. The muscles in his back screamed in complaint over his cramped position. "So. You found me. Congratulations." What the hell was his play? His pillow contained several million dollars' worth of gems. If he left the car and ran, he was more than likely a dead man. He shook the hood of his sweatshirt back and fought to control his raging pulse. "How *did* you find me, anyway?"

"You been gone too long, bro. Don't you remember how Hank used to favor this truck stop?" He indicated the parking lot and the diner beyond. "This here place was one of his favorite distribution points. Now it's mine." He chuckled darkly.

"I remembered. Didn't expect you to look in your own backyard. My strategy ain't working out."

"You couldn't beat me on your best day, little brother. Besides, you think you're the only one who's up on the latest gadgets?" Seth smiled smugly and tapped his gun against the window again.

Great, Seth had bugged him. "Won't do you any good now. I'm meeting the buyer in a couple of hours.

Unless you're goin' out on your own? Your boss man won't like it."

Eyes slit in contempt, his old nemesis studied him. "Don't give a flyin' fuck what Singh likes." He swaggered around the side of the car and scratched his cheek with the muzzle of his pistol. "I got myself to look out for." The gun leveled off, and Seth sighted down the barrel of the pistol.

That ego wouldn't get him very far when Singh figured out the double cross. "I thought you were smarter than that." Beck shook his head. "This guy isn't a small time crook like your daddy."

"Don't talk about Hank." The pistol vibrated in his fist. "That necklace got him killed—they got him killed. Nobody gets that piece but me."

Damn. Seth really was his father's son, taught from cradle to grave that when it came to reckoning, just deserts were always on the menu. "So what now? You gonna kill me like you did fucking Rochambeau?" He held his breath waiting for confirmation.

"Now there's an idea. How 'bout we make this real simple. You open the door and hand off the necklace. And I don't redecorate the inside of your ride."

Beck's guts rolled. Seth had never been one to toss around idle threats. He swallowed audibly. His nerves weren't fake. "Guess that's plain enough, though shooting up the car might draw unwelcome attention." He risked a glance toward the lights, hoping Yosef had noticed his change of circumstances.

Seth canted his head to the side, and a smug smile painted his cruel slash of a mouth. "I ain't worried." He aimed directly between Beck's eyes. "Get out of the car."

The maw of the gun looked as big as a cannon. Beck made a have-it-your-way gesture. "I'm locked in back here. I'll have to get into the front to reach the switch."

Seth wasn't a fool. He frowned and waved his target over the seat. "Don't be stupid," he snarled as the barrel tracked Beck's movements.

Awkwardly, he navigated the seats and dropped behind the wheel. One hand raised, the other froze as he reached toward the lock switch. Grasping for a shred of a chance, Beck grinned and pointed toward the diner. "Never thought I'd say this. But, cheese it—the cops."

Seth hissed out and turned to look. The beat of surprise was all Beck needed. He punched the start button and grabbed the door handle. The engine roared to life as his heel crashed into the door hard. The rigid edge of metal struck Seth square in the groin. The man stumbled away with the impact and swore into the space between them.

Beck palmed the gear shift and slammed the car into motion. Gravel and dirt formed a gritty arch in the air. The small sedan fishtailed, then gained traction on the asphalt. It leaped forward, headed for the bright lights of the coffee shop. He laid on the horn and wished he had one of those giant air horns mounted on the trucks clogging the gas pumps. He got a flash of Yosef's startled face before he screeched to a halt at the wide glass doors. Money flew at the register, and a startled waitress vaulted onto the counter as his friend bolted for the exits. Then the car's back door flew open, and Yosef launched across the seat. Beck floored the gas, and the door slammed shut, barely missing his passenger's heels. Gunshots peppered the back glass as they tore out of the lot into the gathering dawn.

They were back on the road to the interstate before anyone spoke. "Mornin', m'lord." Yosef's face grinned at him in the rearview mirror. The man was a mess, his hair on end as if he'd spent the night in a greasy truck stop diner. Oh, wait... "We need to work on your timing, Becket. I was just about to swill my fifteenth cup of jet fuel." He ran shaky fingers through his tufts of hair. "We *really* must discuss the quality of your uninvited guests. That brother of yours has a dreadfully unfriendly way of showing up where he's least wanted."

"Yeah, he's like that. Used to haul me out of bed by my junk until my arms got long enough to hit back. He's a real piece of work."

Beck's phone buzzed to life in his pocket. He jerked it out and glanced at the screen. He tossed it over his shoulder to his passenger. Yosef snatched it before it hit his head and glared at his driver.

"That's your dream girl," Beck said, his head on a swivel as he stayed alert for signs of Seth. "She's likely wondering where the hell we are. You explain it to her, will you?" He listened to half the conversation as he navigated their path out of harm's way.

"It's Yoyo, darling. No, he's driving. Yeah, we've got it." He paused, then swore a colorful blue streak. "Well, fuck me. No, ducks, we can't come to get you. We're a bit busy at the moment. You'll have to stay put, or I don't know, take a cab to the airport." He looked to Beck for confirmation and received a curt nod. "We'll meet you there once we shake our obnoxious tail. When do you expect your boyfriend?" Another pause. "Right. We'll figure it out. Just keep him on the ground till we get there."

"What—what?" Beck's knuckles were white on the wheel.

"As I predicted, genius, she's out on her ass. The cops have the house staked out, and she's boiling mad. Singh lands around eleven at Kinsey Exec."

Beck rocked his head, rolled his shoulders, and made a conscious effort to loosen his grip on the wheel. "Good, plenty of time to make a plan."

"Plan? We don't need no stinking plan! We go. We trade the goods for Renée. Then it's Bob's your uncle, and we're on our merry way."

Jules had turned him in. He was right—once a good girl... "Yeah, well, I hoped we wouldn't be dodging the law so soon. We're hot as hell now." Beck scrubbed his hand over his face. "Climb up here and bring the backpack, pretty please."

"Bloody wonderful news, that is. Now what? We've got mad-as-a-hatter Seth behind us and cops waiting for us at the other end. My erstwhile girlfriend thinks we ditched her, and yours is leading the charge to throw us in the clink. How do you propose to make this happen again?" Beck's bag clipped his ear as his friend clambered over the seat.

Beck shrugged. "Ever driven a machine larger than this piece of shit?"

Chapter Twenty

Juliette crossed her arms and glared out the windshield. "I can't believe you talked Harry into letting you come along."

Evie pressed the down control on her side window and began searching through her satchel-sized purse. "Nonsense, sugar plum, you underestimate the power of Southern womanhood. The man was putty in my hands." On the console between them, she dumped her bedazzled phone case, wet wipes, perfume, tissues, lipstick, a hairbrush, makeup bag, binoculars, and a package of cigarettes. She grinned at Juliette and brandished her objective—a wicked-looking pistol.

Juliette's mouth dropped open. "Holy cripes! Mama, are you nuts? What the hell is that? And what, in the name of God, is it in doin' in your purse?"

Evie raised her eyebrows and, smooth as glass, ejected and replaced the clip. "This, my darling daughter, is my Beretta. You don't have one? Every girl should, you know. It's part of my emergency preparedness kit." She swept the barrel over the items on the console. "I was considerin' switchin' the grip to a lovely rose color I spied at the last gun show. Then again, you know how I like tradition." She laid the gun in her lap and patted it like an old friend.

Juliette covered her eyes. "I—I just don't know what to say." Did she know this woman at all? First the cigarettes, then the revelation about her ultimate bad-boy fling, and now a gun-totin' mama straight out of the local redneck survivalist group. The laugh bubbling out her mouth sounded a touch crazy. Giving in to a moment's distraction from everything she'd lost didn't feel all that indulgent.

Evie ran a hand through her windblown hair. The sea breezes were picking up. They didn't dispel the heat gathering on the tarmac beyond the chain-link fence separating their parking place from the runways. "I look at it this way; we're here protectin' our interests. Your daddy's so sure he's got all the bases covered. You and I both know your boyfriend ain't likely to come waltzin' into the spotlight wavin' a jolly roger."

She neatly tore the wrapper off her pack of smokes and popped one between her lips—a smooth and practiced movement. Her sparkly lighter flicked to life, and she took a deep drag of the cigarette. A blue-white cloud of fumes spilled out the window. She pointed the glowing end of the smoke toward a gate leading onto the airfield. "See that? It's the only unguarded access point to the whole area unless you count the swampy ground on both sides of the taxiways. If your boyfriend/jewel thief shows at all, he'll need a way in or out. Makes sense he'd use this gate."

Were they playing cops now? "All right, I'll bite. How do you know this exactly?"

"Because, unlike you, I take an interest in the safety of my community. Last year my gun club held active shooter drills out here. We were very thorough. I got to be the disgruntled TSA agent with a grudge. My job was to sneak in and paintball as many people as I could before they put me down." She sounded proud of her role as pseudo-terrorist. "I got eight people, including a retired US Marshall, before they took me out."

Worse than she'd thought. An egotistical, unpredictable vigilante in Evie-clothing.

"Holy crap. So you're not just my mother. You're really Bonnie Parker reincarnated, is that it?"

Her mother's chin snapped up, and Juliette winced. Crazy or not, she had a powerful mom look.

"Sorry, Mama. But come on, what should I do with info like that, pat you on the back? Say sure, go ahead, shoot the only man I've ever lov…"

Criminy, that word again. It kept leaking into her head and out her mouth. Was that the problem? Was that the reason she'd dragged her feet confessing her sins to her parents, to Harry? The reason she couldn't stand the idea of putting him in jail? The reason she secretly admired his allegiance to his friend, his willingness to lay his life—his freedom, his future—on the line for a promise to a dead man?

She forced herself to admit that, despite everything, she believed the unspoken, irrevocable message between them. It was plain as a proverbial bell when he'd trembled as he touched her—when he'd taken her with aching tenderness and searing passion. She'd known it as clearly as if he'd shouted it from the housetops; Becket Ford loved her then, and he loved her now. And God help her; she loved him with the same intensity as she had as a girl. Didn't that make her as crazy as the woman beside her?

What about the necklace? She had to find a way. She couldn't let the stone slip away. That would be unforgivable, not only to her parents but to the world.

And she couldn't tell her mother about its real value, or Evie *would* shoot him in the intensity of the moment.

"All right, Mama, I'll make you a deal. If and when Becket shows, I'll agree to do whatever we have to do—up to and including holding him at gunpoint. You may *not,* however, bust a cap in him or anyone else. Deal?"

"Deal." Evie's eyes narrowed. "Like I would shoot the man." She huffed, expelling another cloud of smoke. "In that case, we should pull up and block the gate, preferably from the inside." She flicked agitated ashes out the window. "That way, there's no lag time between us and the action."

Juliette rolled her eyes and started the engine. "Fine. Go. Push it open. If Harry comes rolling over here, I'm telling him it was all your idea. Maybe he'll arrest you for trespassing." *Please, God.*

Evie gave an excited wiggle and jumped from the passenger's seat. She jammed her pistol in her pocket, trotted to the wide gate, and lifted the latch. Juliette gawked in wonder as her elegantly dressed mother put her shoulder to the wide chain-link panel and muscled it open.

Juliette pulled the Caddy smoothly through the gate and parked at an angle toward the runways, blocking the road out. The distant sound of a jet engine brought her gaze skyward. The bright lights of a small plane blinked at her from the cloudy horizon. It made a swift, sweeping turn over the airport as it lined up for landing. The downdraft and the jet noise washed over her like a desert wind.

Her mother jumped back into the car. "Here we go. I wish I'd remembered to pee before we left the house."

Juliette snorted a laugh. "We're breaking all the cardinal rules now. The world *must* be coming to an end."

****

The temperature under the airport's overhanging upper floor was a couple degrees cooler than the heat waves streaming from the blacktop. The only plus was the shade. "I hate polyester." Yosef flapped the Day-Glo yellow vest covering his orange plaid shirt.

Beck shook his head and settled more comfortably into the seat of the baggage tug. His high school "friend" at the airport had been eager to turn over the keys for a fistful of cash. Turned out, the local boys in blue had been hassling the grounds crew all morning, and his friend was ecstatic to sit out the rest of his shift in a local bar.

"Just try to be inconspicuous and for God's sake put out that fag. We're professionals, remember? Airport personnel do not smoke on the field." He pointed out a fuel truck. "Kaboom."

Yosef took a last drag and ground the butt out on his heel. "Satisfied?" He glanced at his phone. "They should be on the ground in a few minutes. Pashi spotted six cop cars and one SWAT van. The locals are taking this more seriously than we planned, and there's no telling if or when the feds will be here. Probably here already."

"That's good," Beck mumbled and continued his vigil of the runway. "The more, the merrier." Singh wouldn't step foot off the plane and onto US soil. That meant Beck would have to go to him. Hence the whole grounds-crew getup. He'd get on board the jet, make the handoff, and snag Renée. To make it away clean—

chaos worked in their favor. Overzealous cops trying to make a name for themselves guaranteed mayhem better than anything.

"Once he taxies in, I'll roll out and move the baggage cart into position. I figure the pilot will lower the steps, and I'll run up them to greet the bastard. It shouldn't take more than a minute or two for the handoff. Renée may not be able to walk, so if I need to, I'll stash her in the cart and get the hell out of there."

"Over simplistic, if you ask me. Why would the cops let you waltz on board the jet? They're what, just twiddling their thumbs while you're skipping up the steps?"

"O ye of little faith, my friend." Beck flashed his evil grin. He nodded to the fuel truck. "That's where you come in. We need a distraction."

Yosef oofed a breath as a brown cardboard box smacked his chest. "You can't be serious. What's in here, explosives? Check that, where the hell did you get explosives?" He gingerly placed the box in the back of the tug.

Beck pointed to a spot between the anticipated landing site and the maintenance shed where the police had concealed their vehicles. "Don't be a pansy. They're no more than souped-up firecrackers. My buddy uses 'em for fishin'. Just stroll over to the fuel truck and pretend you're headed out to gas up the plane. Splash some juice on the ground and drop the bomb. I know I can count on you to scream like a girl and run like hell. Easy. Nobody gets hurt, and the cops go, '*Holy shit, fire!* Protect and serve, save the women and children.' " He shrugged as if setting fire to a rolling bomb was an everyday occurrence. "You jump behind the wheel of our ride, and we head for the gate I pointed out earlier. No sweat. It's a large-scale version of Three Card Monty. I'll be the queen."

"Right, and I'll be the joker what gets his tail blown off." Yosef patted his pockets for another smoke and glowered at him. "Why can't you be the idiot with the bomb? I'd be a good deal more comfortable that way."

"Can you physically carry an injured girl down the steps and into the cart?"

Yosef started to argue.

Beck stopped him. "I'm just bein' practical, man. As soon as the fire starts, Singh's gonna go apeshit and, I don't know, try to take off with us on board. So I need you to block the landing gear till we get her out of the damn plane. Once that happens, he can stay and fight or fly away home for all I care. I sure as fuck don't want to be on the jet when he does."

"I hope you're right about all this because if I'm not mistaken, that's him about to touch down."

Chapter Twenty-One

"Mr. Singh, we're on final approach to Kinsey Exec., Charleston." Denny's voice flowed into the passenger cabin. Fanish smiled and tightened his seatbelt. He could practically taste victory. His cargo slept soundly on Jasper's stunted shoulder like someone sleeping off a long drunk, one which had left its prints on her face and clothing. She was no longer pretty; gone were the bright, hard glances and the defiant belief she was in control of her destiny. She'd shrunken to a tired rag. He couldn't wait to be rid of her.

"She's supposed to be awake by now." Fanish's brows knitted. She needed to make a suitable impression on Mr. Ford. If he was to keep the upper hand, Becket needed to know she was alive and in danger of losing that status. Pashi's last message indicated a police-free landing site. They couldn't afford delays on the ground. Once Ford was on board and the necklace was in hand—it was back into the air. As far as he was concerned, if the thief and his girlfriend took a high dive onto the runway, it was a win for him. Better yet, over the Atlantic. That was so much the better—no messy ends to tie up.

"She's only sleeping now. The drugs wore off an hour ago." Jasper reached over and patted her cheek.

Her eyelids fluttered, and she moaned out a rusty sound.

"Time to wake up, Renée. It's almost over." He hoisted a water bottle to her lips, and she drank greedily as her eyes opened.

She blinked in confusion until she found Singh. "I hope he kills you." The rebellious spark he'd found so attractive at the beginning was back.

"I'm sure he'd like to try." He brushed his nails casually on his lapel. "Your boyfriend is known for his brash reactions. This meeting of ours will be more along the lines of a peaceful exchange of merchandise. In any case, we won't be on the ground long enough to give him much of a chance. And I have all the protection I need. Isn't that right, Jasper?"

"Yes, sir. Just as you say, we're ready." The water bottle crinkled in his grip.

Renée cleared her throat. "Why are you such a fucking bastard? That's the part I don't get. He was paying off the debt; you didn't need to do this." Her zip-tied hands fluttered down her body like a wounded bird. She inhaled a broken breath. "I'm the one who screwed up, and you didn't need to hurt me to get what you want."

He shrugged a shoulder. "I wanted to be sure he was sufficiently motivated—nothing personal."

"May I ask a question, sir?" Jasper carefully placed the bottle in the cup holder between his seat and Renée's. He waited for Fanish to nod. "Are you certain Ms. Mirin is trustworthy? She's gone rogue in the past."

Fanish flicked away the doubt. "Youthful caprice, Jasper. She knows where her fortunes lie. It wouldn't behoove her to step beyond the bounds of our agreement. She is always aware of the bottom line. As we all should be."

Jasper inclined his head and adjusted his jacket. The hilt of his knife glinted in the light of the port window. He glanced at Renée and rotated his short neck; the bones popped like grease in a wet skillet. She shivered at the sound, and Fanish smirked.

The sunlight rotated to the opposite side of the compartment as they executed a gliding turn. The ground grew closer, and the buildings of the private airfield came into focus. The pilot completed the arc around the airport and back to the runways. The engines vibrated as the landing flaps rose. The wheels rumbled onto the blacktop with a solid jolt of contact. The surging power of the jet's inertia strained against the brakes. Deceleration pitched the passengers hard against their restraints, and he laughed at the frightened faces across from him.

Denny's voice once again filled the cabin. "Welcome to Charleston, Mr. Singh. We'll be refueling for the hop to Grand Cayman. I've prearranged for immediate attention to that. As soon as your business is complete, we can be in the air in a matter of minutes."

Fanish touched the intercom beside his seat. "Good man, Denny. Please keep an eye out for Ms. Mirin. She and our other guest should be arriving momentarily." He palmed his phone and punched in Pashi's number. While he waited for her answer, he stepped across the space separating him from Renée. He gripped her chin and forced her gaze to his. "Be good, and you live through this." His voice was flat and calm. No hope for the future leaked into his words. Her bleak expression brought a smile back to his lips.

"Fanish, darling." Pashi's warm greeting surprised

him. "Good flight?"

"Long flight. Do you have my property?"

"Yes, well, about that. Becket ran into some trouble, but he's here and has the piece on him. He's ready to make the trade for the girl as soon as you reach the refueling point."

His pulse spiked, and his voice dropped menacingly. "I told you to have the goods on you when I landed, Pashi."

"I know, precious. Don't worry, you won't be disappointed. I see you now. I'll be there to greet you shortly." She paused, and her silky, salacious laugh filled his ear. "I can't wait till I'm in your arms again." Her mink-smooth voice soothed him.

"Don't make me regret assigning you this job. I'd be extremely dissatisfied, and you wouldn't enjoy it."

"Now, now, precious. Don't be peevish." Her voice rose excitedly. "Oh, look, there's Becket now. You can't miss him. He's the one in the baggage cart. Kiss you soon, darling." The phone went silent in his hand as the plane jerked to a stop.

****

"Okay. Here we go." Beck punched the start switch on the baggage tractor and held down the brake while Yosef huffed out his displeasure and slid to the ground.

"If I blow myself to bits, I'll never let you forget it." He tucked a handful of firecrackers in his vest pocket and sauntered toward the fuel truck. Yosef cast a covert glance at the jet rocking on its landing gear in the refueling area.

While larger airports used an in-ground storage system, Kinsey Exec. was small enough that the field used the tanker method to refuel. Beck's high school buddy worked for the independent contractor who operated all the ground support services for the privately owned strip. Handy, considering the uptick in security.

He waited for Yosef to reach the back of the tanker, then rolled smoothly toward the jet. The heat coming off the asphalt was like someone had laid down a bed of coals instead of blacktop. The aircraft perched like a sleek bird of prey unhappily forced to the ground.

He maneuvered the tug and canvas-draped cart to the side of the gangway. The servo motors kicked in beside him, and the steps whined to the ground. A uniformed man provided the welcoming committee at the top. He was dressed like an ordinary private pilot, epaulets, sharp creases, sunglasses—all except for the pistol gripped in his hand. The barrel of the gun waved Beck up the stairs.

The spit dried in Beck's mouth. Suddenly his plan felt a good deal flimsier than it had under cover of the airport's terminal building. He refused to allow his hand to quiver as he patted his pocket for the thousandth time. The bulge of the Rochambeau necklace was well camouflaged by his yellow safety vest. He grabbed the backpack and stepped onto the tarmac. A quick glance over his shoulder showed Yosef disconnecting the fuel coupling at the side of the tanker. He got a glimpse of light sparkling off a spray of clear liquid as it splashed on the field. *Right, time to mop this up.*

"Mornin', Denny. Is your boss in?" he asked as the bottom step dipped under his weight. The man sneered at him and moved back slightly. The narrow entrance reminded Beck of a cave's mouth, looming and dangerous. The gangway creaked and swayed as he took each step upward. A draft of cold recycled air met him at the top.

He moved through the doorway and paused till his eyes adjusted to the dimmed light of the passenger cabin. The barrel of Denny's pistol dug into his back. He raised his hands, the backpack dangling from his fingertips. "Easy now. I'm here on business. No need to be pushy."

Singh's voice sounded to his right. "Mr. Ford, nice of you to join us." His grip tangled in Renée's bedraggled mass of red hair, and he wrenched her head back.

Beck's jaw clenched when her face came into view. The bruise covering her blackened eye spread down onto her cheekbone, and her swollen lips looked painfully cracked and dry. Bloodshot eyes pleaded for help as she whimpered in pain.

"That's not necessary, man. I have what you want. Let her go."

"Yes, I'll do that. As soon as you show me the necklace." Singh's expression tightened impatiently, and a muscle ticked in his jaw. "Jasper, hold on to our guest until I've had a chance to inspect Mr. Ford's merchandise, would you?"

The bulldog nodded and took over control of their prisoner. As Singh stepped forward, Beck noticed Jasper's grip on Renée became a stroking caress.

The backpack lost some of the weight dragging on his heart—Renée had an ally. He extended his hand and let the pack swing from one finger. "It's all yours," he said as he held it out toward Singh.

"Unzip it and dump out the contents." Singh

indicated a small table between the seats.

The pack landed with a solid thump on the tabletop. "I'm not stupid enough to pull a gun on you. I've kept my part of the bargain. Now you keep yours." He slid the zipper across the top of the pack and upended it on the table. The burgundy box slid free, and he shook the bag to prove it was empty.

"Open it." Singh's fists opened and closed in coiled excitement.

Beck witnessed the pounding of his pulse above the collar of his shirt and the dilation of his pupils. The man was teetering on the edge of some unavoidable precipice. As though fear and longing had a simultaneous grip on him. The smart thing to do would be to pop the lid on the box and get this the hell over. Then again, he'd stopped being brilliant two weeks ago in the Eggsperience Diner.

Where the hell was his diversion? Playing for time, Beck rested his hand on the leather. "It's quite beautiful, exquisite, really. I can see why you wanted it so badly. I'm sure you'll get everything you deserve by serving your god so faithfully."

Their gazes collided.

"Funny about curses, though, interpreting what they mean can be—chancy."

Singh's once confident gaze flickered. "I don't know what you're talking about." He attempted to cover his slip with a disdainful huff. "I don't have the inclination or interest in discussing theology, Mr. Ford."

"Have it your way, then." Beck shrugged and tapped the box. "This must be worth several million— you're covered either way. Just so there's no misunderstanding, this wipes our slate clean, right?"

Singh jabbed his finger at the box. "Yes, yes. Now open it!" he shouted.

With a flourish, Beck flicked the brass clasp, and the box sprang open. Singh inhaled sharply as the diamonds flashed around the center stone. Even in the ambient light of the cabin, the stone glinted as red as fresh blood. His shaking fingers reached out, and Becket slammed it closed.

"The girl first." Beck's words were deadly quiet.

"I don't give a fuck for the girl, Ford," he growled, glaring at Beck. "Jasper, hand her over."

Renée jerked unsteadily to her feet. Lurching toward Beck, she sobbed, "Thank God."

Fanish's arm snaked out and snapped around her neck. "Denny, let's be on our way, shall—?"

A deafening roar erupted from the runway. The entire aircraft rocked backward, throwing him off balance with Renée sprawled on top of him.

Beck grabbed the table for support and the box as a weapon. He glanced over his shoulder. Denny was clambering to his feet, the pistol aimed unsteadily down the aisle. His co-pilot scrambled out the cockpit door and hit him square in the back. Behind them, a rolling ball of flame obscured the windshield. Denny collapsed to the floor, and the gun flew from his hand. In the same blink, Beck winged the box hard and fast toward the co-pilot, scoring a direct hit to his forehead. Denny flattened beneath his weight.

Jasper lunged forward, grabbed Renée by the armpits, and heaved her off a sputtering Singh into Beck's arms. He grunted as her weight hit him. He scooped her over his shoulder and headed for the door.

Singh surged to his feet and grabbed the gun as Beck stepped past it. "Stop right there, or I swear I'll kill you both."

Beck kept moving.

The gun cocked behind him. "I said stop!" Singh screamed.

Beck hesitated before stepping over the men in the doorway.

"Put her down, Ford."

He froze, just a step from escape. He risked a glance in Singh's direction.

Singh made an aggressive move forward. "I said put her down, or I'll take you out together."

Beck weighed his options. Die here or risk breaking both their necks jumping. He chose the latter and plunged through the open door. A shot rang out, and the bullet pinged off the door frame behind him. He grappled for the handrail and slid down the steps into the super-heated air surrounding them.

Yosef jumped from his crouch between the baggage cart and the tug. His eyes were as wide as saucers as he broke their tumble to the tarmac. "I got you," he yelled and pulled them apart.

Beck leaped to his feet and shoved them both onto the floor of the cart. He jumped behind the wheel, and they jerked into motion.

Above him, a roar of rage poured out of the cabin. It ended in a gurgling scream of pain as Singh cartwheeled out the door. The sun flashed on the hilt of a shiny blade buried in his back.

Chapter Twenty-Two

Evie was striking a light to another cigarette when a giant ball of flame erupted from the other side of the terminal. She stared at the lighter in her hand and dropped it like a hot rock. "That wasn't me, was it?"

"Becket," Juliette cried and grabbed the ignition key to start the Caddy.

"What are you doin', child? We can't go over—" Evie's words chopped off as her daughter floored the accelerator and slammed her back against the seat.

Juliette ignored her shout of fear and burned rubber for the scene of the explosion. They were at least a couple of football fields' distance from the man she loved, and she needed to help him. She refused to believe he was no longer around to need her.

She ignored the road and roared across the open field then back onto blacktop before reaching the end of the terminal building. The flames had subsided into billowing clouds of inky black, and the smell of detonated oil and burning rubber filled the air. In the distance, sirens wailed. Flashing strobes lit the underside of the roiling clouds. As she cleared the corner separating her from the smoke, she swerved to avoid plowing into a small tractor dragging ass for the territory she'd just covered. She pulled hard on the wheel and slammed on the brakes. The tug did likewise, and the canvas draping the sides of the cart brushed her car. She got a quick impression of two people clutching each other on the cart's floor.

Before she could recover and get moving, her door jerked open, and Becket shoved her over the console, pinning Evie against the other door. In the next second, the rear door popped open, and the couple from the baggage cart piled into the back seat.

The sirens were getting closer by the second. Juliette was too stunned to do more than shout in surprised indignation. She was now part of a chase from the rear.

Tire smoke and dust followed him in. "Mornin', ladies. I need to borrow your car. Promise I'll let you out as soon as I can." Becket grinned as he gunned the engine and spun the Caddy to point them back at the wide-open gate.

Evie came alive from her pinioned position and launched herself across her sputtering daughter. She gripped the butt of her pistol in one hand and the wheel with the other. "We're not goin' anywhere with the likes of you," she spewed. Her elbow clipped Juliette's chin.

Beck swore and plucked the pistol out of her hand. The Beretta went end over end into the grass. He struggled to get the pissed-off wildcat away from the wheel while holding on for all he was worth. "Sonovabitch, woman, I said I'd let you go. I've got to get past the gate first."

"Mama!" Juliette yelled through gritted teeth. "You'll get us all killed. Let. Go." One arm gripping Evie's waist, she managed to pluck Evie's grasping fingers off the rim.

"Cops, Becket," Yosef and Renée shouted from the

back. A wave of oncoming cop cars careened around the corner of the terminal.

"Don't worry. They won't catch us. This is where we jump off the cliff." Beck was grinning like a maniac. "We've got the boat Butch and Sundance didn't have."

Hand firmly holding Evie in her seat, Juliette swiveled toward the gate. A familiar gray sedan waited on the outside. A woman stood in the opening, her hand shielding her eyes from the sun. Beck slid into a turn, neatly blocking the hole in the chain link. The Cadillac lurched to a stop, the doors sprang open, and the passengers piled out onto the blacktop.

Evie screamed obscenities and hustled toward the gate. She jabbed the woman in the gut and scrambled to shoulder the gate closed. Pashi shouted back in outrage and shoved in the opposite direction. Yosef clutched Renée's waist and hurried her through the opening.

Juliette gaped in disbelief, her feet rooted to the pavement.

Beck hustled around the car and stopped in front of her. "I left your bait on the jet. Hope it doesn't go up in smoke." He lobbed Evie's keys over the fence, and they clattered to the road out of reach.

She blinked at him for a long second. The wailing police sirens leaked into her brain, and she launched herself against his chest. "Go. Get out of here. I…" Her words jammed in her throat.

He grabbed her face in both hands and slammed his lips down on hers. The kiss was brutal and not long enough. "I love you, Jules. I'll see you again. I promise." He kissed her again quickly and sprinted for the sedan.

Evie relinquished the fight over the gate and threw her hands up in defeat as the group of thieves raced for escape and roared off.

A cloud of dust surrounded mother and daughter as the thundering herd of cop cars came to a halt at the Caddy's side. Harry's shiny bald head popped out of the lead vehicle. "Evie, Juliette, you okay?"

Evie tossed her hands in the air again and gestured frantically down the road. "What the hell, Harry? They're gettin' away. Go after them."

"Yeah. I see that," he yelled back. "Your car is blockin' the damn gate."

"Right. Oh, God, he tossed my keys!"

Juliette's gaze followed Beck's retreating taillights. Her mind reeled; he was running, she'd never see him again, he had the diamond, and she'd finally lost every single thing that mattered. She moved like a rusty puppet as Evie grabbed her shoulders and hurried her to the side of the fence, then ran after her keyring.

"Lord, gimme strength. I need to pee so bad my eyes are floatin'." Evie gasped as she jumped into the driver's seat and opened the way for Harry and his posse.

The black and whites streamed through the gate, and Juliette slumped to the ground. The tears that had blocked her words burst from her eyes. Gone—the word kept repeating in her mind. Her sense of loss all-consuming. She'd failed again. No Becket. No diamond. No career-altering news story, no self-respect. All lost because she had the phenomenally poor judgment to fall in love with a thief. *Stupid, naïve, idiotic fool.*

A gentle hand landed on her shoulder, and she

turned a tear-streaked face to Evie.

"Your daddy's up in the terminal waitin' to yell at us. Come on, sugar, let's go face the music."

Juliette nodded silently and shuddered into her mother's arms.

"There, there, sugar. Don't cry." Evie rocked her and rubbed comforting circles across her back. "We tried our best. It'll work out somehow. You'll see."

Juliette sniffled hard and hid her face against Evie's shoulder. "I screwed this up so bad, Mama. I was so stupid. Now he's running, and it's all my fault. It's all my fault."

"Hush now and stop wiping snot on my blouse." Evie chuckled. "Don't you worry. With our luck, he'll get clean away. Harry's the one chasin' him, right? The man couldn't catch dinner in a catfish pond." She pushed Juliette out to arm's length. "Get in the car, honey. It's time to face the music. Edward's like to have apoplexy by now."

"He'll most likely disown me."

"I doubt that, sugar. Daddy loves you more than any old necklace. Any *two* old necklaces."

****

Beck rocketed out of the airport and took the main highway headed north. Interstate 26 was only a couple miles off. If they made the super slab, the next exit was an open invitation to a hundred different two-lane roads and country lanes. In his book, that meant ample places to regroup and figure out the next step.

Beck growled in frustration at the paltry response of the small sedan. He should have hung on to the big V-eight Cadillac. If he had, he'd be putting the police a safer distance behind them. The exit sign warning of the interstate flashed by, and he glanced in his mirror. Through the spiderwebbed glass of the rear window, he spotted the flashing red and blues heralding his stay in a federal pen. "Not today," he said under his breath.

Pashi fished a scarf out of her bag and wrapped it Grace Kelly style in a chic cover-up over her hair. "This is thrilling, darling. Why didn't you tell me you could drive like this? I would have accepted that job in Monaco last year. We would've had so much fun." She finished it off in a bow at her neck.

"Don't talk to me about jobs. You went way off the rails working for Singh. So sorry about your payday." He barely slowed for the on-ramp, then swerved into light traffic on the broad lanes of the interstate. The next exit loomed at the top of an oncoming hill.

She harrumphed and crossed stubborn arms under her breasts. "I'm here, aren't I?" She jammed dark glasses over her eyes, completing her look. "Where are we going, Oh Lord of the Infallible?"

A snigger came from the back seat. "What? That was funny." Renée stuck her hand over the seat and patted Pashi's shoulder. "Thanks for helping, even if he doesn't appreciate it."

He checked again. The police hadn't made the four-lane. "Oh, I appreciate the hell out of it. I just don't need bullshit at the moment." He made a quick right at the exit and plowed off the highway. His next turn put them on a back road to the same truck stop he and Yosef had gotten to know last night. Not the best choice. The two-lane offered an option, and he took the fork away from Seth's domain.

Slowing to a safer speed, he took a more natural breath. *Think, Becket.* Keep running and risk stumbling across an overzealous hick cop? Plant themselves on the banks of the Ashley River and swat mosquitos till dark? Blend back into Charleston and ditch the car?

He blinked and slapped his forehead. "Jesus, the tracking device." He jerked the car to a dusty stop and shouted for Yosef's help. "You still have that bug finder in your kit? We need it."

Yosef jumped to join him. He rummaged through his bag in the trunk and came up grinning with a black rectangle the size of a package of cards. "I should have been an Explorer Scout." He flicked on the power and, in a matter of minutes, plucked the small transmitter into the light. "I hate insects of all kinds. Especially the ones who attract vermin." He dropped the device and ground it to pieces in the dirt.

"Good work, professor, that should deflate whatever Seth's got on his mind. We've got to get off the road. If I remember correctly, Jules's folks used to have a fishing cabin out this way." One that he and their adventurous daughter had taken full advantage of when they needed privacy. The Rochambeau penchant for holding on to property made it a good bet they'd kept the place. Finding it was another story. "Look for a sign sayin' *The Rookery*. We should be safe there for a while. It's around here somewhere." They hopped back into the car.

Yosef huffed. "Oh, great. Another old family haunt?"

"Nope. Just a place to regroup. I need to make some calls so we can get the fuck out of here. New York is a long way off."

"I can help you there," Pashi piped up. "I have a friend who owes me a ride in his shiny new helicopter.

Interested?"

"You couldn't have mentioned this before? Like while we were at the airport?"

"Now what good would that have done? He's in Savannah, and besides, he wouldn't be expecting a crowd, if you know what I mean. Just let me handle it."

Yosef grumbled about a "wealth of men following her trail like a pack of hounds," and she rounded on him.

"Are you jealous, Yoyo darling? If so, what have you done about it, hmm? I'm not a mind reader, you know."

He swallowed audibly. "Well, I…" She tsked, and he clamped his mouth shut. He made a what-did-I-do gesture, and his palms popped open in apology. "Sorry?"

"Never mind," she hissed and flopped back in her seat. Her arms formed angry armor across her chest.

"Damn, it's like a freaking soap opera in here," Beck grumbled. "Just watch for the sign. We should get off the road."

Half an hour of aimless turns and country back roads found them on the same path past the infamous hot-spot truck stop from the night before. Options were nonexistent. Cursing his idiot self for getting lost, Beck fought the urge to sink into his seat as they rolled past the lot.

"Ooo, darling," Pashi chimed, "I could use half a mo in the loo. Pull in, won't you?"

"No!" he and Yosef exclaimed.

"Whyever not?"

Beck glanced at her. "Because we've got enough troub…" Past her shoulder, his gaze locked on the grill of a black SUV pulling onto the road behind them. "Oh, motherfucker. Seth." He floored the gas, and they jumped forward. Pashi shrieked in alarm, and Yosef cursed the fates for hooking him up with the fool behind the wheel.

Would they ever get a break? The wall of greenery on both sides of the car was an emerald smear past their windows. The big chrome grin on the SUV filled his rear window. The cracked-ice effect of the splintered glass amped up the threat level. Beck pushed the car for every ounce of power; he began a zigzag weave across the road. If the enormous black muscle behind them gained position and pushed them off the pavement into the trees—someone would die today. Seth had other ideas.

They crested a small rise, and Beck's move into the oncoming lane narrowly avoided a poor sap on a rusty green tractor. He swerved away, and the farmer's face became a mask of shocked terror as he dove off his seat for refuge in the ditch. The SUV wasn't as quick to recover. The noise reached them like a scream as Seth clipped the lumbering tractor's fender, and they skidded into a spin. The force of the impact sent a shower of chrome and black metal into a missile-choked cloud of deadly debris. The farm vehicle, floundering like a wounded animal, shuddered into the weed-covered verge and up onto the bank.

The SUV poised on two wheels until the centrifugal force of the spin overcame it, and gravity won out. The momentum brought it crashing to the pavement in a sickening shriek of metal on asphalt.

A shout of success rose from the back seat. Their cheers changed to screams as Beck slammed on the brakes. Dust filled the car when they slid to a stop on the roadside.

Yosef shoved his shoulder hard. "Go, go, go. Don't stop for that bastard. He could have killed us last night, remember?"

Beck shouted back. "Christ, man, don't you think I know that? He's my brother. I have to see, to get to him." His chest constricted as if a colossal fist clutched his heart and wrung the breath from his lungs. Not again, not another brother dead by his hand. The smell of the seawall choked him, and the roar of crashing waves filled his mind. He threw open his door and stumbled to the pavement. His feet beat a tattoo as he raced toward the smoldering carcass of Seth's car.

Someone moved in the driver's seat. A face dripping blood emerged from the blown side window. Beck's pace slowed. Seth's gaze met his, and the relief was like a sweeping dose of cold water. He lurched forward to pull his brother from the wreckage. The smell of unspent gas made it hard to breathe.

"Get the fuck back, Becket." Seth's voice was as sharp as the broken glass littering the pavement. "I caught you, bro." His lopsided grin was a white slash on his gruesome face. "You never could outrun me."

"Let me get you out of—" A *whoomph* filled his ears. The world contracted and then expanded like a trampoline pushed to its limit. A wall of heat and sound stopped his dive before he could reach for his brother. The force of the blast knocked Beck halfway to his car. A rolling cloud of billowing flame and heat gorged on the air around him as he landed.

Chapter Twenty-Three

"Honey lamb? Did you hear me?" Evie's voice was like someone calling from far off. Juliette knew she should answer. It simply wasn't important enough to pull her back from the comforting blankness of staring out her bedroom window. Beck had disappeared into the wind, and the diamond with him. His face plastered the wanted lists. Harry's dogged determination to find him was tinged by disappointment when last they'd spoken. In her heart she accepted that no last-minute Hail Mary's or sudden revelations would lead to Becket's capture.

She drew in a shuddering breath and pushed away from the window. "I heard you. I'll be out in a second." The silk lining of her dress caressed her legs as she bent to scoop the delicate beaded clutch off her dressing table. The crystals winked at her from the pale pink beneath them. They reminded her of tears, and her eyes threatened to mimic them. She paused before opening her door. *No more tears for Becket Ford, not tonight.*

She turned the knob and pulled open her door. Her mother, swathed from head to toe in muted silver, stood in the hall.

"You're positively regal, Mama."

Evie blushed. "This ol' thing? I've had it for years. You can't go wrong with the classics, though, can you?"

"There's my girls." Her father spoke up from behind his wife. "Classic beauty and class all rolled into one." Since the whole firestorm of news stories and hounding reporters had dropped off, her father had relaxed into acceptance. She hardly even noticed his lingering disappointment anymore.

He scooted his wife out of Juliette's door and crooked a tuxedo-covered arm out to his side. "Shall we?" Over his shoulder, he grinned at his daughter. "Race you to the elevator?"

Evie laughed and slapped his arm. "Edward, don't you dare! I'll break my neck in these heels."

His full belly laugh rolled over Juliette like sunshine after a hard rain. She fell into step beside them and linked her arm through his. "I love you, Daddy. Thank you for forgiving me."

"Nothing to forgive, sugar plum. The heart wants what the heart wants. Ain't no gettin' round it. That boy will get his comeuppance. Mark my words."

She gulped back a sob and let him usher them into the ornate elevator.

She struggled to find a balance between the gains and the losses. Rochambeau, Inc. had experienced an unprecedented uptick in business as a result of the publicity. She didn't understand why people would flock to their doors as a result of their failure to keep their most prized possession under their own roof. Some of it was curiosity. The rest? Who knew, perhaps their notoriety was newsworthy enough that Rochambeau would lend the buyers personal panache—the store that had been robbed by an infamous thief and lived to tell the tale. The public didn't know the gritty details of how it went down or the price she'd paid. She hoped they never would.

As it was, since she'd agreed to stay on, it was good to be needed in a real way. It gave her a degree of pride to bask in the unexpected gratitude of her parents. They'd finally gotten what they wanted—her, home for the foreseeable future. And she would move heaven and earth to make it worth their while. After all, she *had* managed to lose the most elusive and incredible gem in the history of the known universe. That was a debt she'd never be able to repay.

As they reached the ground floor, the murmur of the guests at the cocktail party reception was like an army of bees swarming beneath the antique cypress floorboards of the store. The hum and buzz of two-hundred people strained the confines of the showroom to past capacity. Her staff was in full black-tie party regalia. They handled their posts behind the counters, indulging every full wallet that wanted to take home a sample of local history.

Unsurprisingly, the ruby cases were doing a land-office business. Chet's boys had been hard-pressed to put together smaller versions of the Rochambeau ruby and diamond necklace for the occasion. She had no doubt they'd be sold out by the end of the night.

On a raised dais, near an honest to God podium, the dignitaries huddled in conversation. How her father had managed to get the mayor and the Smithsonian rep to show up was beyond her. The only offering her family had was a copy of the real thing. According to her daddy, the publicity was spurring considerable growth in ticket sales for the exhibit, and they were only too happy to capitalize on it.

Edward cleared his throat and waded into the

throng. He paused long enough to grin at his girls and whisper, "Showtime."

Evie nudged her into the crowd. "Go show off your dress, honey, and work your way to the front. Daddy has no idea about his cake. When I give Gabby the signal, she and Chet will wheel it in from the shop. I want you front and center for the candles. He'll never be able to blow them out by himself." A mischievous grin split her face.

Juliette pasted on her best debutante smile and moved into the mass of humanity choking the showroom. She shook hands, fielded questions about the story of the decade in gossip-loving Charleston, and dodged several overzealous customers. She hadn't broken character once. *That was a win, right?*

She was about to step onto the dais when was she almost knocked off her feet by a ringing swat to her backside. She whirled on the culprit. A man wearing a rumpled tux and a lopsided grin faced her. A red wine stain marred the crushed ruffles at his chest.

He gave her a leering bow. "Do pardon me. I realize that appeared inappropriate." His eyes hid behind thick, tinted lenses perched on a bulbous nose. He sucked back saliva and ogled her chest. "I assure you there was a mosquito the size of a water buffalo about to assault you." His accent was straight out of Downton Abby. The man, however, would have blended better in the slums of Victorian Cheapside.

"I see," she said. She struggled not to sneer while looking down her nose at him. Honestly, some people had all their taste in their mouths. "Lucky me, then. I suppose my thanks are in order."

She stuck out her hand, and he took it. His grip was

unsurprisingly clammy. She pulled back, but not before he managed to swipe his middle finger across her palm. The rude gesture sent a sickening shiver over her skin. A breath of relief slipped from her when he released her.

His crumb-encrusted moustache twitched. "I'm James Paulson of Paulson, Smythe, and Blaine Auctions, in London. Perhaps you've heard of us?"

"Sorry, no." She backed up a step and half turned toward the dais. "If you'll excuse me, the ceremony is about to start."

"Of course, my dear." Another formal bow. "Be sure to tell old Eddy I'd like to speak to him when he has the chance." He raised a flute of champagne to his lips, and the hairy brush beneath his huge nose trailed a spray of droplets.

"I'll do that, Mr.—Paulson, was it?"

He nodded and toasted her with his glass. She gave him a ghost of a smile and stepped up on the platform. Her father took her hand and wrapped his arm around her waist. She leaned into him and whispered in his ear, indicating the man at the bottom of the steps.

Edward glanced over her shoulder. "What man, sugar?"

She turned back, and Paulson was gone. A quick survey of the crowd revealed no bespectacled, hairy-faced perverts in shabby tuxedos. She shrugged and made a mental note to google his company later. The whole incident left a quivery sense of unease.

Her father squeezed her waist. "He'll catch up later. Don't worry about it. This crowd is fixin' to drink us out of house and home. Let's get this party started." He drew her to the center of the platform. The mayor and the head of the Smithsonian's gem collection shook her hand like old friends.

Edward stepped to the fore and tapped the microphone on the podium. He cleared his throat and looked out over his audience. "Ladies and gentlemen, thank you all for coming." He waited while the people settled in to listen. "As I'm sure you're aware, this is a rather unusual reason for a party." A smattering of laughter swept the crowd, and he held up his hand. "My family has had a busy month. There's no need for me to detail the challenges we've faced. Y'all woulda had to be livin' under a rock to miss all the news coverage we've gotten. Like any good story, there was a homecoming, tears and laughter, and personal loss. There was international intrigue and the capture of some less-than-savory characters."

Juliette stiffened at his side, and he squeezed her hand reassuringly.

"As my mama always used to say, 'It ain't over till it's over,' and this story ain't finished yet." He paused and turned to the dignitaries beside him. "There's no need to introduce our mayor, Jim Tunny." He swept his hand out to the barrel-chested politician next to him. "He's already tapped most of you for a contribution, I expect."

The crowd laughed as the mayor waved and showed his empty pockets. Catcalls erupted when a single quarter rolled to the edge of the stage.

Edward chuckled and slapped the man on the back. "Next, I'd like to introduce the head of the Smithsonian's gem collection, Mr. Saul Wilborn. He's come all the way from D.C. to accept our offering for the upcoming exhibit called *Royal Blood*."

The representative glad-handed Edward and nodded to the crowd.

"Considering the extraordinary circumstances concerning the necklace, Mr. Wilborn has graciously agreed to accept the piece we have on display here today in place of its sister." He indicated the raised display case where the copy rotated on a lighted pedestal.

Juliette struggled to keep her smile in place. The light playing off the stones made her eyes sting, and her lips tipped downward. She blinked hard and concentrated on her father.

"My daughter, Juliette, has been invaluable in the appraisal and inspection of this piece. If you will, darlin', I'd like you to model it for the folks."

She blanched; her mouth took on a stubborn line. Didn't he realize what it represented to her? Hadn't she lost enough over it?

He patted her shoulder and raised a hand to Chet standing guard beside the case. "Please bring it up here so the photographers can get a good shot of it on her neck, will you?"

Chet made a show of unlocking the case and pulling on a pair of white cotton gloves before lifting the jewels from their rotating throne. He placed the necklace on a silk-lined tray and walked to the dais; the crowd parted in front of him like the Red Sea before Moses. Juliette was mildly surprised that the strains of "Pomp and Circumstance" weren't playing over the sound system.

He winked at her as he stepped up to her side and set the tray on the podium. He lifted the necklace and moved behind her as she gathered her hair to the side to allow him access. The clasp snapped into place, and the cold, heavy weight of the jewels settled on her neck. A murmur of appreciation rose from the audience as the lights trained on the stage set off an explosion of glittering sparks from the diamonds swathing the brilliant pomegranate center stone.

Juliette blinked as a battery of camera flashes filled her eyes.

"Push back your hair," one of the photographers called, and she turned toward the voice. As she moved to comply, several long blonde strands caught in the clasp, and she winced. She slid a finger beneath the clasp and slipped it along the connector rings to free her hair. As she did, a slight roughness brushed the pad of her fingertip. She hesitated and repeated the movement. Her whole body locked up, then lurched as her pulse stampeded into a gallop.

It was there, the nicked joint Chet had called out to her in the shop. The tiny key to unlocking the original from the fake. "Daddy?" She could barely breathe. She pressed the red diamond against her chest. Her redemption, her future warmed against her skin. She turned disbelieving eyes to her father.

He winked at her. "I told you everything would be all right," he whispered and kissed her cheek.

He turned a blinding smile to the crowd. "Ladies and gentlemen." Ever the showman, he made a sweeping gesture to the necklace and the woman wearing it. "Marie Antoinette's gift to my family and the woman who discovered the hidden treasure it is."

He waited for raucous applause to die down. "For over three hundred years, the center stone was revered as a bold and beautiful ruby. That is until my brilliant daughter got her hands on it. As in all the best stories of buried treasure, she found that its true riches lay undiscovered." He beamed at her. "Tonight, my family and I are proud to introduce to the public—the Earth's rarest and most spectacular creation." He paused for effect. "The Rochambeau Red Diamond." The triumph on his face was rivaled only by the chandelier-rattling cheers filling the showroom.

****

By the time Juliette finished the transfer of their necklace to the Smithsonian's transport team, she was more tired than she'd ever been. Considering how intense the last few days had been, that was an accomplishment. The showroom was empty, and her parents had retired to their bed. Her feet screamed at her even though she'd changed out of her finery and into capris and sandals. The fairy-tale ball was over, and her handsome prince hadn't bothered to show.

The presentation of the necklace was impossible to top. However, the expression on her father's face as the giant pile of frosting and candles rolled into the room had been just as good. He'd been overjoyed, and her mother basked happily in the glow of a well-sprung surprise.

She keyed the security pad and trudged up the stairs to the hollow sound of the tall grandfather's clock striking midnight. The mellow chimes called out a reminder of time's relentlessness, and she found herself wishing the transition from complacency to reality wasn't so jarring. She was sad they'd had to make all the changes. Unfortunate and unavoidable upgrades that reflected the world they lived in now.

She toed off her shoes, walked barefoot across the

landing, and turned down the darkened hall toward her bedroom. Her fingertips skimmed the smooth plaster of the wall as she avoided the small table that flanked the attic door. She groaned, noticing a dim glow beneath the narrow opening. She wanted to ignore it in favor of the call of her mattress. Old buildings being what they were, she didn't dare risk an electrical fire started by a malfunctioning light socket. More than likely, she was the one who'd left the light on anyway.

Was it only a few days since she'd last been up there? Her confession to Harry seemed like forever ago. So much had happened—the airport, the explosion, the chase, Seth Santos's death, the arrest of the buyer and his men, the ceremony. It was all a blur of emotion—from cloying sadness to lighter-than-air exaltation. No wonder her mind had issues settling on one problem at a time. Sleep, when she managed to talk herself into it, would be a welcome escape.

Her feet dragged as she climbed the stairs up to the attic. She reached for the dangling light cord and froze.

Outlined in the moonlight of the fan window, Becket leaned against the sill.

Her blood was singing in her veins as he stepped away from the window and glided toward her. How had she never noticed the sleek way he moved? The shadows peeled off him as though he were walking through a portal.

"Jules." His voice was a dark, sweet salve on her aching soul.

"What are you doing here, Beck?" *Where the hell have you been?*

He stopped a foot from her. "I needed to know you were okay." He shrugged, and his hands left his pockets. "And I brought you this." Her turquoise scarf twined through his outstretched fingers.

He stepped under the light, and her gaze moved from the scarf to his ruffled shirt. A stain turned the fabric a dull red. Her gaze snapped back to his. Visions of the rude Englishman downstairs popped into her mind. Not just a thief—a master of disguise as well.

"Mr. Paulson, is it?" She peeled the souvenir from his hand and peered over his shoulder. "Where are your cronies? Masquerading as customers?"

"I expect they're basking on a beach somewhere by now. It turns out I have friends in low places."

She struggled to drum up some anger that they'd gotten away and couldn't. "Want to tell me how you managed the switch, or should I just make it up to suit myself?" Her voice was smooth.

"Ask your daddy."

"What's my father got—?" She didn't get the chance to finish.

"Yeah. He believes you've got more than a high school crush on me. Is that true?" He inched forward.

Was it true? She'd been tripping over that four-letter curse for days. "You're the one who pulled out the L-word. Did you mean it?" She copied his movement. The heat from his body warmed her suddenly chilled arms. If it was true, where did that leave her? Continually yearning for the ghost of a man on the run?

He raised a hesitant hand, and his knuckle lightly stroked her cheek. The touch streaked all the way to her core. Before he could drop his hand, she caught it in hers. A slight tug brought him even closer. Her palms landed on his hard chest. At least he wasn't running now.

His hands flexed into place on her hips and splayed across her lower back. Those arresting gray eyes bored into hers. A wealth of conflict and fragile hope swam in them. "I meant every word, Jules. I have always, will always, love you." His rumbling voice vibrated through her palms and into her battered heart.

She pulled the scarf around his neck. "You're still a thief," she whispered. Could she do this? Did it even matter?

"I am." He pulled her tight against him. His dimples winked into being. He leaned forward and kissed her forehead, a soft brush of the lips. "Interpol sees my skill set as a valuable asset. We made a deal."

Her eyes fluttered closed, and her brow wrinkled. "I don't understand. You're what, free to go? Working undercover? Constantly on their chain?" She tightened the scarf below his Adam's apple and drew his face toward hers.

He laughed and ran a finger between his neck and the noose. "When you put it that way, it doesn't sound very appealing. I'm on their payroll for the next five years. My time, aside from their requirements, is my own as long as I don't revert to type."

"Well, aren't you just special." She released the scarf and pushed away from him.

He held her fast. "The other alternative was never seeing you again. I couldn't bear that. I need you, Jules."

Her eyes stung, and she studied his Adam's apple. "You do?"

His touch was featherlight as he tilted her chin up. "Yes, you stubborn, beautiful girl. I love you, and I'd like to know I'm not out there alone. Will you take another chance on me? Help me be the man you believe I can be. That's the only way it's gonna happen, you know."

Why was she holding back? She'd loved him since she was seventeen years old. As the boy he was then and as the man he was now. She even loved the man she knew he would become.

Juliette grabbed the bold-colored memory in her fist and kissed him hard. "Yes, Becket, I'll do everything in my power to make an honest man of you."

A smile, as bright as the sun, lit his face. His arms banded her to his chest, and he whirled them into a laughing spin. She held on for dear life—the attic filled with the effervescent joy of their most precious acquisition—a future.

A word from the author...

I can't resist the call of a great story. As the child of a world-class machinist and a frustrated artist, I learned early on the joy of creating handcrafted jewelry. Each piece, like every customer, has its own tale to tell. You'll find them, collected like pearls in a strand, inside my steamy contemporary romance and edge-of-your-seat romantic suspense novels. Like my one-of-a-kind pieces of jewelry, the heroines in my books are rare, desirable, and priceless. Their hearts can only be won by sexy, formidable heroes.

~*~

Find me online at:
http://JayneYork.com

Thank you for purchasing
this publication of The Wild Rose Press, Inc.

For questions or more information
contact us at
info@thewildrosepress.com.

The Wild Rose Press, Inc.
www.thewildrosepress.com